THE FOUR
—— WHO ——
ENTERED PARADISE

BY HOWARD SCHWARTZ

Poetry
Vessels
Gathering the Sparks
Sleepwalking Beneath the Stars

Fiction
A Blessing Over Ashes
Midrashim
The Captive Soul of the Messiah
Rooms of the Soul
Adam's Soul
The Four Who Entered Paradise

Editor
Imperial Messages: One Hundred Modern Parables
Voices Within the Ark: The Modern Jewish Poets
Gates to the New City: A Treasury of Modern Jewish Tales
The Dream Assembly: Tales of Rabbi Zalman Schachter-Shalomi
Elijah's Violin & Other Jewish Fairy Tales
Miriam's Tambourine: Jewish Folktales from Around the World
Lilith's Cave: Jewish Tales of the Supernatural
Gabriel's Palace: Jewish Mystical Tales

Children's Books
The Diamond Tree
The Sabbath Lion

THE FOUR
—— WHO ——
ENTERED PARADISE

a novella by
Howard Schwartz

with an introduction and commentary by
Marc Bregman

illustrated by Devis Grebu

JASON ARONSON INC.
Northvale, New Jersey
London

Some parts of *The Four Who Entered Paradise* were excerpted in the following journals and anthologies: *The Sagarin Review* and *Skywriting* and *Gates to the New City: A Treasury of Modern Jewish Tales* (Jason Aronson Inc., 1990).

The three tales in Appendix I are reprinted from *Adam's Soul: The Collected Tales of Howard Schwartz* (Jason Aronson Inc., 1993). The tale in Appendix II by Marc Bregman is reprinted from *Gates to the New City* (Jason Aronson Inc., 1990).

This book was set in 11 and 14 pt. Bembo by Alpha Graphics of Pittsfield, New Hampshire, and printed by Haddon Craftsmen in Scranton, Pennsylvania.

Library of Congress Cataloging-in-Publication Data

Schwartz, Howard, 1945–
    The four who entered paradise / by Howard Schwartz ; with an
introduction and commentary by Marc Bregman ; illustrated by Devis
Grebu.
        p.   cm.
    Includes bibliographical references.
    ISBN 0-87668-579-3
    1. Akiba ben Joseph, ca. 50-ca. 132—Fiction.   2. Jews—
History—70-638—Fiction.   3. Tannaim—Fiction.   I. Bregman, Marc.
II. Title.
PS3569.C5657F68   1995
813'.54—dc 20   94-24520
                                                           CIP

Manufactured in the United States of America. Jason Aronson Inc. offers books and cassettes. For information and catalog write to Jason Aronson Inc., 230 Livingston Street, Northvale, New Jersey 07647.

For Marc Bregman
and
Arthur Kurzweil
H. S.

For Alice
D. G.

Four sages entered Paradise: Ben Azzai, Ben Zoma, Elisha ben Abuyah, and Rabbi Akiba. Rabbi Akiba said to them: "When you reach the stones of pure marble do not exclaim 'Water, Water!'" Ben Azzai looked and died. Ben Zoma looked and lost his mind. Elisha ben Abuyah cut the shoots. Only Rabbi Akiba ascended in peace and descended in peace.

The Talmud

We were fashioned to live in Paradise, and Paradise was destined to serve us. Our destiny has been altered; that this has also happened with the destiny of Paradise is not stated.

We were expelled from Paradise, but Paradise was not destroyed. In a sense our expulsion from Paradise was a stroke of luck, for had we not been expelled, Paradise would have had to be destroyed.

Franz Kafka

Contents

Preface
Howard Schwartz

The brief and enigmatic legend of the four sages who entered Paradise was the first Jewish legend to capture my imagination. The mysterious fate of the four sages haunts all those who learn it. What, after all, did Ben Azzai see that caused him to look and die? What did Ben Zoma see that caused him to lose his mind? Why did Elisha ben Abuyah become an apostate, and what does it mean that he "cut the shoots"? And how did Rabbi Akiba "enter and depart in peace," or, as it is also stated, "ascend and descend in peace"?

In 1976 I began to weave a midrashic fantasy, in which the journey of the four sages was inspired by their desire to recover the Book of Raziel, a mysterious and prophetic book said to have been given to Adam by the angel Raziel. I sought inspiration in the legend of the four sages and the various related legends found in the Talmud, the Midrash, and, above all, the *Hekhalot* texts that describe heavenly journeys. As time went on, I saw that the legend of the four sages represented the mystical tradition within Judaism from its earliest inception until the kabbalistic era, and even beyond, into the teachings of the Hasidim.

Along the way to Paradise I became distracted. There were so many beautiful legends I stumbled across, so many jewels to recover. Each of them beckoned to me. In time I lost the thread of the fragile narrative I had begun to weave, and for more than ten years I put the story of the four sages aside and pursued other captivating legends and tales.

Finally, with the encouragement of Marc Bregman, who lives and breathes the Midrash, and Arthur Kurzweil, editor-in-chief of Jason Aronson Inc., I returned to my oldest story and tried to discover for myself what it was that happened to the four sages so long ago. The story that follows is my report of their journey as it took form in my imagination. Like Rabbi Akiba, who witnessed all the miracles of Paradise and returned unharmed, may you enter and depart in peace.

Introduction

Marc Bregman

Some stories seem to be inexhaustibly intriguing.[1] In the vast expanse of rabbinic literature—sometimes referred to as "The Sea of the Talmud"—no story seems to have evoked more discussion and commentary than the famous story of the four sages: Ben Azzai, Ben Zoma, Elisha ben Abuyah, and Rabbi Akiba.[2] For this enigmatic tale, preserved in several different versions in classical talmudic and early Jewish mystical literature, is clearly a key text for the study of Jewish mysticism in late antiquity (roughly from the end of the biblical period until about 500 C.E.).[3] Not only has this mystical tale continued to elicit controversy among Jewish scholars throughout the Middle Ages and into modern times, but this provocative story has also inspired Jewish storytellers, who have told and retold this famous story and its related traditions, each in their own way, according to the genius of their creative imagination. The most recent, and perhaps the most expansive and imaginative, in this time-honored tradition of retelling is *The Four Who Entered Paradise* by the well-known Jewish poet, writer, and anthologist Howard Schwartz.

I have no intention of trying to resolve the many scholarly controversies concerning the original meaning of the core story and the complex debate over the historical development of its many variants and offshoots.[4] My purpose is much more modest: to briefly chart for the reader some of the ways in which this enigmatic tale has evolved, from its earliest appearances in rabbinic tradition, through Jewish mystical texts, and on into modern times. However, as we shall see, the scholars' efforts at interpreting a text and the storytellers' seemingly different techniques of recounting a tale sometimes intersect in surprising ways.

TALMUDIC VERSIONS OF THE STORY OF THE FOUR SAGES

Several versions of the story are found in Tannaitic tradition,[5] that is to say, as part of the Oral Torah taught by the rabbis who lived in the period leading up to the compilation of the Mishnah in the first third of the third century. Three of these versions are found in three separate talmudic works as part of what David Halperin has called the "mystical collection."[6] In each of these works this collection of traditions serves to explicate the term *merkavah*, "chariot" in Mishnah *Hagigah* 2:1, which places restrictions on the exposition of three potentially dangerous biblical passages: "One may not expound the Forbidden Sexual Relationships (found in Leviticus, chapters 18 and 20) with [as many as] three persons, nor the Work of Creation (Genesis, chapter 1) with [as many as] two, nor the [Work of the] Chariot (Ezekiel, chapter 1) with [even] one, unless he were wise and understands from his [own] knowlege."

In the context of the extensive discussion of the Mishnah it becomes clear that *merkavah* is more than simply a term for the divine chariot seen by the Prophet, in the opening vision of the Book of Ezekiel, but a conceptual term or code word denoting the secret, mystical lore of ancient Judaism. In the course of the often highly allusive discussion of this concept, the story of the four sages is related[7]:

[Tosefta]

Four entered *pardes*.[8] Ben Azzai and Ben Zoma, Aher and Rabbi Akiba.

[Babylonian Talmud adds]

Rabbi Akiba said to them: When you arrive at the stones of pure marble, do not say: Water, Water! For it is said, "The speaker of lies shall not endure before My eyes" (Psalms 101:7).[9]

[Tosefta]

One looked and died. One looked and was smitten. One looked and cut the shoots. And one ascended in peace and descended in peace. Ben Azzai looked and died; about him Scripture says, "Precious in the eyes of the Lord is the death of His saints" (Psalms 116:15). Ben Zoma looked and was stricken. About him Scripture says, "Have you found honey? Eat what is enough for you, etc." (Proverbs 25:16). Elisha [Aher] looked and cut the shoots; about him scripture says, "Do not let your mouth lead your flesh to sin, etc." (Ecclesiastes 5:5)

[Palestinian Talmud adds]

Who is Aher ["other"]? Elisha ben Avuyah, who used to kill the masters of Torah. And not only that, but he would go into the school-house and would see children sitting before the teacher and would say: What are these sitting and doing here?! This one's trade is builder, this one's trade is carpenter, this one's trade is hunter, this one's trade is tailor. And when they heard this they would abandon [study] and leave [school]. About him [Aher/Elisha] scripture says, "Do not let your mouth lead your flesh to sin, etc."[10]

[Tosefta]

R. Akiba ascended in peace and descended in peace;[11] about him Scripture says, "Draw me, we will run after you, etc." (Song of Songs 1:4)

On the one hand, the similar wording of the basic story suggests that all the versions stem from a shared source that circulated, orally or in some rudimentary written form, as part of Tannaitic tradition. This basic story of the four sages seems represented in its simplest narrative form, among the texts that have come down to us, by the Tosefta

version. In the other two versions, the basic story has been elaborated
in different ways that may reflect the different editorial styles of these
other works. In the Palestinian Talmud, several highly imaginative stories have been inserted,[12] clearly by some later redactor of the text, to
explain why Elisha is referred to by the derogatory alias *Aher* ("the
Other").[13] In the Babylonian Talmud, Rabbi Akiba not only departs
unscathed from the enigmatic adventure, but warns his three companions how they might avoid one of its primary dangers. Without going
further into the complex question of how the different versions evolved,
it is clear that even within classic talmudic literature the process of retelling and elaborating the story of the four sages had already begun.[14]

The various interpretations of this highly elliptical and enigmatic
tale turn on the various possible meanings of the word *pardes*, which
the four sages are said to have entered. Two basic approaches have
developed. The first approach interprets the word *pardes* according to
its normal, well-attested meaning in both biblical and rabbinic Hebrew, as "orchard." According to this interpretation, the "orchard" is
a metaphor for some kind of dangerous pursuit after knowledge, perhaps theosophical knowledge of God (*gnosis*), the goal of Gnosticism,
one of the major religious–intellectual movements in late antiquity.
Read this way, the story serves as a warning that only one in four
learned seekers managed to survive this mental quest unharmed.[15] The
other basic approach interprets the word *pardes* as related to the Greek
paradeisos meaning "paradise."[16] Read this way, the beginning of the
story tells us that the four sages attempted what is known as a "heavenly ascent."[17] That is to say, Rabbi Akiba and his three companions
engaged in something more than purely mental inquiry. Their enigmatic story tells of some sort of ecstatic, mystical adventure actually
experienced by the four sages.[18] The versions of the story found in
the Tosefta and the Palestinian Talmud may be read as describing a
purely intellectual quest. But whoever added Rabbi Akiba's warning
to his three companions in the Babylonian Talmud clearly seems to

have understood the story of the four sages as a legend of their having "entered paradise," that is, their attempt to make an ecstatic ascent to the heavenly realms and the dangers they encountered in this mystic adventure.[19]

This reading of the story of the four sages as a "heavenly journey" is further developed in the ensuing discussion of the details of the story in the Babylonian Talmud. It is instructive to compare the "down-to-earth" explanation of why Elisha ben Abuyah was referred to by the derogatory alias *Aher* ("Other") found in the editorial addition to the story in the Palestinian Talmud, with the "celestial" explanation of Elisha's sin found in the Babylonian Talmud (*Hagigah* 15a):

> Aher cut the shoots; about him Scripture says: "Do not let your mouth lead your flesh to sin, etc." (Ecclesiastes 5:5). What [did he see that led him to sin]? He saw that permission had been given to Metatron [one of the most important and puzzling angels] to sit and write down the merits of Israel. Aher said: It is taught that on high there is no sitting [out of respect for God]. . . . Perhaps—Heaven forbid—there are two [divine] powers![20] They led Metatron out and flogged him with sixty fiery lashes[21] [to show he was no more powerful than the other angels . . . but in return] permission was given to Metatron to erase the merits of Aher. A heavenly voice proclaimed: "Return, O backsliding children" (Jeremiah 3:14)—except for Aher.

In following the evolution of the story of the four sages, it is significant to note that in both the Talmuds, the sin of Elisha is "explained" using the storyteller's method of adding supplementary narrative material to the expanding initial tradition.[22] The hermeneutic mode employed here and elsewhere could be characterized as telling a story to explain a story.

As we shall see, the Babylonian Talmud's interpretation of the core story as a tale of mystic ascent has been highly pervasive. This approach has been adopted not only by many interpreters, ancient[23] and mod-

ern,[24] but also by those who continued to retell the story from ancient times until now.

HEKHALOT LITERATURE

It is not surprising that the story of the four sages, understood as a key
rabbinic legend of mystic ascent, should find expression in early Jewish mystical texts known collectively as the *Hekhalot* (or *Merkavah*) literature.[25] As its name implies, this genre of literature deals largely with
the "heavenly journeys" of various personalities through the celestial
"palaces" (*hekhalot*) that are related to or are actually part of the "divine chariot" (*merkavah*). One of these personalities is none other than
Rabbi Akiba, who, according to one *Hekhalot* text,[26] relates:

> Four we were who entered *pardes*. And these are they: Ben Azzai and
> Ben Zoma, Aher and I, Akiba. Ben Azzai looked and died; Ben Zoma
> looked and was smitten; Aher looked and cut the shoots. I ascended in
> peace and descended in peace. And how was it that I ascended in peace
> and descended in peace? Not because I am greater than my companions;
> but my deeds caused me [to succeed where my companions failed]—to
> fulfill what the sages taught in the Mishnah, "Your deeds will bring you
> near and your deeds will put you at a distance" (Mishnah *Eduyot* 5:7).
>
> Rabbi Akiba said: When I ascended on high I left a sign on the pas-
> sageways to the heavenly firmament more than the passageways to my
> home. And when I arrived behind the celestial curtain (*Pargod*), the an-
> gels of destruction came and sought to push me away until the Holy
> One, blessed be He, said to them: My sons, leave this elder alone for
> he is worthy to gaze at my glory. About him it says, "Draw me, we
> will run after you, etc. [the King has brought me into his chambers]"
> (Song of Songs 1:4).
>
> Rabbi Akiba said: When I ascended on high, I heard a heavenly voice
> that came forth from under the Throne of Glory and speaking in the

Aramaic language, in this language. What did it say in the Aramaic language, in this language? Before the Lord made Heaven and Earth he established . . . a passageway to go in and out[27]; He established His immutable name. . . .

The most consistent difference in this version is that here the story is recounted as a first-person narrative, told from the perspective of Rabbi Akiba who adds that it was his "deeds" that permitted him to ascend and descend in peace, in contrast to his less fortunate companions. These "deeds" are apparently related to his foresight in leaving some sort of "sign" during his ascent to the heavenly realms. The idea seems to be that Akiba marked his trail[28] so that he would be able to remember the passageways (*mevo'ot*)—more than the passageways to his own home[29]—leading through the heavenly firmament (*rakia*), that is, the various "palaces" (*hekhalot*). He alone reached the ultimate goal of the mystic ascent, to see beyond the celestial curtain (*Pargod*) and enter the actual presence of the Holy One. Like other *Merkavah* mystics, including even Moses, Rabbi Akiba encounters angelic opposition but is found worthy to gaze at God's glory and thus be saved by divine intervention. From the continuation of the passage, with the words that issue from under the Throne of Glory, it seems that Rabbi Akiba alone correctly understood that these divine passageways had been established not only for entering but also for leaving the heavenly realms. And so upon entering he had the foresight to leave a "sign" (*siman*).[30] This sign, which Akiba left on the "passageway," seems to be related to God's "immutable Name," since both were established "before the Lord made Heaven and Earth." It may be that in this and similar *Hekhalot* passages, Rabbi Akiba's particular fame in talmudic literature, of being able to interpret "every jot and tittle" of the letters of scripture,[31] is extended to a theurgic ability to make use of the letters of the Divine Name[32] to return from the heavenly journey unscathed, where others failed.[33]

It is also not surprising that the *Hekhalot* authors, who were particularly concerned with the "heavenly journey" and its dangers, elaborate on Rabbi Akiba's specific warning, "When you arrive at the stones of pure marble, do not say: Water, Water!" (as found in the Babylonian Talmud, see above). Let us focus our attention on one example of the expansion of this motif in another passage from the *Hekhalot* literature[34]:

> Rabbi Akiba said: Ben Azzai succeeded in reaching the gate of the sixth palace. He saw the splendor of the air of the stones of pure marble. He opened his mouth twice and said, "Water, water." Instantly they cut off his head and threw upon him eleven thousand iron axes. This is to serve as a sign for all time, that one must not make an error at the gate of the sixth palace.

At first glance this looks like an imaginative elaboration of the Babylonian Talmud's version of the story of the four sages, designed to explain the death of Ben Azzai by linking it to Rabbi Akiba's warning. However, in an extensive discussion of the "water test" motif, David Halperin has argued that this motif developed independently in the earliest layers of the *Hekhalot* tradition and was only later combined with the story of the four sages.[35] If this is indeed the case, we have here an interesting analog to the way in which Howard Schwartz, in his modern retelling of the story of the four sages, has creatively combined this talmudic tale with another esoteric motif, which as we shall see also plays a role in the *Hekhalot* literature—the motif of the secret book.

THE BOOK OF RAZIEL

The Four Who Entered Paradise, as narrated by Howard Schwartz, opens with Rabbi Akiba's strange and disturbing dream of a secret book lost in the sea. As the opening chapter continues, Rabbi Akiba consults with his three companions, each of whom it turns out also had related dreams. Let us eavesdrop for a moment on their opening conversation, at the moment Rabbi Akiba begins to understand the meaning of his own dream:

> "My own dream is starting to become clearer to me. The clue is the secret book inscribed on sapphire which we sought. Do you have any notion of what that might signify?"
>
> "Of course," said Ben Azzai, "there is the tradition of the sacred Book of Raziel, which the angel Raziel revealed to Adam, which was said to have been engraved on sapphire."
>
> "Exactly!" said Akiba. "And this very Book of Raziel must be what we are seeking."

In Schwartz's retelling of the story of the four sages, the search to recover the lost Book of Raziel becomes the primary motive for their heroic quest to enter Paradise.

Just as the story of the four sages is based on classical talmudic sources, so too the motif of the lost, secret Book of Raziel is based on ancient Jewish tradition as Ben Azzai suggests.[36] A work with this title was actually published only at the beginning of the eighteenth century.[37] But the legend of a secret book given to mankind by the angel Raziel already makes its appearance in an early Jewish mystical text, particularly concerned with magic, which was known in antiquity by various names.[38] The Prologue to this book alerts the reader to its extraordinary antiquity and the remarkable way in which it was preserved:

> This is the book, Mysteries of Wisdom, which was revealed to Adam by Raziel the angel.[39] And Noah inscribed it upon a sapphire stone. . . . And he learned from it how to do wondrous deeds, and secrets of knowledge. . . . And he placed the book in a golden cabinet and brought it first into the ark. . . . And when he came forth from the ark, he used

the book all the days of his life, and at the time of his death he handed it down to Abraham, and Abraham to Isaac, and Isaac to Jacob, and Jacob to Levi, and Levi to Kohath, and Kohath to Amram, and Amram to Moses, and Moses to Joshua, and Joshua to the elders, and the elders to the prophets, and the prophets to the sages,[40] and thus generation by generation until Solomon the King arose. And the Books of the Mysteries were disclosed to him and he became very learned in the books of understanding. . . . For many books were handed down to him, but this one was found more precious and more honorable and more difficult than any of them. Happy the eye that will look into it. Happy the ear that will probe its wisdom. For in it are the seven firmaments and all that is in them. From their encampments we shall learn to comprehend all things, and to succeed in every action, to think and to act from the wisdom of this book.

We do not know if the original readers of this book of celestial and magical mysteries were convinced of its authenticity by this rather extravagant preface. But we do know that the legend of the secret book handed down from hoary antiquity did enjoy great popularity.[41] For example, the Book of Jubilees[42] tells of an astronomical writing "which the ancestors engraved on stone" that existed already in the time of Noah (8:1–4). And Noah himself is said to have copied the medical wisdom he learned from angelic beings into a book that he gave to his son, Shem (10:10–14). Another early tradition tells of books taken from the Lord's storehouses and given to Enoch by a scholar archangel whose name may originally have been Raziel.[43] Rabbinic tradition speaks frequently of a Book of Adam.[44] This legend is clearly related to the beginning of Genesis, chapter 5, which introduces the (priestly) history of humanity, from the creation of man to the flood, with the superscription: "This is the book the generations of Adam (*sefer toledot adam*)." However, in typical midrashic fashion, this verse has been understood as if it spoke of "Adam's book of generations." And mythopoesis takes over to weave the legend of a book in which Adam recorded all future human generations, which he was shown by God.[45] One version of this tradition runs as follows: "As Resh Lakish said: What is written 'This is Adam's book of generations' (Genesis 5:1) teaches that the Holy One, blessed be He, showed him each generation and its interpreters, each generation and its sages. When he got to the generation of Rabbi Akiba, Adam took pleasure in the teaching of Rabbi Akiba."[46]

It is significant that the Book of Adam is said to record reference to the generation of Rabbi Akiba. For, as we have seen, it is Rabbi Akiba alone who ascended to Paradise unscathed, according to talmudic tradition. And it is Rabbi Akiba and his Tannaitic contemporaries who are the exemplary heroes of the celestial ascent traditions typical of *Merkavah* mysticism. Ultimately, this esoteric doctrine was also thought to have been preserved in a secret book that is the key to success in the *Merkavah* mystics' quest[47]: "Everyone who deals carefully with this book . . . the fathers of the world pray for his vitality and give him entry to paradise [*gan eden*]."[48]

In our contemporary world, such a lavish promise about any book might sound a bit bombastic. But it is fair to say that the reader of Schwartz's *The Four Who Entered Paradise* is in for a remarkable tour back through the Garden of Eden and on into the celestial realms! To reveal any more at this stage[49] would be to give away too much of the mystery that awaits.

ABOUT THE AUTHOR—A PERSONAL MEMOIR

It has always seemed to me symbolically significant that I first met Howard Schwartz—not in our mutual home town, St. Louis—but rather in the holy city of Jerusalem. Our first meeting in 1977 lasted for many hours. From the first moment, I was captivated by his forte for making traditional texts come alive. And he bombarded me with questions, most of which I could not answer but only suggest where one might search for bibliographical information. As our friendship developed, Howard told me of his project to retell, in novelistic form, the famous talmudic story of the four who entered paradise and I became familiar with the numerous black notebooks he filled to overflowing with notes and sketches for the developing scenes and chapters. This was at a time when Howard had already established his reputation as an important new Jewish poet and was just beginning his second, related career as anthologist and reteller of a vast variety of Jewish tales. In subsequent years I was continually amazed at the cornucopia of articles, poems, stories, and books that flowed from his fertile mind. During these years I often asked about what I referred to as "the fate of the four." At one point, I even assumed a pen name and composed my own brief version of the story, in a humorous attempt to remind him that the four sages were still waiting for his assistance in returning to paradise.[50] Perhaps this is what did the trick. To my delight, Schwartz—now a well-established reteller of Jewish tales[51]—returned to the talmudic tale that had first stimulated his remarkable creative imagination. I am honored that Howard has seen fit to incorporate some of the ideas that emerged in the dialogue that subsequently developed between us. The result is this master storyteller's first book-length retold Jewish legend, *The Four Who Entered Paradise*. May you find their heavenly ascent as elevating and enchanting as I have.

NOTES

1. In the Introduction, and in the Thematic Commentary appended at the end of the novella, I have tried to address a broad spectrum of foreseeable audiences. The Notes and Selected Bibliography are provided primarily for

those interested in pursuing specific points; here too I have attempted to cite English-language publications wherever possible. I am sure that, like myself, many readers will recognize that my discussion of the core story of the four sages and the many other traditional themes and motifs woven into the novella only begins to explore the richly allusive tapestry of Schwartz's *The Four Who Entered Paradise*.

2. Yehudah Liebes, *The Sin of Elisha—The Four Who Entered Pardes and the Nature of Talmudic Mysticism* (Jerusalem: Academon, 1990) [Hebrew], p. 1.

3. See Louis Jacobs, *Jewish Mystical Testimonies* (New York: Schocken, 1978), p. 21.

4. Moshe Idel is currently preparing a comprehensive study of medieval interpretations of this talmudic legend. For the time being see his article, "An Early Kabbalistic Interpretation of the Story of Entering Pardes," *Mahanaim* 6 (1993): 32–39 [Hebrew]. Also see the Selected Bibliography in this book.

5. See below for a composite presentation of the versions found in Tosefta, Palestinian Talmud, and Babylonian Talmud. A fourth version of the story is found in *Song of Songs Rabbah* 1:4, introduced by an Aramaic technical term (*tamman tenenan*), which usually indicates a citation from the Mishnah. This version is similar in some respects to the version found in the Palestinian Talmud (see below, n. 10), and in other respects to a version found in the *Hekhalot* literature (see below, n. 26).

6. *The Merkavah in Rabbinic Literature* (New Haven, CT: American Oriental Society, 1980), chap. 3, pp. 65–105; *The Faces of the Chariot—Early Jewish Responses to Ezekiel's Vision* (Tuebingen: Mohr-Siebeck, 1988), pp. 28–30.

7. Based on *Tosefta Hagigah* 2:3–4 (Lieberman ed., *Mo'ed*, p. 381). Extensive additions unique to the parallel versions found in the Palestinian and Babylonian Talmuds are printed in smaller type. Synoptic presentations of the parallel texts may be found in David Halperin, *The Merkavah in Rabbinic Literature* (New Haven, CT: American Oriental Society, 1980), pp. 86–87, and in C.R.A. Morray-Jones, "Paradise Revisited . . . Part 1: The Jewish Sources," *Harvard Theological Review* 86 (1993): 210–215.

8. For a discussion of this key concept, see below.

9. Babylonian Talmud, *Hagigah* 14b.

10. Palestinian Talmud, *Hagigah* 2:1 (Venice ed., 77b). A version of this

story about Elisha appears in *Song of Songs Rabbah*, see above n. 5. A second story, about how Elisha informed against his fellow Jews, causing them to violate the biblical prohibition of labor on Sabbath, follows here in the Palestinian Talmud.

11. An alternate reading found in some versions is: "Rabbi Akiba entered in peace and left in peace."

12. In all three works additional stories are added—outside the framework of the story—to elaborate on the behavior, character, and intellectual leaning of the various sages.

13. On the use of *Aher* as a derogatory alias for the heretical sage Elisha ben Abuyah, perhaps to indicate his gnostic apostasy, see: Gedaliahu G. Stoumsa, "Aher: A Gnostic," in *The Rediscovery of Gnosticism: Proceedings of the International Conference on Gnosticism at Yale, 1978*, ed. Bentley Layton [Studies in the History of Religion: Supplememts to *Numen* 41] (Lieden: Brill, 1980–1981), vol. 2, pp. 808–818; David Halperin, *Faces of the Chariot*, pp. 31 ff. especially n. 21; Yehudah Liebes, *The Sin of Elisha* [Hebrew], pp. 12 ff. On the use of *aher* ("other") in later Jewish mysticism to indicate "evil," compare the term *sitra ahra* ("the other side," i.e., cosmic evil); see Gershom Scholem, *Kabbalah* ("Basic Ideas: The Problem of Evil"), pp. 123–128.

14. On the process of telling and retelling typical of *Aggadah* (Jewish legend), see Joseph Heinemann, "The Nature of the Aggadah," trans. Marc Bregman, *Midrash and Literature*, ed. Geoffrey H. Hartman and Sanford Budick (New Haven, CT: Yale University Press, 1986), pp. 41–55.

15. The "metaphorical" approach to *pardes* was favored by nineteenth-century scholars, such as Gratz and Joel, and with considerable variations by more recent scholars, such as Urbach, Fischel, Halperin, Frankel, and Goshen [see the Selected Bibliography at the end of the book for details]. See also S. Krauss, "Outdoor Teaching in Talmudic Times," in *Exploring the Talmud*, vol. 1, *Education*, ed. Haim Z. Dimitrovsky (New York: Ktav, 1976), p. 333: ". . . T.B. *Hagigah* 14b, the verb 'entered' is obviously a metaphor, just as is the expression '*Pardes*'." A previous novelistic treatment of the story of the same four sages, Milton Steinberg's *As a Driven Leaf* (Northvale, NJ: Jason Aronson, 1987) can be seen as yet another example of this nonmystical approach, since it studiously avoids portraying the sages' quest for knowledge as an entry into "paradise."

Steinberg's attempt at historical realism is, in some ways, a mirror image of Schwartz's fantastical depiction of the sages' heavenly ascent.

16. It should be noted that this meaning is only rarely attested elsewhere in rabbinic literature; see the parable cited in Sifra, *Behukkotai, perek* 3, section 3 (ed. Weiss, p. 111b) in which *pardes* is analogous to "the future paradise" (*gan eden le-atid lavo*). However, compare the different parable cited in *Tanhuma* (ed. Buber), *Shemot* 10, p. 6, in which it is specifically stated that *pardes* is analogous to "this world." On the development of the term *pardes/paradeisos* from a Persian word referring to a royal enclosed garden (e.g., the Hebrew text of Nehemiah 2:8), via a term for orchard (e.g., the Hebrew and Greek [Septuagint] texts of *Song of Songs* 4:13), to a term for paradise (e.g., the Septuagint to Genesis 2:8), see *Theological Dictionary of the New Testament*, vol. 5, pp. 765–766, s.v. *paradeisos*. In the New Testament (Luke 23:43, 2 Corinthians 12:4, Revelations 2:7) and in patristic literature, *paradeisos* normally means "paradise." As noted by Halperin, *Faces of the Chariot*, p. 32, the Qumran fragments of the original Aramaic text of the Book of Enoch use *pardes kushta* ("garden of righteousness") for paradise; see his extensive discussion of the term *pardes*, pp. 31–37.

17. From among the vast literature on this topic, see Allan Segal, "Heavenly Ascent in Hellenistic Judaism, Early Christianity, and Their Environment," *Aufstieg und Niedergand der romischen Welt*, II, Principat, vol. 23,2 (Berlin: de Gruyter, 1980), pp. 1333–1394, esp. pp. 1388–1394 (bibliography, pp. 1388 ff.); Ioan Petru Culianu, *Psychanodia, I—A Survey of the Evidence Concerning the Ascension of the Soul and Its Relevance* (Leiden: Brill, 1983); Martha Himmelfarb, *Ascent to Heaven in Jewish and Christian Apocalypses* (New York: Oxford University Press, 1993). For heavenly ascent in Christianity, see Morton Smith, "Ascent to the Heavens and the Beginnings of Christianity," *Eranos-Jahrbuch* 50 (1981): 403–429 and the article by C.R.A. Morray-Jones on Paul's ascent to Paradise (2 Corinthians 12), forthcoming in *Harvard Theological Review*.

18. The two approaches that have developed to the understanding of the *pardes* in the story of the four sages are a prime example of the model proposed by Tzvetan Todorov, *The Fantastic*, trans. Richard Howard (Ithaca, NY: Cornell University Press, 1975). As summarized by Eric S. Rabkin, *Fantastic Worlds—Myths, Tales, and Stories* (New York: Oxford University

Press, 1979), p. 465: the fantastic is the moment of hesitation in which a reader cannot decide whether something odd in the text should be taken metaphorically (making the work "marvelous") or literally (making the work "uncanny"). On the conflicting opinions of the post-talmudic commentators as to whether the sages' entry into the celestial paradise was real or imagined, see below, n. 23.

19. The difference between these two fundamental approaches to the story of the four sages mirrors in an interesting way the difference between two basic approaches to Jewish mysticism in general. The earlier approach, up to and at least partially including the seminal work of Gershom Scholem, tended to emphasize the theoretical–intellectual aspects of Kabbalah; more recent research, particularly since the revolutionary research of Moshe Idel, has tended to emphasize the experiential–ecstatic aspects of Jewish mysticism. See Moshe Idel, *Kabbalah—New Perspectives* (New Haven: Yale University Press, 1988). For a retrospective overview, see Elliot R. Wolfson, "Forms of Visionary Ascent as Ecstatic Experience," *Gershom Scholem's Major Trends in Jewish Mysticism 50 Years After—Proceedings of the Sixth International Conference on the History of Jewish Mysticism*, ed. Peter Schaefer and Joseph Dan (Tuebingen: Mohr-Siebeck, 1993), pp. 209 ff.

20. See Alan F. Segal, *Two Powers in Heaven—Early Rabbinic Reports about Christianity and Gnosticism* (Leiden: Brill, 1977), pp. 60–73.

21. On this punishment for celestial beings, see Halperin, *The Merkavah in Rabbinic Literature*, pp. 169–172, who argues that this detail points to a fourth-century Babylonian milieu for the story.

22. For an extensive discussion of this passage as the core story about the sin of Elisha, see Liebes, *The Sin of Elisha* [Hebrew], pp. 29 ff. Compare 3 Enoch, chapter 17, in which this story about Elisha/Aher is retold from the perspective of Metatron as a first-person narrative.

23. For the further development of this approach in the *Hekhalot* literature, see below. Rashi to *Hagigah* 14b, s.v. ". . . entered *pardes*" comments: "they ascended to heaven by use of the Name [of God]." However, compare Tosefot, ad loc.: "'. . . entered *pardes*'—as if [*ke-gon*] by the use of the Name [of God], but they did not really ascend; rather it seemed to them that they had ascended; and thus it is interpreted in the *Arukh*." This is indeed in line

with the interpretation given by Rabbi Nathan of Rome in his talmudic lexicon [see *Arukh Ha-Shalem*, ed. Alexander Kohut, vol. 1, p. 14], s.v. *avnei shayish tahor*: ". . . but they did not ascend on high, but rather in the chambers of their heart they saw and contemplated. . . . This is the interpretation of Rav Hai Gaon." On the evolution of this psychological–spiritual approach to the entry into *pardes* and *Merkavah* mysticism generally, in geonic and medieval Jewish thought, see Elliot R. Wolfson, "Merkavah Traditions in Philosophical Garb: Judah Halevi Reconsidered," *Proceedings of the American Academy for Jewish Research* 57 (1990/1991): 179–242, especially pp. 216 ff. and see further in the Thematic Commentary following the novella, n. 26 (on out-of-body experience) and p. 160 (at end on psychology and soul). However, compare Rabbi Nathan's comment on the talmudic story of the four sages in his lexical comment on *pardes* [*Arukh Ha-Shalem*, ed. Kohut, vol. 6, p. 413]: "It is called *pardes* because of its similarity to the Garden of Eden which is hidden away for the righteous. So that place is a place in the clouds in which the souls of the righteous are bound [*tzrurot*]." As noted by Kohut, this comment is copied from Rabbenu Hananel's commentary on *Hagigah* 14b. It is significant to note that in the continuation of his comment there, Rabbenu Hananel adopts the approach of Rav Hai Gaon to the story of the four sages who entered *pardes*: ". . . but they did not ascend to heaven; rather they contemplated and saw by means of the understanding of the heart. . . ." On readers' ambivalence about the reality of experience described in a literary text as a key characteristic of the "fantastic," see above n. 18.

24. See, for example, the writings of Bousset, Neher, Scholem, Schaefer, Morray-Jones, Liebes, Idel, and Dan listed in the Selected Bibliography at the end of the book.

25. See the classic discussion of this material by Gershom Scholem, *Major Trends in Jewish Mysticism* (New York: Schocken, 1941), pp. 40–79, and the recent reevaluation by Peter Schaefer, *The Hidden and Manifest God—Some Major Themes in Early Jewish Mysticism* (Albany: SUNY, 1992).

26. From a *Genizah* fragment (Cambridge, Taylor-Schechter K 21/95) published by Rachel Elior, *Hekhalot Zutarti*, Jerusalem Studies in Jewish Thought, supp. I (1982), pp. 38–41; the text quoted is also found in Schaefer, *Geniza-Fragmente zur Hekhalot-Literatur* (Tuebingen: Mohr-Siebeck, 1984),

§88, lines 5–6. English translations are found in Halperin, *Faces of the Chariot*, p. 203 (VI), and Morray-Jones, "Jewish Sources" [see Selected Bibliography], p. 198. The parallels are conveniently presented in Schaefer's *Synopse zur Hekhalot-Literatur* (Tuebingen: Mohr-Siebeck, 1981), §388 and on. More than a dozen passages in the various *Hekhalot* texts relate in some way to the story of the four sages who entered *pardes*. See Halperin, *Faces of the Chariot*, pp. 199 ff., for an English translation of a number of these sources (particularly those related to Rabbi Akiba's water warning) and a discussion of the evolution of these sources. For a recent attempt to present the *Hekhalot* versions of the story in a more synthetic way, see Morray-Jones, "Jewish Sources," p. 195 ff.

27. The phrase "to go in and out" has been added from the parallels, see Schaefer, *Synopse* §348. On this passage see Gershom Scholem, *Jewish Gnosticism, Merkavah Mysticism and Talmudic Tradition* (New York: Jewish Theological Seminary, 1965), pp. 77–78.

28. On the folk motif of tokens left to mark a trail, see Stith Thompson, *Motif Index of Folk-Literature* (Copenhagen-Bloomington: Indiana University Press, 1955–1958), H88.

29. Compare "You shall bind them for a sign [*ot*] on your hand . . . and you shall write them upon the doorposts of your house and on your gates" (Deuteronomy 6:8–9, 11:18–20). I am tempted to suggest that the idea of leaving a sign (*siman* or *ot*) on the passageways (*mevo'ot*) may be based on some kind of underlying wordplay on *mavo* ("passageway")—*ot* ("sign"). In ancient times, private homes were often attached "apartments" arranged along public passageways or alleys (*mevo'ot*). Note that 3 Enoch 22B:1, in describing the approach to the seventh hall ("holy of holies"), speaks of a bridge placed over a river that extends "from one end of the passageway (*mavoy*) to the other," while the continuation in verse 4 speaks of "paths of firmament heaven" (*shevilei rakia shamayim*).

30. On the relationship between such "signs" (*simanim*) and the "seals" (*hotamot*) that the *Merkavah* mystic uses to overcome angelic opposition, see Menahem Kasher's *Torah Shelemah*, vol. 22, pp. 187 ff.

31. See, for example, Babylonian Talmud, *Menahot* 29b.

32. On the name of God revealed to Rabbi Akiba when he "descended to the Chariot" and that he taught to his disciples after he descended in peace

from his own heavenly ascent, see *Hekhalot Zutarti* (ed. Rachel Elior, lines 15–19) (Schaefer, *Synopse* §337); Schaefer, *Hidden and Manifest God*, p. 68; Joseph Dan, *The Ancient Jewish Mysticism* (Tel Aviv: MOD Books, 1993), p. 82. On Rabbi Akiba's use of the Divine Names in other parts of *Hekhalot Zutarti*, see Schaefer, *Hidden and Manifest God*, pp. 57, 145–147.

33. See chapter 6 of the novella for a narrative expansion of my interpretation of this *Hekhalot* text.

34. Schaefer, *Synopse*, §410 (MS New York); English translation taken from Halperin, *Faces of the Chariot*, p. 201 (IID).

35. *Faces of the Chariot*, pp. 199 ff. and particularly p. 206; for further recent bibliography on the "water test" and a sympathetic evaluation of Halperin's discussion, see Schaefer, *Hidden and Manifest God*, p. 38 n. 122.

36. See Ginzberg, *Legends of the Jews*, vol. 1, pp. 90–93, 154–157, and the notes in vol. 5, pp. 117–118, 177. In the version of this legend published by Ginzberg in *Ha-Goren* 9, pp. 38–41, the envious angels throw the Book of Raziel into the sea; but God commands Rahab, the angel of the Sea, to restore it to the understandably distraught Adam. On the Book of Raziel, see also Robert Graves and Raphael Patai, *Hebrew Myths: The Book of Genesis* (New York: McGraw-Hill, 1966), p. 53.

37. See Joseph Dan in *Encyclopaedia Judaica*, vol. 13, cols. 1592–1593, s.v. Raziel, Book of, who notes that this book contains extensive quotations from the much earlier work mentioned below. For the beginning of the Book of Raziel, in which the angel gives the book to Adam, see Menachem Kasher's *Torah Shelemah* to the end of Genesis, chap. 3, vol. 2, section 244.

38. See Mordecai Margalioth's introduction (pp. 56–62) to his edition of this work, *Sepher Ha-Razim—A Newly Recovered Book of Magic from the Talmudic Period* (Jerusalem, 1966)[Hebrew]; a translation of Margalioth's text and a brief abstract of his introduction is available in *Sepher Ha-Razim—The Book of Mysteries*, trans. Michael A. Morgan (Chico, CA: Scholars Press, 1983). This same work, reconstructed by Margalioth, was also known as the Book of Raziel (*Sefer Raziel*); both names appear at the beginning of MS Kaufman, the best of the complete manuscripts. Margalioth understands "The Book of Raziel" to be an indication, as it were, of the work's angelic "authorship"; see his introduction, pp. 48–49, 59. See also Menahem Kasher's comments

in *Torah Shelemah*, vol. 22, pp. 188 ff.; and H. Merhavia, in *Kiryat Sefer* 22 (1967): 297–303.

39. This is the reading of the Cairo *Genizah* fragment (Jewish Theological Seminary, Adler 2750/4), which according to Margalioth, pp. 58–59, preserves the more original version of the beginning of *Sefer HaRazim*. The continuation is paraphrased from the Margalioth edition, pp. 65–66. A more complete English translation of this text may be found in *Sepher Ha-Razim*, trans. Michael A. Morgan, pp. 17 ff. Note that in the tenth-century Irish work, *Saltair na Rann*, which is based on earlier sources, Adam is given mystical secrets by Raphael (possibly a mistake for Raziel); see the reference to Graves and Patai, *Hebrew Myths* (below, n. 43).

40. Morgan, in his translation of this text, p. 19, calls attention to the similarity to *Avot* (1:1). Compare Schaefer, *Synopse* §676 (*Merkavah Rabbah*), cited by Schaefer, *Hidden and Manifest God*, p. 109.

41. For a general survey of this theme, see Wolfgang Speyer, *Bucherfunde in der Glaubenswerbung der Antike mit einem Ausblick auf Mittelalter und Neuzeit* (Hypomnemata 24) (Gottingen: Vandenhoeck & Ruprecht, 1970).

42. Composed apparently between 161 and 140 B.C.E. See *The Old Testament Pseudepigrapha*, ed. James H. Charlesworth, vol. 2, p. 44.

43. See 2 Enoch (Slavonic Apocalypse of Enoch) 22:11–12. Margalioth, in his Introduction to *Sepher Ha-Razim*, p. 56 n. 5, argues that the otherwise unexplained name of this archangel in the Slavonic text, Vrevoil/Vereveil or Pirviel, may be a corruption of Raziel. See also, Graves and Patai, *Hebrew Myths*, pp. 53, 119 (on Raphael as an error for Raziel, see there p. 81).

44. See Ginzberg, *Legends of the Jews*, vol. 7 (index), p. 17, s.v. "Adam, books of, details concerning."

45. For a number of versions of this legend, see *Genesis Rabbah*, chap. 24. For an extensive survey of the parallels, see the notes by Theodor in the Theodor-Albeck edition of this work, pp. 232–235, and in Menachem Kasher's *Torah Shelemah* to Genesis 5:1, secs. 2–16.

46. Babylonian Talmud, *Sanhedrin* 38b.

47. On the secret "Book of *Merkavah* Mysticism," see Schaefer, *Hidden and Manifest God*, pp. 72–73.

48. Schaefer, *Synopse* §426 (*Hekhalot Zutarti*).

49. For continued discussion of other traditional motifs and the psychological structure and literary character of Schwartz's work, see my Thematic Commentary appended after the novella.

50. Reprinted in Appendix II to this volume; originally published under the *nom-de-plume*, Moshe ben Yitzhak HaPardesan, "The Four Who Sought to Re-enter the Garden," in *Gates to the New City—A Treasury of Modern Jewish Tales*, ed. Howard Schwartz (New York: Avon, 1983), p. 279. In the same volume (pp. 274–309 and notes, pp. 673–677) Schwartz collected a number of other modern retellings related to the core story of the four sages by M. J. Berdichevsky, Milton Steinberg, Arthur Waskow, Cynthia Ozick, and several of his own preliminary sketches subsequently incorporated into the present novella (one of which, "The Four Who Entered *Pardes*," is reprinted in Appendix I to this volume). For a recent poetic version, see "Four Entered the *Pardes*," in Shirley Kaufman, *Rivers of Salt* (Port Townsend, WA: Copper Canyon Press, 1993), p. 7.

51. On Schwartz's technique of expansively retelling traditional sources, see my survey review, "The Art of Retelling," in *The Jerusalem Post* Magazine, August 12, 1994, p. 20.

THE FOUR
—— WHO ——
ENTERED PARADISE

1

Rabbi Akiba's Dream

On the eve of the ninth of *Av*, the day of mourning for the destruction of the Temple, Rabbi Akiba ben Joseph had a strange and vivid dream. In the dream a great quaking shook the world and he saw a blazing star fall from the heavens and disappear into the sea. After that he found himself sailing in search of a lost treasure. This treasure included a sapphire jewel on which a secret book had been written, and it was this jewel, in particular, that Akiba sought.

Among the sailors with whom he sailed, Akiba recognized only three: Simeon ben Azzai, Simeon ben Zoma, and Elisha ben Abuyah. And at night, when the decks above grew quiet, Akiba and his companions studied an ancient map. They felt certain that if they could decipher the map, they would learn the location of the treasure. But in all the centuries since the map had been found floating in an ancient urn, no one had found how to decipher it. Even the symbol designating the treasure was unknown, as was the relationship of the map to the ocean floor.

Long ago the other sailors had abandoned the map. They simply dove beneath the surface and dug in the ocean floor. And though they had not found any trace of the precious sapphire, sometimes they did recover a beautiful pearl. But the four of them were determined to decipher its secret.

Now, once more, Akiba found his eyes tracing the familiar lines of the map. Sometimes it was a map, and sometimes a mirror. Once, when it was a mirror, Akiba saw himself wandering in a labyrinth, lost in a tangle of possible turns. Then, just before waking, he drew his eyes back and saw the map as if for the first time. It took the form of the letter *Bet*, as it is elaborately inscribed in the opening letter of a scroll of the Torah, with four flourishes on top of it, forming a crown. And Rabbi Akiba could not understand how he had ever failed to recognize it.

When he awoke, Rabbi Akiba recalled every detail of this dream and wondered about its meaning. Surely it was significant that his companions had been the two Simeons and Elisha ben Abuyah, for it was with them that he often studied the Mysteries of the Torah. Although they had been meeting for almost ten years, they had delved so deeply into the first verses of Genesis that they were still discussing them, for those verses were at the heart of the Mysteries of Creation.

Then Rabbi Akiba recalled that it was the day of mourning for the Temple that lay in ruins in the center of Jerusalem. It was the fiftieth year since the Romans had torn down its sacred walls. Somehow Rabbi Akiba felt that his dream must be linked to that tragic anniversary.

That morning everyone assembled beside the ruins of the once magnificent Temple built by King Solomon. And while they were praying, there was a terrible sign: a fox was seen roaming through the ruins, and this sight reduced all those assembled to tears, for it confirmed the verse *For the mountain of Zion, which is desolate, the foxes walk upon it.* Afterward only Rabbi Akiba was able to derive from this sign a message of hope, by pointing out that since this tragedy had been prophesied and fulfilled, so too would the prophecy that one day the Temple would be rebuilt. Had these words come from anyone else they would have been ignored. But since they came from Rabbi Akiba they served as consolation.

As everyone returned to their homes, Akiba signaled for the three sages to follow him. Only to these three could he reveal his grief about the sign in the ruins that morning.

Of the three, Simeon ben Azzai was the youngest, and his devotion to the Torah was legendary. It was said that the words of Torah were as fresh for him as they were on the day they were received from Mount Sinai. He was betrothed to Rabbi Akiba's daughter, and probably no other was on such intimate terms with Akiba.

The second Simeon, ben Zoma, was famous among all the sages for his scholarship, yet he also had distinctly mystical leanings. It was this combination of diligence and mysticism that so attracted Akiba, who also shared these characteristics.

The third sage, Elisha ben Abuyah, Akiba recognized as a true seeker, one who did not accept traditional knowledge until he had verified it for himself. That such a nature could lead to danger was apparent to Akiba, yet among all his associates there was none other who had the instincts of an explorer as did Elisha, and Akiba was grateful that they had become close.

Now Akiba revealed the reason he had brought them together. He told them his dream and asked for their help in trying to interpret it. That is when he learned that each one of them had also remembered a vivid dream, dreams that somehow seemed related to his own.

Ben Zoma said: "In my dream I was drawing a map, and as I finished, I flew up in the air and saw it come to life beneath me. I was flying over an orchard, and when I descended into it I saw a tree from which hung four kinds of fruit, unknown to me among the fruits of this world, each shining like a sun in itself. Then the earth quaked, and three of the fruits fell from the tree. And I thought to myself: if only these fruits had not fallen. And then a voice spoke forth from heaven and said: 'They would still be there but for three finger-breadths.' Then I awoke."

Then Ben Azzai said: "I dreamed that I had forgotten how to speak Hebrew, and I was especially upset that I could not understand the meaning of the word *Bereshit*. Later I decided to enter the letters of the alphabet, one by one, in order to remember the language. But I had gone no further than the second letter, *Bet*, when I found myself in another place, standing outside the gate of a garden. And from there I peered inside and saw that it was a garden of exotic fruit trees and flowers of colors that can only be imagined. So too was it filled with the songs of many birds, that seemed to blend into a beautiful harmony. And as those vivid colors called me closer, the gate swung open, but just as I was about to step into the garden, it disappeared, and I found myself awake, in my room."

The last to report his dream was Elisha ben Abuyah: "In my dream we found ourselves in a cave known as the Cave of the Elders, in which the priceless jewels of our exiled kingdom had been concealed. These jewels had somehow multiplied over the ages, until the day the cave had been violated, and now the sacred jewels were missing. We were the last of the Elders, whose sole duty had been to guard these treasures. The location and even the knowledge of the existence of the cave was a closely held secret. And for ages there had been a legend told among the Elders that foretold the evil that would descend should the jewels, so closely guarded, slip from our grasp. Thus we were shattered to discover that they were missing. Now we faced the end of our lives with the prospect that even the secret location of the cave would itself be lost when we passed out of this world."

When the four sages had finished relating their dreams, Ben Zoma attempted to tie the dreams together. He said: "It is surely significant that in Elisha's dream precious jewels had been stolen, and in Akiba's dream they were being sought. Surely these jewels represent the sacred teachings we have spent our lives attempting to preserve and transmit. Furthermore, in two of the dreams a map plays an important part, and in two dreams the letter *Bet* appears. Finally, both Ben Azzai and I dreamed of a garden not unlike the Garden of Eden, from which Adam and Eve were expelled. Along with the sign of the fox this morning, it is apparent our kingdom is in grave danger and that these dreams are signs from the Holy One, Blessed be He, warning us to take action to preserve the treasures of our kingdom from oblivion."

Without exception the sages agreed with Ben Zoma's interpretation, and then all at once Rabbi Akiba began to speak: "My own dream is starting to become clearer to me. The clue is the secret book inscribed on sapphire which we sought. Do you have any notion of what that might signify?"

"Of course," said Ben Azzai, "there is the tradition of the sacred Book of Raziel, which the angel Raziel revealed to Adam, which was said to have been engraved on a sapphire."

"Exactly!" said Akiba. "And this very Book of Raziel must be what we are seeking."

"How is that possible," asked Ben Zoma, "since that book was among the sacred treasures destroyed with the Temple? Long before that, the original sapphire on which it was engraved was lost, but Noah brought the parchment, inscribed by Enoch, with him on the ark. In this way the book was preserved until the Temple was destroyed. But when the parchment burned the book was lost, and with it, it is said, the gift of prophecy."

"But wait!" cried Akiba. "The parchment burned, but the book was not destroyed." Ben Zoma and the others did not follow at first. Akiba continued. "Do you recall the rest of the tradition about the Book of Raziel? Although it was first revealed to Adam by the angel Raziel, the book itself was said to have been created on the first day of creation, and held in waiting until the day it was revealed."

"Yes!" exclaimed Elisha. "It is said to have been contained inside the first letter of the first word of the Torah. That word is *Bereshit*, 'in the beginning,' and the letter is *Bet!*"

The sages all drew in their breath at the same time. The mystery was beginning to be revealed.

Akiba continued: "Now, since the legend tells us that the Book of Raziel existed even before it was revealed, it follows that it continues to exist: that even though the parchment burned, the letters flew back to the place where they were first revealed.

"This, as we know, was the fate of the letters inscribed on the tablets of the Law. For when Moses saw the golden calf, he threw down the tablets. But before they struck the ground, the holy letters took flight, flying up into heaven. Likewise, the letters of the Book of Raziel surely also took flight when the Temple burned. It is now up to us to seek them out where they can be found, and that place is Paradise! The people of Israel are in grave danger—the presence of the fox this morning makes that all too certain. I feel that a long exile is imminent. The gift of prophecy must be restored if we are not to be the last of the Elders, as in Elisha's dream, and carry to the grave the secrets we have spent our lives attempting to preserve. We must go in search of the Book of Raziel, wherever that search may take us, even if it be into Paradise!"

For a long time the others sages were silent. The quest Akiba proposed was impossible to comprehend. At last Ben Azzai said: "But how can we find our way to Paradise? Surely the answer can be found in the map of the letter *Bet*!"

Rabbi Akiba then spoke the words they were all thinking: "It is known that the whole world was created through the letter *Bet*. Nor should it seem strange that such a map was brought into being, for when a king builds a palace he employs an architect. The architect does not build the palace out of his head, but uses plans and diagrams. Similarly, God must have consulted the map He had created in order to be certain that His creation followed the original plan in every respect. Since the world was created out of words, and since words are made up of letters, it follows that the first letter should contain all those that follow, and the first letter of the Torah is *Bet*. As in my dream, we must regard this letter as the map that will lead us to a place where no living man has set foot since Elijah was taken up into Paradise."

From that time on the four sages meditated on every aspect of the letter *Bet*. Not even to the second letter of the first word of the Torah, *Bereshit*, did they progress, but always came back to the *Bet*. They formed it in their minds before they retired at night, in the hope that additional dreams might reveal more of its secrets; and they thought of it on waking, that they might meditate on it all day. But the task seemed so hopeless that Akiba often recalled the sailors in his dream, who abandoned the mystery of the map and instead chose to dive to the bottom at random, hoping to discover the treasure by chance.

After forty days and nights of such solitary meditation they met together to see if they had made any progress in deciphering the map. Ben Azzai spoke first; he was anxious to set out on the journey and could not understand the confusion of his colleagues. "If the letter *Bet* is a map, as we believe, it must have a specific relationship to the surface of the earth. Our task must be to first discover this relationship, and once we have located a single place in this world that is indicated on the map, it will direct us to where we want to go."

Ben Zoma, on the other hand, was of the opinion that they would be foolish to start their search in this world, since the Book of Raziel no longer existed there. "No," said Ben Zoma, "if we are to search for a link between the map and this world, it will only be because such a place exists to connect this world to the next."

Elisha ben Abuyah agreed with him: "This map links our world and Paradise. Therefore it can be said to exist in both places at the same time. Somehow we must travel from this world to that one. In terms of the map, we have to move from the outside of the letter *Bet* to the *dagesh*, the dot at its center, which is surely our destination, although there is no apparent path to take us there.

"But let me propose a way in which we might succeed in making this journey—it was suggested to me by Akiba's dream, in which the letter appeared not only as a map, but also as a mirror. Indeed, let us approach this map as if it were a mirror. Our task, then, is to peer inside the mirror to find out where we are intended to go. Our first problem is to find out how to look inside the mirror, and once we do, how to find our own reflection among all the mysteries it reveals."

It was Rabbi Akiba who saw how to make use of all these suggestions: "First," said Akiba, "Ben Azzai is right in insisting that we locate one place on earth that is designated on the map. And such a place, I believe, can be found. Try to follow my reasoning: At one point *all* of creation, not only the Book of Raziel, was contained in the letter *Bet*. For the light streamed out through the open side of the letter, illuminating all of creation. Since the Book of Raziel reveals everything that has been or will be, and since the book was once contained within the letter *Bet*, the letter itself can be said to contain a map of all creation. Therefore, if we begin our explorations on earth, as Ben Azzai proposes, we will in fact be selecting a place that is shown on the map, although we may not know where. Then we can seek out a place that can take us from this world to the next, as Ben Zoma has suggested, and Elisha has revealed where Paradise is indicated on our map of the letter *Bet*."

"For now," Akiba continued, "I suggest that we begin our journey by choosing a place on earth we feel certain to be designated on the map —as it exists as a map of the route to Paradise. Now one such place exists in the world, the cave in which not only Abraham, Isaac, and Jacob and their wives are buried, but also where our first father and mother, Adam and Eve, are said to be at rest."

Ben Zoma interjected: "The cave of Machpelah at Hebron?"

"Yes," said Akiba. "I first thought of this cave when Elisha related his dream of the Cave of the Elders, and since then it has become even more apparent to me that this is the best place for us to begin. Remember: we know that the soul of every man and woman who dies must pass through the Garden of Eden on the way to Paradise, and we also know that each and every soul must first pass through the Cave of Machpelah in order to reach the Garden of Eden. Furthermore, the letter *Bet* itself confirms this approach, for it is closed on all sides, except for the front, like a cave. So let us travel to this cave, taking our map of the letter with us, in the hope that Ben Azzai is right that we will find the path to the gates of Paradise there. But first, a warning: even if we do succeed in traveling the path from the Cave of Machpelah to Paradise, who is to say that we will be permitted to pass beyond the gates? As you know, after the expulsion of Adam and Eve from Eden an angel was placed outside the Gates of the Garden, who holds the ever-spinning flaming sword. Only those permitted to enter Paradise can pass beyond that point, while all others will be consumed in the flame. Now is the time for us to consider that even if some or all of us gain admittance, there is still a chance that none of us will ever return."

Here Akiba stopped speaking. Nor did any of the others attempt to reply to his speech. For each one considered what Akiba had said in silence, and each knew that the silence was an assent, for now that they had begun their quest none of them was willing to turn back.

2

The Cave of Machpelah

So it was that in order to reach Paradise, where they hoped to recover the sacred Book of Raziel, the four sages, Ben Zoma, Ben Azzai, Elisha ben Abuyah, and Rabbi Akiba, first journeyed from Jerusalem to Hebron, to the sacred Cave of Machpelah. The cave was located at the end of a field, its entrance guarded by an iron door that dated from the time of our forefathers. The doorkeeper was an old Jew who assumed they had come to visit the burial place of the Patriarchs Abraham, Isaac, and Jacob and their wives. He directed them to cross two empty caves and then to descend twenty-four steps in a narrow passage, in order to come to the six tombs on which the names of the Patriarchs and their wives are engraved.

Each of the sages purchased a candle from the old man and they passed through the outer caves as he had directed them. Inside they saw by the light of the candles that these caves were filled with stone boxes containing bones that had been brought there because the cave was a holy resting place. When they reached the tombs of the Patriarchs they stopped to pray, and afterward Rabbi Akiba took out the map of the letter *Bet*, which he had inscribed on parchment, exactly as he had remembered it in his dream, and held it up to the candle. To progress any further in the cave without guidance was impossible; there in the inner chamber all passages seemed to come to an end. Yet Akiba also knew that the bodies of Adam and Eve were believed to have been laid to rest in the Cave of Machpelah. In fact, Abraham was said to have discovered the cave while chasing after a calf he planned to slaughter for the three angels who had come in disguise to visit him. That is when he discovered the bodies of our first parents there. He knew that at the time of the resurrection of the dead those buried in that cave would be the first to rise up, so he wished to be buried there himself, and eventually purchased the cave and the field that surrounded it from Ephron, for four hundred silver shekels.

Akiba still held the map up to the light, but he could find no clue that would guide them in continuing their journey. Finally he put down the candle and sat down, placing the parchment in front of the tomb of Abraham. It was then that the miracle they had been awaiting came to pass. Although the map was no longer illumined by the light, it continued to glow by itself in the dark. Ben Zoma was the first to notice it. Then all the others saw that a light, growing steadily brighter, was emerging from inside the map. Soon the *dagesh*, the dot inside the letter *Bet*, itself began to glow apart from the parchment, and all of the sages, knowing that they were witnessing a miracle, were speechless.

As Akiba bent over the map, what he saw in the glowing mirror of the *dagesh* was a beautiful garden, with a river winding through it. The current of the river seemed to carry him downstream, until he reached its mouth, where he saw three women, who looked like sisters, and sometimes seemed to blend into a single figure, seated outside the entrance of a cave. Akiba beckoned the others to look into the map. They too saw the mirror and the garden reflected inside it, and when the vision faded it was replaced by another, of the four sages traveling downstream in a small wooden boat. Akiba pointed out the sign on the side of the boat—it was the letter *Bet*!

And no sooner did the sages raise their eyes from the map than they saw the light it cast illuminating the tomb of Abraham, and while they watched the tomb was transformed. It grew young and old, large as the planet they stood on and small as the star that rose above it in the sky. Then they realized that the Patriarch sleeping inside it was both dead and alive, and ruled that sacred place and all those who entered within its boundaries. And they understood that all of them must pass beyond that tomb, that there was no other choice, that this was precisely the route they needed in order to complete their quest; moreover, that this route was their destiny.

Now the map no longer revealed any visions, yet it continued to glow. It was Elisha ben Abuyah who understood that it could now serve to guide them through the cave. And as he lifted the map, the light it cast lit up a small passage at the back of the inner cave, and one by one the four sages crawled through to the other side. And as they passed through it, somehow they passed out of this world into the next, for they had indeed passed beyond the tomb, although they did not know it.

Now, no sooner had they crossed into this secret cave than they saw two beautiful bodies stretched out on their couches, candles burning at the head of their resting places, while a sweet scent pervaded the cave. Adam and Eve! The four sages stood back in awe. The sight of the perfectly preserved bodies of our first parents along with the first, unforgettable fragrance of Paradise was too much to comprehend. For in that one whiff they experienced, one at a time and yet all at the same time, a tide of sweet scents. So too did they gaze at the face of Adam, whose features they had often tried to imagine. Rabbi Akiba first saw the face of his father, and then the face of every man he had ever known. And each of the other sages, too, saw his own father's face in the face of the first father and then the multiple faces of all mankind.

Whispering to the others, Akiba recalled the legend

about Adam bringing Eve into the cave and wanting to go further because he had caught the scent of Paradise, but stopping when a heavenly Voice called out, "Enough!" Therefore Adam and Eve were buried there, so that they could be as close to Paradise as possible. None of the sages would have been surprised had the same Voice called out to them, but the map continued to glow, so they knew they were destined to journey further into the cave.

Now the letter began to glow with a light so bright it was no longer possible to look at it directly, as if it were reflecting a hidden sun. The sages saw that the light it cast led directly to a passage near the ceiling of the cave, which they could reach by climbing up the side. Ben Azzai, the youngest of the four, assisted the others in reaching this passage. Then he followed after them as they descended to a stream that flowed slowly through the center of the new passageway. There they saw an astounding sight: a small wooden boat, the same one they had seen in the mirror of the map, inscribed with the letter *Bet*. This letter must have been engraved with a pen of fire, for the flames still burned there, although it did not cause the boat to be consumed.

A new scent arose from the wood of the boat, also an unforgettable fragrance, for it had been formed from one of the cedars that grew in the Garden of Eden. That is when they noticed that the boat had no oars. "How are we to guide ourselves without any oars?" asked Ben

Azzai. But even as he asked he knew the answer: they must let the current carry them. So without any further questions the sages slid the boat into the water and climbed inside it. Almost at once the slow current began to move the boat downstream, with no sound filling the air except for the sweet singing of the waters.

The four sages were gently rocking back and forth to the motion of the boat, almost hypnotized by the subtle calling of the current. Then Ben Azzai happened to peer over the side and was so startled by what he saw that he almost caused the boat to tip over. At last he regained his composure and was able to speak: "When I glanced down into the water I saw eyes staring at me from beneath the surface—whether of angels or demons I cannot say." Then all of the sages looked into the water and observed a succession of strange images: an animal taking form out of a flower, and a child transformed into a cat. Then many houses, like those in Jerusalem, appeared and were just as quickly torn down, to be replaced by more ancient houses, and these were soon replaced by still more ancient ones. For a time the four sages were certain that a whole ancient city existed beneath the surface, but these images also disappeared.

The frightening visions continued: Elisha saw a tree that had been torn free from its roots; Ben Zoma looked into a vast abyss that seem to break open beneath them, less than a hand's breadth beneath the boat; Ben Azzai saw himself standing before a fiery gate; and Rabbi Akiba saw a scroll of the Law that had lost all its letters.

Shortly after this Rabbi Akiba concluded that they were being carried on the River of Dreams and that the visions rising to the surface were among the multitude of dream images that come to every man and woman while they sleep. The other sages agreed, and they decided they would gladly spend a little time sleeping. Then, choosing Ben Azzai as their guard, the others began dreaming almost before their eyes had closed.

They dreamed of unknown forests, of roots clasped by the earth that grew around them, and of giant rocks for whom a man's lifetime is but an instant. In a single night all of them experienced a month of dreams, and at the same time they listened to unknown songs whose meaning remained hidden. These songs always came back to the beginning and started over again.

Waking uncounted hours later, Akiba found the meaning of the songs revealed in the patterns of the currents rising to the surface of the waters. Even Ben Azzai, their guard, was asleep. Rabbi Akiba looked at his three companions floating in a small boat down the River of Dreams and recalled that it was taking them to Paradise. And as he studied the walls of the caverns he began to recognize patterns repeating themselves, similar forms that could be perceived beneath the natural formations, like a series of crystals. Then Akiba closed

his eyes, for he could no longer discern whether he was
dreaming or awake, nor was he certain that it mattered.
For he had given himself to this venture like a dreamer
to a dream; he was a vessel blessed with wine that bore
the fragrance of Paradise.

When Rabbi Akiba opened his eyes again he realized
at once that they must have floated a great distance. He
had no idea how long they had been sleeping, but now
they were drifting through a forest that grew inside the
cavern. No longer were the rough walls of the cavern
illuminated; now the walls were concealed behind a thick
growth of vines, shrubs, and trees, and the boat barely
made its way beneath the branches that hung low across
the River of Dreams. This transformation startled Akiba
and alerted him to possible dangers. He fought off the
sleep that had gripped him so strongly and shook the
others one by one until they managed to drag themselves
awake. They knew that they must be alert to face whatever dangers lay ahead, but with sorrow they recalled
that they had been deeply immersed in dreams, and now
they would never know how those dreams would have
ended.

While they had been floating down the river they had
been surrounded by silence. The only sound had been
that of the current. Now the cries of many birds echoed
around them, and the rustling of leaves filled the air.
Finally Elisha noticed that their map, resting on the floor
of the boat, had begun to glow again, and soon the light

emerging from the map illumined the forest surrounding them. Ben Azzai, whose sense of direction was impeccable, expressed amazement at the presence of the forest, for, as he pointed out, they had been traveling south, and there could be nothing above them but the wasteland of the Sinai desert. But Akiba had already considered this problem, and he readily replied: "Not wasteland, but an inverted forest, with all the foliage underground!" This concept, so strange at first, was soon accepted by the others as the only logical explanation, unless they had slept much longer than they had realized and had been carried to another part of the world.

The sages did not meditate on this question long, however, because they discovered since waking that they were quite hungry: they had not eaten anything since they had entered the Cave of Machpelah. And now that the thought of hunger had entered their minds, the sages explored the trees that surrounded them on all sides and saw the branches were heavy with every kind of exotic fruit. So abundant was the harvest that they simply needed to reach out and pluck whatever fruit struck their fancy, without even needing to stand up in the boat. They said the blessing over the fruit, as well as the *Sheheheyanu*, the blessing recited over something new: "Blessed art Thou O Lord our God, who has given us life, sustained us, and brought us to this moment." Then the sages delighted in discovering the new tastes of the fruits, and ate their fill.

Soon after this Ben Zoma saw a honeycomb in the hollow of a tree and plucked it as their boat floated past. He tasted the honey, and it was so good that he could not put it down. Rabbi Akiba said: "Have you found honey? Eat what is enough for you." But Ben Zoma could not stop eating, so delicious was it, and he did not heed Akiba's warning. And before long it was all gone.

It was then that the sages noticed for the first time that a dim light was entering the cavern, suggesting they were soon to emerge into daylight. So too did a faint melody drift to their ears. Not long afterward their boat rounded a corner and they were able to discern that the strange river was about to exit from the cavern. The four sages climbed out of the boat, lifting it from the water and setting it down at the side of the cave, for when they would return. Then, with both excitement and trepidation they stepped out of the cave and found themselves in an overgrown forest, surrounded by trees, vines, and a multitude of small plants. So dense was the forest that the sages could find no path to follow. There was only the woods, growing thick and wild wherever they looked.

3

A Faint Melody

After all that had taken place in the Cave of Machpelah and on the River of Dreams, the sages grew accustomed to putting themselves in the hands of destiny. But now there seemed to be no clues to guide them. Akiba, however, had been aware of the faint melody they had first heard in the cave, mixed with the songs of the birds, and now that they had emerged from the cave the melody was clearer. He pointed this out to the others, and after listening intently they all agreed that the voice they heard stirred their souls and made them want to follow it. And since no other possibility presented itself, Akiba suggested that this faint melody might be the clue they needed, and the sages proceeded to make their way through the forest in search of the source of that haunting song.

Before long the song became discernibly louder, and at the same time the wind that carried it to them also brought the fragrant scent they had first encountered on discovering the resting place of Adam and Eve. But now the fragrance was much stronger, though still delicate and inviting. And the combination of the alluring voice and aroma that proceeded from the same direction drew the sages on. At first it seemed as if the song were a wordless melody, but eventually they were able to discern words, which they later discovered to be a secret psalm of King David. For David had not revealed all of his psalms to the world, but had kept ten of them secret, revealing them only in the World to Come. But of course the sages did not know this. They only marveled at how well the lyrics and melody fit together, as if they had been created at the same time, as, indeed, they had been.

So it was that the four sages made their way through the forest, using the voice as their guide until they came to a clearing where they saw a young woman who was seated on the edge of a clear pool, holding a child. She was very beautiful, with long, black hair and pale skin, and a high, clear forehead. While she sang, she wove a golden garment, and when the sages came close enough to see it, they saw themselves reflected within it, as if it were a mirror, and their lives passed before them, from the time they were born until that very moment.

And when this vision ended, the sages knew that she who wove that garment must be blessed indeed. Just then the young woman looked up and saw the sages, and she stopped singing. But the melody had been so beautiful

that all the sages wanted her to continue, and Ben Azzai
spoke for them all when he said: "We did not intend to
interrupt your song." As she turned toward them, the
sages saw a pearl that seemed balanced in her long hair,
which was swept away from her forehead. The sages
were so awed by her exceptional beauty that all of them
averted their eyes. She smiled at this gesture of modesty
and said: "You are welcome in this kingdom. I have
known for some time that you would be coming, and I
have awaited your arrival. Although wandering spirits
are quite common here, the approach of the living is
quite rare, and the birds have reported your arrival to
everyone who makes his home here."

At this explanation the sages grew afraid, for they had
almost forgotten that they were in a world whose ways
were foreign to them. But the mention of wandering
spirits brought them back to their task by reminding
them of the route souls must take on their way to Paradise. And Rabbi Akiba decided that he would raise the
question of how the sages might find the way to the
Garden of Eden, the next stage of their journey.

The young woman continued to speak, introducing
herself as Neshamah and her child as Kohava. She told
them that she lived with her two sisters in a cave not far
from the pool. In turn the sages introduced themselves,
and as they spoke, each became aware that this young
woman reminded him of someone very close. Ben Zoma
thought he saw something in her features that reminded

him of his mother; Elisha thought he saw a resemblance to his sister; and Ben Azzai thought he recognized something of his betrothed, who was Akiba's daughter. For Akiba, though, the resemblance was quite miraculous, for he recognized features and gestures that reminded him of his mother, his wife, and his daughter. And with this recognition, each sage secretly felt love and affection for this young woman similar to the emotions they felt for the loved ones she resembled.

After the sages had introduced themselves, each of them urged Neshamah to continue singing her song. And as she sang, they again observed the pearl she wore in her hair. They now saw that it was quite extraordinary, suspended as if it were a sun or moon in itself, glowing with a light of its own.

While Neshamah sang, her song uplifted the spirits of the four and carried them across the forest to the place they sought, Paradise. Hearing that song, they knew with certainty that its melody must have had its origin there. For her voice and the melody awoke in them a great longing for Paradise, such as they had never before known.

When Neshamah had finished singing, the sages were silent, and their souls glowed like the map of the letter *Bet* when they were being carried by the currents down the River of Dreams. Finally Rabbi Akiba told Neshamah of their quest and asked if she could guide them to the gates of the Garden. But no sooner were these words out of his mouth than the fabulous pearl that was balanced above her forehead flew out of her hair and fell into the pool. "The pearl!" cried Neshamah, and the four sages, who only a moment earlier had sensed that their entrance into Eden was imminent, saw their chances disappear as the pearl sank out of sight to the bottom of the pool. At that moment a remarkable transformation took place: both the sky and the waters grew dark, so that in a moment the daylight had disappeared and night seemed to fall. Now Neshamah began to sob over the loss of her pearl, and the sages tried to console her, by saying they would gladly try to retrieve it once the waters became clear and the daylight returned.

But Neshamah could not be consoled, and from her sobbing the sages understood that only the recovery of the pearl could bring back the light, for it was the soul of the moon itself. The sages saw that Neshamah was too distraught to help them, so they discussed the matter among themselves. They decided to simply dive into the pool and search for the pearl there. Ben Azzai, the youngest, quickly offered to do so, and the others agreed to let him go because they all wanted to console Neshamah as soon as possible.

Moments later Ben Azzai dove into the water. It swirled around him and washed him with its freshness. For even though the water was dark, it was drawn from the deepest and purest springs in existence. Now Ben Azzai was looking for a single glowing pearl, but instead he saw three bright objects at the bottom. Drawing a long breath, he dove all the way down. It was a long dive, which seemed to take years, and yet, all that time, he never felt short of breath. At last Ben Azzai reached the bottom and scooped up the three glowing stones. One of them, he felt sure, must be the pearl.

Then Ben Azzai turned upward, and the moment he did his head emerged from the pool, as if the waters had evaporated around him, and he climbed out of the pool with the gems in his hand. The others greeted him, anxious to know if he had succeeded. But when Ben Azzai opened his hand, they saw no pearl among the three gems he had recovered. Instead, there was a carnelian, a topaz, and an emerald, which were among the precious gems worn on the breastplate of the High Priest.

When Ben Zoma saw this, he climbed into the pool and took a deep breath. He submerged as did Ben Azzai, and likewise he saw three glowing gems on the floor of the pool and recovered them. But they, too, did not include the pearl. Rather they consisted of a turquoise, a sapphire, and an amethyst, which were also among the precious stones of the breastplate.

Elisha ben Abuyah fared as did the others, and brought back gems of jacinth, agate, and crystal. But the pearl was still missing.

Soon Rabbi Akiba found himself diving to the bottom of that pool, and all the way down it felt as if he

were diving into the depths of his soul. He likewise recovered three more glowing gems, though the pearl was
not among them either. They were beryl, lapis lazuli,
and jasper. But together those gems constituted all twelve
gems of the breastplate. Just as the sages realized this, the
missing pearl suddenly reappeared in Neshamah's hair.

"It's back!" Ben Zoma cried. And Neshamah looked
at her reflection in the pool and saw that the pearl had
indeed been restored. And she smiled at the sages and
said: "By this you have proven yourselves worthy of
entering the Garden. For the precious gems you have
recovered have been lost in the pool a long time. Put
them in a safe place, and keep them close to your heart.
They will protect you on your journey. As for me, I
will be more than happy to become your guide. But first,
drink from the spring beside the pool, which is its
source." Now until then the four sages had not seen the
spring. But when Neshamah pointed it out to them, they
saw there was a beautiful spring hidden behind some
nearby bushes. So too did they now hear the waters of
the spring for the first time. Neshamah led the sages to
the spring, and there they saw the water bubbling up
from below. And those were the purest waters they had
ever seen, so pure they were transparent.

Then the sages put the jewels away, and one by one
they bent over that spring, cupped water in their hands,
and took long drinks. That was the purest water they

had ever tasted, for those were the primordial waters that were created on the second day of creation. That long drink satisfied a thirst so deeply felt they had almost forgotten it. Their thoughts became as clear as those waters, and when they sat up and looked around, they saw that they were no longer in a forest, but in another place, whose dimensions were only beginning to become clear. Neshamah saw their confusion and said: "Now that you have tasted these living waters, you will slowly begin to see what has so far been hidden from your sight. You must know that you are *already* inside of Eden, but have yet to reach the Garden that can be found within its boundaries, as it is written, *A river went out of Eden to water the Garden*. For Eden and the Garden are distinct. All this was hidden from you until now as if behind a veil, but now you have proven yourselves worthy of having your eyes opened."

As Neshamah's words began to sink in, the sages had their first glimpse of the light of Paradise, which glowed like an aura around her and illumined every tree and flower they saw. Ben Azzai was the first to point out that they themselves were surrounded by this same aura, a divine presence that hovered over everything, touching yet not touching, like a dove hovering over its nest.

With every passing minute the eyes of the sages saw more of the world that had been hidden from them while they were within its midst. Looking up into the night sky they were astonished to find not one but two moons.

At first they thought the second moon might only be a reflection of the first in the clouds that floated beside it. But as the veil was lifted from their eyes they saw that it was, in fact, a second moon, whose place was right beside the first. The sages asked Neshamah about this, and she said: "The second moon exists, as you can see, but it is invisible to almost everyone unless they have the good fortune to glimpse it from the right angle, when the proper constellations are in place. And even then it remains a mystery, for the second moon is the exact opposite of the first, waning when the other waxes, and waxing when the other wanes. But once it has been sighted, this second moon can always be seen again, and any question asked in its presence will be replied to in a dream that will be delivered that same night."

As Neshamah spoke Elisha happened to look down and saw that he and the other sages were each casting two shadows. The first looked familiar, while the second was much lighter. Neshamah saw that he was perplexed by this extra shadow, and she said: "Do not be disturbed, Elisha, that you have seen your second shadow. It has always existed, but like your soul it was invisible to you until now. Nor could you have seen it until this stage in your journey."

Then all of the sages looked down and marveled at their second shadows, which grew darker in their vision and soon seemed as natural as one shadow had seemed before. Now, too, the sages became aware of occasional sounds in the winds, sometimes quite close, and sometimes far away, and they were accompanied by a strange rustling in the trees. Finally the sages began to perceive faint shapes moving through the forest, sighing as they traveled from place to place. "Are these some kind of spirits?" asked Ben Zoma. Neshamah replied: "Yes, these are wandering souls that have passed, as you did, through the Cave of Machpelah and down the River of Dreams. Like you, they are searching for the gates of the Garden of Eden. But because their eyes were closed to their souls when they were among the living, now it is the fate of their souls to wander blindly in endless circles. But because your eyes were open to the way of the Torah, you were able to follow the signs of the hidden Torah, which is the path of truth. That is how you reached this place. For the knowledge you seek is the key to Paradise."

Hearing these words, the four sages realized that they had somehow crossed over to the World to Come and had truly found their way into Eden. That is when they understood that they too were souls wandering in that world. And they wondered if they would ever return alive to the world of men. But now the quest called them, and the image of the Book of Raziel was fixed in their vision. At the same time, the fate of those wandering souls haunted them, and they vowed never to be blind to their own souls.

Nor had they forgotten their quest. Even as they looked around at the unearthly beauty of Eden, with sacred lights glowing all around them, the reaches of heaven remained before them, waiting to be explored, and the Book of Raziel still glowed like a bright star in their vision, with the knowledge and hope it would bring to a weary world. Neshamah saw that the sages were filled with the wonders of Eden and the calling of their quest. She smiled at them and said: "Now I must go, and you should let yourselves sleep, for tomorrow will be a memorable day."

As she said this the sages realized they were tired, though not exhausted, by any means, for the desire to sleep in Eden is sweet, not bitter, and sleep is as welcome as are the fragrant, sacred flowers whose beauty surrounded them. But Ben Azzai had one last question for Neshamah: "Please tell us who you are and how you came to be here in Eden."

She replied: "Just as you are the sons of men, I am a daughter of the Bride, as are my sisters. We make our home in Eden. For many years we have known that you were coming. We have been awaiting your arrival for a very long time. And that is all for now. Good night."

Then Neshamah walked away, leaving the four sages filled with wonder as they lay down on the soft moss and closed their eyes for their first night's sleep in Eden.

4

The First Night in Eden

A s they slept, dreams came to each of the sages, leaving deep imprints on their souls. Ben Azzai dreamed that he flew from his body and floated beside the blossoms at the top of a tree, then dove into the earth and lay still while his body stood guard above him. Ben Zoma dreamed of a magic tortoise, a creature possessed of such supernatural power that it lived on air and needed no earthly nourishment. Its shell was pure white, with the flaming letter *Bet* inscribed on it. Elisha dreamed that he was sailing on a river with the other sages, and that they threw out their nets like fishermen to probe the treasures that floated beneath the surface. Then they followed the river to its source and discovered that it branched into two paths, one ending in fire, one in ice. As for Akiba, he dreamed of a bird whose feathers were woven of moon rays, whose heart was a living opal, and whose wings in flight echoed the crystalline music of the stars.

Rabbi Akiba, wakened by the sound of wings, was the first to open his eyes the next morning. At first he thought he was still dreaming of the magical bird. Then he saw three young eagles circling above him, their soft feathers drawn around them, gray and white. As he watched, Akiba saw something quite strange: sometimes the three eagles seemed to blend into one, while a moment later he saw all three again soaring side by side. This happened several times before the eagles landed on the other side of the rock that stood next to the pool of living waters, where the sages had first found Neshamah. Then Akiba saw Neshamah and two other young women who bore a close resemblance to her emerge from behind the rock and come toward the place where the other sages were still sleeping.

Akiba quickly woke the others. All of them found it hard to believe that they had reached the Land of Eden. They told each other their dreams, and then they went to greet Neshamah and her sisters, whom she introduced as Ruah and Nefesh. Akiba saw that the three sisters sometimes seemed to blend into one figure, who was somehow more complete than any one of the three by herself. This he linked to the three eagles, and he understood that the sisters had the power to alter their form.

It was while they were greeting the sisters that the sages first became aware of the prayers drifting toward them from every direction: one blessing followed another, rising and falling, floating beside the blossoms. At the same time the sages also became aware of bright bodies of light scattered around them, in trees, in the air, and on the earth, which were the source of these prayers. Then the knees of the sages became weak, and Ben Zoma confessed that since they had begun their journey they had lost track of time, and that it must surely be the Sabbath, judging from the prayers that pervaded the air—and the bodies of light that seemed to be their source, were they angels?

"Yes," said Neshamah, "it is indeed the Sabbath. But you need not fear that you have been remiss, for in Paradise the Sabbath is celebrated every day of the week, with both the souls of the righteous and the angels offering prayers to the Holy One, blessed be He. It is just that now your eyes have been opened enough for you to perceive the prayers floating around you."

"Likewise," she continued, "the bodies of light you have begun to see are angels, whose presence will become more apparent after you have drunk again from the sacred waters. Eventually you will be able to communicate with them even as you do with us—for you should know that outside of Eden even we would be invisible to you, but now you have purified yourselves enough to see us."

"But tell me," asked Ben Azzai, "why yesterday did the sighs of the wandering spirits fill my ears and today those sighs are nowhere to be heard and the air is pervaded with prayers?"

Then Ruah said: "That is because as your ears began to open, along with your eyes, you were first able to detect the wandering souls, for your perceptions yesterday were more human than divine; you had more in common with the lot of the suffering than the grace of the blessed. But by now you have begun to transcend your bodily bondage, and your ears no longer listen for sighs of unhappy souls, but instead have opened to the prayers of the blessed."

"And now," said Neshamah, "you should know that for the rest of your stay in Paradise you will be spared all bodily hungers and need only concern yourselves with the hungers of your souls. I think you will find that all but the sacred fruits have grown invisible, and to sustain yourselves you need only drink once a day from the streams throughout Eden. They are all fed by the same source flowing out of the sacred Tree in the center of the Garden."

With that the sisters offered the sages gourds from which to drink, and one by one they sipped the living waters, knowing, as they did, that their eyes would continue to open. Soon it would be their destiny to explore those parts of Paradise that are concealed from all except those who are truly counted among the blessed.

The sages saw that Neshamah was holding a robe that she was repairing. The cloth of the robe was of a thin, luminous material that looked like it had the consistency of light. The sages asked her if the robe was her own, and Neshamah replied that it was robe of the *Shekhinah* that she had been wearing at the time the Temple was destroyed. The Bride of God, who is also the Sabbath Queen, had been greatly reluctant to abandon the Temple that was her home, and did not depart until the flames had entered her very dwelling place, the Holy of Holies. Then, as she rose up, a spark of the flames caught the hem of her gown and it began to burn. By the time she had returned to her heavenly home nothing remained of the robe but a single thread, but this was enough to reconstruct the robe. For a single thread remaining from the old garment sufficed to give the new one the essence of the old. Neshamah had worked on repairing the robe since then, and now the work was approaching completion, for with every stitch she took she connected the upper and lower worlds and brought them closer.

The sages marveled at this account of the robe and began to realize how fortunate they were to have arrived in that realm of the blessed. "And now," said Neshamah, "to protect from having the veil fall over your eyes again, it is required that each of you plant a seedling or flower, which will root you to the earth of Eden forever. For the sacred fruits and plants of Eden never die unless, Heaven forbid, someone plucks one of them. But in the history of Eden that has only happened once, when the serpent tempted Eve into disobeying the command of the Holy One, blessed be He. For the fruit that she picked was from the Tree of Souls, and because of her error the souls of many generations were torn from the Tree."

Reminded of the consequences of that single act, which still reverberated in the world, Ben Azzai became frightened and asked the sisters how they could avoid harming those sacred plants.

"Ah," said Neshamah, "you will easily distinguish the sacred plants of Eden from the others because of the light that glows from within them. These sacred plants are closely tied to the fate of beings both living and dead, and to their families and future generations. For their souls can flourish only as long as these sacred plants continue to grow, but should they be plucked, terrible damage would be done. Look around you now and see if you can recognize them." And when the sages raised their eyes, they saw glowing lights scattered all around them, arising from plants and flowers and fruits wherever they turned. As they gazed in amazement, Ben Zoma became uncomfortable, afraid that in their ignorance the sages might have damaged some of those sacred plants before the veil was lifted from their eyes. He shared this fear with Neshamah and she replied: "There is no need to worry—like the other secrets of Eden, these plants were quite invisible to you while your eyes were closed, and beyond harm. It is only now that you must take care not to damage them." And all of the sages assured her that they would take the greatest care with those plants. Then, one by one, each of them kneeled reverently and said a prayer, then planted a seed in Eden and thus rooted himself in the World to Come. And each of those seeds sprouted at once, breaking open like shattered vessels, and a glorious light shone forth.

After that, the four sages followed the sisters on a winding path. Along the way they noticed a structure that was only beginning to materialize for them, but already was stunning in its beauty and almost blinding in its brightness. Elisha asked Neshamah what it might be, and she said: "That is a hidden palace, secret and unknown, a palace of longing that is closed to all but the Messiah. On the night of *Rosh Hodesh*, when there is a new moon, the Messiah enters that palace. He lifts up his voice, and weeps, and two tears fall from his eyes into the Ocean of Tears. That is the ocean that holds all the griefs of the Jews. Nor will the Messiah be able to come until all those tears are dried."

And Ben Azzai said: "How can that Ocean of Tears be dried?"

Neshamah replied: "Only the Holy One, blessed be He, has that power."

As they accompanied the sisters, the sages were aware of how close they felt to them. And Ben Azzai said: "We have come here searching for the Book of Raziel. But even if we were to proceed no further, it would be enough. For we have seen divine wonders and have been fortunate enough to find our way into Eden, where we met you."

The sisters were moved by these words, as were the other sages. Neshamah said: "Surely you must be counted among the righteous to have found your way here. No book is held in such high esteem in heaven as the Book of Raziel, because here it is known that the book is actually the Hidden Torah. For there is the revealed Torah, which God dictated to Moses at Mount Sinai. But there is a hidden Torah as well. Tell me, what is the one thing you would most like to read about in the Hidden Torah?" And the sages thought deeply on this before they spoke. At last Ben Zoma said: "I am seeking the Mysteries of Creation, for ever since I was a child I have longed to know the secrets of how the world came into being."

Then Ben Azzai said: "Once, when I was studying Torah, a flame surrounded my body, and I heard the words of the Torah as they were spoken at Mount Sinai. And when I opened my eyes I saw the chariot in the vision of Ezekiel, and a bolt of electrum passed through me, and for a long instant my soul flew from my body. And I heard a voice say 'Rise, for magnificent palaces and golden beds await you in Paradise.' Ever since I have pursued the Mysteries of the Chariot, for they haunt me night and day. It is these I would hope to find in the Hidden Torah."

Elisha ben Abuyah was the third to speak: "I have

always been drawn to seek knowledge of God, for God is the source of all knowledge. Yet the Mysteries of the Godhead are well hidden. Surely these mysteries would be revealed in the Hidden Torah."

At last Rabbi Akiba said: "The Torah is the map and charter given to us by the Holy One, blessed be He, and it is our duty to study that map and let it guide us as we make our way in the world. It was by following the path of the Torah that we came to be here, and it is the light of the Hidden Torah that we seek."

And Neshamah smiled a great smile, so that her whole being seemed to be illuminated. And she said: "Let your words be for a blessing." And the sages replied: "Amen."

Then Ben Zoma said: "You have been so good to us and made us feel at home in this world. Tell me, is there some way that we could help you?"

And Neshamah said: "You have already helped us, simply by pursuing your quest. But there is one thing I would ask of you. If you succeed in entering the Garden, seek out sparks of the primordial light. This is the sacred light that was created on the first day of creation, when God said, '*Let there be light.*' That light shone from ten vessels of primordial light that the Holy One sent forth at the beginning of time. Their light was all pervasive, and in it Adam could see from one end of the universe to the other. But when Adam and Eve tasted the forbidden fruit, all but one of the vessels of that primordial light shattered, and the holy sparks were scat-

tered throughout the world. A great many fell on the
Holy Land. But the real treasury of these sparks is hidden in the Garden of Eden. Each of these sparks bears a
great blessing. Gather as many of them as you can, and
take them with you. They will make the way easier for
you."

These words thrilled the four sages, for they longed
to glimpse that primordial light, which had been hidden for so long. And now they knew that this light could
aid them in their quest. And Rabbi Akiba asked: "And
what shall we do with those sparks?"

Neshamah said: "If you can, give them to the Messiah. For the more sparks that are gathered for him, the
sooner his footsteps will be heard in the world."

The thought that they might in this way contribute
to the coming of the Messiah stirred every one of the
sages. And they assured Neshamah that they would
search for those sparks everywhere, and that they would
take any that they found with them. God willing, they
would personally give them to the Messiah.

At last they arrived at a gate that was guarded by two
angels, standing back to back, with swept-back wings
that were almost touching: one spinning a sword of
flame, the other guarding the way to the Tree of Life.
Here the sisters told the sages that they must continue
on their own, and gave them one last word of advice:
not to hesitate when an opportunity arose to pass through
the gate, or they would not be permitted to enter. It

was then that the sages gazed upon the terrible countenance of the angel facing them, and the fiery circle of its sword. And they wondered at the face of the other angel, which they could not see. Frightened, the sages turned to look back and found that the sisters had gone, and all they saw were three eagles disappearing into the distance.

Confronted with that fiery sword, the sages did not know what to do next. To try to pass that sword while it was spinning would surely mean death. Indeed, because the reflection of the flaming sword was so bright, three of the sages shielded their eyes or turned away from it. Only Rabbi Akiba dared to look directly at it. There he saw a mirror that reflected the sages as they stood before the gate. This discovery gave Akiba an idea—he told Ben Zoma to give him the map of the letter *Bet*, and when Ben Zoma took it out they found the *dagesh*, the dot inside the letter *Bet*, glowing brightly, reflecting the light of the flaming sword as if it were a mirror. Akiba held up the map and the reflection from the flaming sword was directed back upon the angel that spun it. Blinded for an instant, the angel stopped spinning the sword. Akiba whispered for the sages to enter quickly, without hesitating, and they slipped beneath it into the Garden, for that flaming sword was itself the gate. And only an instant later the cherub uncovered his eyes and resumed spinning the sword. That is when the second angel, who guards the way to the Tree of Life, saw the four sages, and they were afraid for their lives.

But instead of casting them out, the angel said: "Welcome, rabbis. Your coming here has been foretold for many generations." So it was that the second cherub welcomed them inside the garden, for he only kept out those who were forbidden to enter, and he had long known that the day would come when he would welcome the four sages into Paradise. For their mastery of the Torah was often spoken of on high. It was said that they had pierced the secrets of the Mysteries of Creation as well as the Mysteries of the Chariot, and by following the hidden light of the Torah they had reached that sacred place.

5

The Garden of Eden

Now as soon as the sages set foot in the Garden of Eden, they realized that they had entered a world both very foreign and yet strangely familiar. Just as the sisters had warned them, they each perceived the Garden in their own way. For they saw not just one Garden, but four, with paths that led in divergent directions. Yet because of their trust in Rabbi Akiba, they agreed to let his vision guide them, even when it conflicted with their own. For Rabbi Akiba had a sure instinct for following the right path.

Now when they first entered the Garden, it seemed dark to their eyes, as if it were night. Only little by little did their eyes adjust, and the hidden forms of the Garden reveal themselves. Then the sages saw that the Garden resembled a beautiful orchard, with many trees bearing exotic and fragrant fruit. As they were walking in the Garden, Elisha saw something glowing. He reached beneath a leaf and brought back a glowing spark, and when he showed it to the others, Ben Zoma said: "Surely that is one of the sparks that Neshamah told us to search for. You have been blessed to find it." The others agreed, but Ben Azzai wondered how Elisha would carry it. So Elisha explained that from the moment he had touched it, it had remained with him.

After that the sages searched for those sparks in every crevice and under every leaf, and they found them scattered everywhere in the Garden. And each time they came close enough to touch a spark, it remained with them, brightening the world around them, bringing it into greater focus. Then Ben Azzai reminded them of the words of Isaiah: *Behold, all of you kindle a fire and surround yourselves with the sparks. Therefore you are only walking in the light of your own fire and in the sparks you have kindled.* And now these words echoed for the sages in a completely new way, and they knew that Isaiah also knew the secret of the sparks.

Now the very act of gathering those sparks gave the four sages the greatest pleasure, for they saw how each spark they gathered was holy. And in the aura of those sparks, the four sages found themselves fully immersed in a sacred world, so that they were never tempted to turn from the path of righteousness.

Now Rabbi Akiba noticed that the number of sparks they found increased when they went in one direction and decreased when they went in another. He brought this to the attention of the other sages, and Ben Azzai said: "Do you remember the words of Neshamah? She said that the true treasury of sparks lies in the Garden of Eden. I thought she was referring to the abundant sparks we have already found. But perhaps there exists such a treasury of sparks."

And Rabbi Akiba said: "That is exactly what I was thinking, for those same words of Neshamah had come back to haunt me."

Elisha then said: "If such a treasury exists, surely the sparks can lead us to it. Let us follow the path they form."

Then the four sages peered across the Garden of Eden and saw that the scattered sparks did indeed form a path, which they now beheld for the first time. They followed that path and it led them to a cave. Sparks could be seen floating out of that cave, spreading across the Garden. At first the sages were reluctant to enter that cave, because it seemed to be such a holy place. But when they remembered that the sparks could not only aid them in their quest, but could assist the coming of the Messiah, they realized they could not turn back.

Now they had to crawl for a long distance through a passage filled with those sparks. At last they came to a large cavern, and there they saw a Holy Ark. But when they opened the doors of that Ark, expecting to find a scroll of the Torah, the sages found instead a large, glowing vessel of light. The sight of that beautiful vessel left them speechless, and they saw how it cast forth a multitude of sparks, while its own light was undiminished. Then Rabbi Akiba understood that it was the one vessel of light that had not broken, but had been preserved in that Ark. And that, surely, was the treasury of sparks.

As they stood in the presence of that divine vessel, the four sages felt its holy light surround them and purify their souls. And they opened their arms and collected armloads of sparks. And when they looked at each other, they saw that each of them was surrounded by an aura. And Rabbi Akiba said: "Surely we are fortunate to have stood in the presence of this holy vessel. For now I am certain that our souls have been purified enough that we will be permitted to enter into the heavenly realms. And without our having found it, we might never have progressed any further." And all of the sages agreed that finding that unbroken vessel had strengthened their faith and filled them with holiness.

Then Rabbi Akiba closed the Ark, and the four sages made their way out of that sacred cave. And when they emerged from that cave, they found that their sight had been transformed, and they could not only see everything in the Garden, but to the ends of the universe. When they discovered this, the sages were tempted to focus their attention on the world they had left behind. But Rabbi Akiba quickly warned them not to do this, for they might be distracted from their quest. The others recognized that he was right, and after that they kept their eyes focused solely on the Garden and paid close attention to everything they encountered there.

Now that they had emerged from the sacred cave, the sages began to see angels everywhere, ascending and descending, hidden in the branches of trees, singing and praying, and guarding over them. So too did the four discover that not only had their eyesight improved, but their hearing as well.

At first they heard something that sounded like whispering nearby, though they could not make out the words. But as they listened closely, they began to understand what was being said. In this way they learned that they could overhear the angels, as well as the heavenly voices that came forth from time to time. Much to their surprise, they found that the angels were whispering about their quest, and how it was being spoken of in every heavenly palace. This reminded them of the urgency of their mission, and they knew that they must find a way to ascend on high. But even though they had come much further than they had ever imagined possible, all the way into the Garden of Eden, they had no idea how they might proceed from there.

At last Rabbi Akiba decided that they must try to make contact with the angels. And no sooner did he speak of this to the others than they heard an angelic voice say: "Until this moment, you were not ready to become our partners in this world, but now the time has come to greet you." The sages looked around, and there before them stood an angel, face to face. All of them were struck dumb, except for Rabbi Akiba, who said: "We are overwhelmed in the presence of such a holy being as your-self. Please, tell us who you are."

The angel said: "I am Shamshiel, guardian angel of the Garden of Eden. I have been sent to guide you in the Garden. I was with you from the first, but until you had gathered enough of the holy sparks, you could not com-municate with me." Then the four sages knew that they were blessed indeed, and they were grateful to Neshamah for telling them to search for the scattered sparks.

After that Shamshiel accompanied them everywhere and revealed the mysteries of the Garden to them. One of the strangest sights was a vast number of sleeping angels. Elisha asked about this, and Shamshiel said: "Yes, these angels spend much of their time sleeping. But no matter how long they may sleep—one hundred, two hundred years—ten centuries is not too much—the first to wake up takes the torch that has been handed down, adds a drop of oil to the lamp, blesses the eternal light, and then recalls the name of every other angel. And one by one, as they are remembered, they wake up."

Just then one of the sleeping angels did awake and did exactly as Shamshiel had said, recalling every angel's name. And, indeed, as they were remembered, they did wake up. Then the sages knew that for those angels there was nothing more beautiful than memory.

Now the sages noticed that some of the angels had come to clean and sweep. As the sages looked around, they saw leather soles and straps lying in the grass in the

Garden, and sometimes even whole sandals. And they wondered how they had gotten there. Rabbi Akiba asked for an explanation, and Shamshiel said: "These sandals came from Jews who danced with the Torah on Simhat Torah. For just as Sandalphon weaves crowns out of the prayers of Israel for the Holy One to wear on His Throne of Glory, so does he make crowns out of the sandals of those who dance with the Torah."

When the four sages heard this, they were so over-joyed that they kicked up their feet in dancing until all of their sandals had flown off their feet. And they saw how the angels collected those sandals and put them together in a bundle for the angel Sandalphon. Now as soon as their sandals were off, the sages discovered, to their great pleasure, that they could fly. All they had to do was to turn their thoughts toward where they wanted to go, and in an instant they would find themselves there. Just as the sages were making this discovery, Shamshiel took flight, and Ben Azzai told the others to hurry, so that they might follow him, for he wanted to know where he might lead them.

As they flew above the Garden of Eden, the sages were astonished at its great size. For it stretched in every di-rection as far as they could see, no matter how high they flew. At last they came to realize that the Garden of Eden was infinite from the inside, even though it appeared to be much smaller from without. That is when they under-stood that they had truly reached the *Olam ha-Ba*, the

World to Come. For there time and space are infinite and eternal, as is the Holy One Himself, blessed be He.

At last Shamshiel alighted in a beautiful orchard and told them that the time had come to see the Tree of Knowledge. Now when the sages learned this, they trembled with fear, for they had not forgotten the fate of Adam and Eve. The angel saw their trepidation and said: "Know that no one who enters this Garden can go any further until they have stood before the Tree of Knowledge." And when they heard this, the sages realized that there was no turning back.

Thus the Angel led the four sages to the tree whose forbidden fruit changed all of history. But when they reached that tree, each of the sages saw something else.

What Ben Azzai saw was a tree that burned without being consumed. And when he saw it, he felt certain that Moses must have seen not a burning bush, but a branch of that very tree. And when he looked upon those branches burning eternally in that flame, Ben Azzai suddenly felt the immortality of his soul, and he became supremely happy. Yet when the vision vanished he broke out into sobs, for the illusions of existence had been torn from his eyes, and afterward he was able to see only the forms behind reality, the seams of creation, but not the forms of creation themselves.

As for Ben Zoma, he saw a tree of unimaginable beauty, which bore a single fruit that glowed as brightly as the sun. So bright was it that he had to shade his eyes, and he understood that the single fruit represented its Creator, the Holy One, blessed be He.

Elisha ben Abuyah saw two trees growing there, a Tree of Life and a Tree of Death. For each seed of the Tree of Life also contains a seed of the Tree of Death, so closely are they entwined. In fact, he saw how it is impossible to have one without the other, for that is the way the Holy One had brought them into being. Then Elisha understood how from the seed of Isaac came both Jacob and Esau. For Jacob traced his descent from the Tree of Life, since it is written, *The Torah is a Tree of Life to those who cling to it.* But Esau traced his descent to the Tree of Death, for it was said that he had the countenance of the Angel of Death.

As for Rabbi Akiba, he saw a tree bearing a unique, jewel-like fruit, which glittered like precious gems and glowed with a light from within. That light illumined every corner of the garden, and Rabbi Akiba saw first-hand how the light of knowledge illuminates the world. Nor could he understand how anyone could pluck that precious fruit.

After each sage had his own vision of the Tree of Knowledge, the angel Shamshiel revealed one of the greatest secrets of the Garden: that the Tree of Knowledge contains a hidden gate. At first the sages could not see it, but then the map of the *Bet* began to glow brightly,

and its light revealed a gate. The sages could barely believe their eyes and turned to the angel Shamshiel, who
said: "The book you have been seeking lies beyond this
gate, which is known as the Gate of Knowledge, and
the key is in your hands." Then Rabbi Akiba realized
that the map of the letter was the key to the gate, and
as he held it up, the mirror of the map shone brightly
on the gate, and it flew open. An instant later the sages
found themselves inside a glowing cloud, where a bright
aura surrounded their bodies and glowed from every
face. So too did they hear the echo of the Ten Com-
mandments as they were given at Mount Sinai, and they
fell to their knees in awe. And Rabbi Akiba said: "Surely
this is the cloud that carried Moses into the heavens to
receive the Torah, for the words of the Torah still echo
in this place." And Rabbi Akiba covered his eyes and
led the four sages in saying the *Shema*, for the Holy One
had seen fit to let them enter there. And as they pronounced the final word, "One," the cloud began to
ascend on high.

6

The Palaces of the Patriarchs

So it was that the four sages found themselves carried in a cloud, ascending into Paradise. The duration of the ascent was a great mystery, for everything seemed timeless.

There in the cloud Rabbi Akiba looked down at the map and saw that the mirror of the *dagesh* was still glowing. The other sages gathered around, and there, in the mirror, they saw the history of the world unravel, from the very beginning, when *God said, Let there be light.* And for the whole six days of creation they remained peering into that map, as they witnessed the Mysteries of Creation. All that time they remained as if in a trance, until the mirror of the map went dark.

Then, after putting away the map, Rabbi Akiba discovered that it had left an imprint of itself inside the cloud, a sign in the firmament. For now that it was in Paradise, that celestial map was gaining even greater powers, as it drew nearer its source. Rabbi Akiba marveled at that sign, and a wonderful idea occurred to him. He said: "Look at how the image of the *Bet* remains fixed in the firmament even when the map has been put away. Perhaps we can leave signs in this way that could guide us back to the world. For how else will we be able to find our way back from such a high place?" The other sages were delighted with this discovery, and after that Rabbi Akiba made signs wherever they went, as it is written, *And this shall serve you as a sign.*

At the end of the sixth day the cloud came to a rest and began to dissolve. The four sages found themselves floating in the upper reaches of Paradise. The heavens seemed to open infinitely before them. There they saw a multitude of glorious palaces shining like stars, each of them seeming to beckon them closer. At first they were tempted to seek out the closest palace, but then they saw a flock of angels flying through the heavens, and they followed them, for now they too knew the secrets of flight in that sacred realm.

In this way the four sages eventually ascended through the palaces of heaven, and Rabbi Akiba left the sign of the *Bet* wherever they went. By following that angelic flock, they came to the palaces of each of the great *ushpizin*, the seven patriarchs who appear as guests at the *sukkah*, each of whom—except for Isaac—has a heavenly palace of his own.

The first palace they arrived at was that of King David, where they found both sages and angels crowding around the king as he sang the psalms, accompanying himself with a harp. That is when the sages learned the secret melodies of the psalms, which had long been lost. They stayed there, as if in a trance, until King David had completed all of the psalms, for they hungered to know each and every sacred melody.

Afterward King David looked up and saw the four sages and beckoned them to come closer. And the sages were thrilled to stand in the presence of the legendary king, who had conceived of building the Temple on earth and had written the psalms. And King David said: "Welcome, Rabbis. Your journey here has been foretold for a long time. Know that the gates of heaven have been opened for you, so that you might complete your quest. May you enter and depart in peace."

The sages all greeted King David and bowed low in his presence, and thanked him for his blessing. Then Rabbi Akiba said: "My master and teacher, we have come here in search of the Book of Raziel. Can you assist us?"

King David said: "I am only allowed to tell you this much: The book contains the secret of God's Name. Only one of you is permitted to learn the Name, for this secret may only be known by one *tzaddik* in every generation."

Then King David bid the sages goodbye and wished them success on their quest. The sages reluctantly took their leave, for they longed to gaze upon the countenance of King David. Once more they followed the angels until they reached the palace of Joseph, more beautiful than that of any Pharaoh. There Joseph held court like a king, and when it was announced that the four sages had arrived, Joseph had them brought before him. When they reached his throne, the sages saw that Joseph was peering into a silver cup—the very cup that he had hidden in the saddlebags of his brother, Benjamin—the cup with which he divined. And when Joseph looked up, he greeted them and said: "Know that we in this world have awaited your arrival as anxiously as I awaited the arrival of my father Jacob when I was the Prince of Egypt. In the oracle of the cup it is revealed that the book you are seeking is within reach, but remember, only one of you can read in it."

Then Joseph indicated that the audience had ended, and the four sages took their leave, weighing the oracle. It bode well for their quest, but they wondered who among them would be permitted to read in that sacred book. And with these thoughts, the four sages ascended to the very palace of Moses.

There they found that a great gathering of angels and the souls of departed sages had assembled in his presence, for Moses was the most honored teacher on high. All of the patriarchs and sages sat at his feet listening. The four sages came as close as they could, but the light that glowed from the face of Moses was so great that they had to avert their eyes. And Moses said: "God created man out of two elements, the body and the soul. For the body he gathered dust from the four corners of the earth, and *breathed into his nostrils the breath of life*, which is the soul. For this reason, the soul is eternal. But being made of matter, everything else consists of chaos and void. Therefore everything on earth has chaos at its root, except for the immortal soul. Indeed, all of existence was created in this way. Thus the worlds on high and below exist because of God's belief in them. Should that belief ever waver, for as much as an instant, all of the worlds would come to an end. Likewise, our existence depends on our belief in God, as well as God's belief in us. Should our faith ever waver, we would know the fate of wandering souls, who circle the worlds endlessly." Then the four sages knew that Moses was as honored in heaven as he was on earth, and just as Moses taught the ways of the world during his lifetime, so now he taught the ways of heaven.

Now it was surely no accident that the sages had received that teaching, although they did not fully understand it. Just then Ben Zoma glanced at the marble pillar beside them, and it seemed to consist of waves, and he was tempted to cry out "Water, water!" but he controlled himself in that sacred palace. And when he told the others about this, they understood the words of Moses and understood that they could only remain on high as long as they maintained their faith, and that if doubt entered in, it would be too late. For just as that marble pillar had begun to dissolve in Ben Zoma's vision, so would they be cast out of heaven if they did not have the faith to sustain them in that place.

Bearing the important teachings of Moses in mind, the four sages left the palace of Moses and continued their ascent. This time they reached the palace of Aaron, the brother of Moses.

The four sages identified themselves to the angelic guards outside the gates, and they were brought into Aaron's presence at once. Aaron was wearing the garb of the High Priest, except that the breastplate was missing. He came forward to greet the sages and embraced them as if they were long-lost friends. Then he said: "We have been waiting for you to come here for longer than you might imagine. Come with me, and let me show you something."

The four sages followed Aaron to the heavenly Ark of the Tabernacle, which Aaron opened. There they saw a breastplate hung over the mantle covering the scroll of the Torah, suspended between the two Trees of Life, as the wooden poles that hold the Torah are known. But all of the stones in the breastplate were missing. When they saw this, the sages suddenly perceived the true purpose of the precious stones they had recovered in the bottom of the pool, when they had been searching for Neshamah's pearl. And they knew, at once, what they must do. They took out the jewels and showed them to Aaron. He signaled for them to proceed, and then each of the sages, in turn, put a row of those stones back in the breastplate. Ben Azzai replaced the first row, Ben Zoma the second, Elisha the third, and Rabbi Akiba the fourth.

As soon as the last jewel had been replaced, Aaron put on the breastplate and said: "It is a great blessing to have recovered these precious stones. For at the time of the destruction of the Temple, they fell out of the breastplate, and a great river of tears washed through Paradise and carried off those stones to the pool where you recovered them. Without them the oracle of the breastplate, known as the *Urim* and *Tumim*, could not be used, and the art of divination was lost. And now the *Urim* and *Tumim* can again be used for divination."

Then Aaron stood before the four sages wearing that array of holy stones and asked them in turn what they saw. Each of the sages peered into that breastplate and saw that the stones had begun to glow. Only Aaron, among all those assembled there, knew how to interpret that oracle. And Aaron asked the four sages: "Tell me what you see when you peer into the breastplate." As each of the sages gazed into the *Urim* and *Tumim*, a vision took form in his sight. Ben Azzai was the first to reply: "I see the Temple in all its glory, before it was destroyed." And Aaron said: "That is not the Temple on earth, but the celestial Temple on high. You will find your destiny there."

Then Ben Zoma peered into the breastplate and said: "I see the world as it was before it was created, when *tohu* and *bohu*, chaos and void, reigned supreme." And Aaron said: "You will find your destiny there. "

Then Elisha reported what he saw in the breastplate: "I see an orchard that is also a garden." And Aaron said: "You will find your destiny there. "

Finally it was Rabbi Akiba's turn, and he said: "I see letters flying in every direction, forming themselves into holy names." And Aaron said: "Each of you will share in the glory of recovering the lost book. But it is only Rabbi Akiba's destiny to read in its pages."

Each of the sages was deeply moved by the visions they had seen and the prophecies of Aaron that had accompanied them, especially the prophecy that they would succeed in their quest. So too did they accept that it was Rabbi Akiba who was destined to delve into the sacred Book of Raziel, for that was his divine fate. Then they gratefully took their leave of Aaron and departed from that palace.

—— 7 ——

A Heavenly Ladder

As they emerged from the palace of Aaron, the sages saw something that looked like a beautiful rainbow, arching upward through the heavens. But as they approached it, they saw that it was a heavenly ladder, with angels ascending and descending. Then the sages knew that it must be the ladder that Jacob had seen in his dream. And they too climbed that ladder, along with the angels, and at the very top of it they found tents of such great beauty that no palace could compare to them. And Rabbi Akiba said: "Surely these are the tents of Jacob, as it is written, *How goodly are thy tents, O Jacob.*" And that, indeed, is what they were.

Now there were twelve tents that formed a circle around one central tent. And the four sages saw that a long line of angels had formed outside that tent, with angels coming and going. Now the four sages wondered about this, and they joined the line. And when at last they entered it, they saw that there was someone asleep inside. And when they saw his imposing features, they knew it could be none other than Jacob himself, as it is written *behold this dreamer cometh*. But what was most remarkable was that while Jacob was dreaming, his dreams rose up as visions, and each of the angels who witnessed one of those dreams then carried it off to deliver it to the world of men. And blessed would be he who received one of the dreams of Jacob. For when that person awoke he would find that his faith had been restored, for it bore the imprint of the faith of Jacob, which was perfect.

When the sages came out of the tent of Jacob, they saw the world in a new way. Now they saw how God's purpose pervaded everything, and they saw this purpose reflected as clearly as in any mirror. Then they understood how Jacob's life had been transformed after his dream of the ladder reaching from earth into heaven. For after that he saw how everything in this world, without exception, was linked to the next.

After that the four sages desired to travel to the palace of Isaac, but they did not know where to seek it. Just then they saw a golden dove ascending on high. That dove was so indescribably beautiful that Rabbi Akiba knew it had to be a sign, and he signaled for the others to follow it. The golden dove led them to a beautiful palace and perched on the branches of a tree outside it. The sages felt certain it was the palace of Isaac, but the angel guarding its gate told them that they had reached

the academy of Shem and Eber. Now they were delighted to reach that legendary academy, which was the
first of its kind. Still, they wondered why the golden dove
had led them there. And when they told the angel that
they were seeking the palace of Isaac, the angel said:
"Isaac does not have a palace of his own, but you will
find him here, for this is where he makes his home."

The sages were relieved to know they had come to
the right place after all. But they could not understand
why Isaac would not have his own palace. Elisha asked
about this, and the angel said: "This academy was once
Isaac's home in heaven. For when his father, Abraham,
raised the knife above him at Mount Moriah, Isaac's soul
took flight. While his body lay on the stone altar, his
soul ascended on high, rising up through the palaces of
heaven. And the angels brought Isaac's soul to the celestial academy of Shem and Eber. There he remained for
three years, studying the Torah. In this way Isaac was
rewarded for all he had suffered in that moment of great
fear, when his soul took flight.

"So too were all the treasuries of heaven opened to
Isaac: the celestial Temple, which has existed there since
the time of the creation, the Chambers of the Chariot,
and all of the palaces of heaven; all the treasuries of ice
and snow, as well as the treasury of prayers, and the treasury of souls. There Isaac saw how he had descended
from the seed of Adam. So too was he permitted to see
the future generations that would arise from the seed of

Abraham. Even the End of Days was revealed, for no mystery of heaven was deemed too secret for the pure soul of Isaac.

"During all this time Abraham remained frozen in place, the knife in his upraised hand. But to him it seemed but a single breath. Then the angel spoke: *"Lay not thy hand upon the lad,"* and at that instant Isaac's soul returned to his body. And when Isaac found that his soul had been restored to him, he exclaimed: *"Blessed is He who quickens the dead!"* And when Abraham unbound him, Isaac arose, seeing the world as if for the first time, as if he had been reborn.

"Then, after his death, Isaac chose to return to the heavenly academy where he had been taught. Now it is he who teaches here. And sages and angels flock from every corner of Paradise to hear his teachings."

Ben Zoma said: "Could we sit at the feet of our father Isaac?"

"Surely," said the angel. "Follow me."

Then the sages saw that every corner of that great academy was filled with the souls of the greatest sages and a multitude of angels. There they saw Isaac seated at a table, his eyes closed. For while he was blind in the world of men, in heaven he could see much better with his eyes closed. And in his teachings he reported back on all the mysteries that took form in the darkness, secrets that were unknown even to the angels.

Now when all those present saw the four sages, they

made a path for them, which appeared to the sages like
the parting of the Red Sea. Then the angel who had
brought them there led them to the very front, so that
they did indeed sit at the feet of Isaac.

Just as they were seated, Isaac began his *D'var Torah*.
His subject that day was the passage in Genesis, *This is
the book of the generations of Adam*. And Isaac said: "What
book does this refer to? To the book that was brought
to Adam by the angel Raziel while he was still in the
Garden of Eden. When the angel tried to read from that
book, Adam fainted. Therefore the angel left the book
with him, for its mysteries were too great for him to
absorb at once.

"But where is that book? It was passed down through
the generations. I received it from my father, Abraham,
and I gave it to my son Jacob. In this way it survived
until the destruction of the Temple. Then its pages
burned, but the letters rose up on high. But those letters are beyond the reach of those who make their home
in heaven, for only one of the living can recover that
book."

When the four sages heard these words, they understood why they had been guided to that place, for the
task of recovering the Book of Raziel required the aid
of the living. So too did they learn from Isaac's words
that they must be close to fulfilling their destiny and
recovering the lost book.

The four sages left the Academy of Shem and Eber

filled with admiration for Isaac, who had surely revealed that teaching because of their presence, even though he was blind. And they knew that they must remain on the path that had brought them there, and that path led directly to Abraham.

Before departing from the Academy of Shem and Eber, the sages asked the angel who had led them to Isaac where the palace of Abraham could be found. The angel pointed upward, to a sky crowded with stars, in which one glowed brighter than all the rest. And the angel said: "Do you see that star? That is the palace of Abraham."

So the four sages set out for that distant star, and in the blink of an eye they found themselves standing before a palace of light. All of the walls of the palace, as well as its roof and its pillars, consisted of light, which shone with a holy radiance. Now the four sages had only arrived at the gate, when Abraham himself came out to greet them. He was wearing a white robe, and a glowing jewel hung from his neck. He warmly welcomed the sages and invited them to be his guests. And the sages saw firsthand that everything they had learned about the modesty and generosity of our father Abraham was true. Tears of joy ran from their eyes, for they realized how blessed they were to stand in the presence of Abraham, whose path they had so closely followed. For Abraham had established the path of the righteous for all generations, and the way of the Lord.

Abraham told them that he had heard tidings of their

journey from three angels, who had recently visited him. And Elisha asked: "Can you tell us, father Abraham, what angels these were?" And Abraham said: "Yes, those were the three angels who visited me by the terebinths of Marmre, where they prophesied Isaac's birth—none other than Michael, Gabriel, and Raphael. These angels told me that they had heard whisperings about your quest from behind the *Pargod*." And when the four sages heard this, they knew the urgency of their quest, for those angels are only sent on the most important missions. But even more amazing to the sages was the hint that the Holy One Himself, hidden behind the *Pargod*, was concerned about their attempt to recover the lost book.

After that, Abraham regaled the sages with wonderful stories, one after another. This surprised them, for they had always imagined Abraham to be taciturn. But now they realized that he was a great storyteller. One of the stories he told them was about a quiver of letters:

"Before the three angels who visited me took their leave of my tent, they gave me a great gift. It was a quiver, which appeared to be filled with arrows. But when I looked more closely, I saw at once that it was not an ordinary quiver, nor were its arrows like any I had seen. The quiver was shaped like a scroll, and at the end of each arrow was a single letter. There were twenty-two letters that fit inside the quiver, and five final letters that rose up above it.

"The angel Michael, who gave the quiver to me, told

me to take it with me on my journey to the Holy Land. I replied that I would gladly carry the quiver and the letters that fit within it; but perhaps I could leave behind the five letters that stood out, to lighten my load. The angel said no, that was not possible, but I would be permitted to fold the five letters so that they would fit inside the quiver like the others. And that is what I did, knowing that at the End of Days the letters would be restored to their original shapes.

"In the days that followed I studied each and every one of those letters, even those that had been folded, and inscribed them on rocks I passed in my long journey into the Land. So too did I name each letter at the moment I first inscribed it, and later I formed the letters into words and assigned each word a meaning. At that time I did not know that the names of the letters and the meanings of the words were being revealed to me from on high."

And when they heard this tale, all of the sages were delighted, for now they knew how Hebrew, the language of the angels, had been introduced in the world of men. Then Abraham told them the tale of his journey to Egypt:

"There was a famine in the land, and Sarah and I went down into Egypt to sojourn there. While we were crossing the desert a sandstorm arose that circled us like a whirlwind and everything was blotted out in our sight. When the storm subsided we found that our food had

been scattered, our water spilt, and we were lost between
Kadesh and Shur in the Egyptian desert. There nothing
flourished, and there was nothing to guide us, for all the
landmarks had been buried beneath the sands. At last,
when our thirst was such that the Angel of Death appeared before our eyes, I stopped and prayed, and soon
a white bird appeared on the horizon and flew directly
toward us. When this bird reached me, it dropped a
single seed from its beak, which fell at my feet. And I
cradled the seed and kneaded the earth to make it ready
and planted the seed while it was still damp. And before
the sun had set a tree grew up in that place and bore
fruit. Then I knew that my covenant with the Lord
would be fulfilled."

The sages marveled at this tale, and Rabbi Akiba said:
"Surely that white bird was the dove of Noah, as it is
written, *And the dove came to him at eventide.* And Abraham
said: "Yes, that was the very same dove, and the seed it
brought me was a seed from the Tree of Life, for that
seed gave us new life."

Now the sages were very curious about the glowing
jewel that Abraham wore around his neck. And Ben
Zoma asked him about it. Abraham said: "I found this
jewel in a cave when I was a child, and I have worn it
ever since. It serves as a healing stone and also as an astro-
labe. But most of all I use it to divine."

And Abraham beckoned each of the sages to come
forward and peer into the glowing stone. Ben Azzai went

first, then Ben Zoma, then Elisha ben Abuyah, and Rabbi Akiba went last. And each of them saw flaming letters take form inside that jewel, and there they each read a single word. Afterward Abraham asked them to tell him what word they had read there. Ben Azzai said: "I read the word 'throne' in those flaming letters." Ben Zoma said: "I read the word 'water.'" Elisha said: "I read the word 'shoots.'" And Rabbi Akiba said: "I read the word 'peace.'" Abraham said: "Your fate lies in the words you have read: Ben Azzai will *behold my Lord seated on a high and lofty throne.* Ben Zoma will *see the spirit of God hovering over the face of the waters.* Elisha will *hear the voice of the Lord God walking in the Garden.* And Rabbi Akiba will *come again to my father's house in peace.*" Each of the sages weighed these words ever so carefully and saw many meanings in them. And they kept those verses in mind, for they knew that they contained the secret of their fates, if only they could decipher it.

At last the four sages took their leave of Abraham, and before they departed he gave them a great blessing that seemed to lift their burdens and make the path before them as clear as their purpose. And in that moment each of them felt that their lives had been fulfilled, and they gave thanks to the Holy One, blessed be He, who had showered them with such abundant blessings.

— 8 —

The Celestial Garden

Now when the four sages had passed beyond the palaces of the patriarchs, they reached the celestial Garden. For the earthly Garden of Eden is mirrored in a celestial one. And when the sages entered it, they found themselves in a garden of stars as vast as the universe.

The sages peered at that garden of stars for what seemed like years. Indeed, they became bewildered by it, for it was also a labyrinth of stars. It was Rabbi Akiba who recognized the danger of becoming lost there, for everything they gazed upon was a world in itself. And as the other sages began to drift toward those enticing worlds, Rabbi Akiba called out for them to close their eyes. Now they were reluctant, but they did as he asked. And as they closed their eyes, they each had a vision in which they were present for the Giving of the Torah at Mount Sinai. There was thunder and lightning, and the heavens split open to reveal the mysteries of the Torah.

And among the 600,000 assembled there, the four sages recognized each other, for they were standing side by side. And they saw the flaming letters of the Torah, as Moses held the tablets up for the people to see, and they witnessed a luminous aura reflected from his face. At that instant the vision ended and each of them began to sob, for that vision of the Giving of the Torah had so moved them. Then they knew that their lives together had been fated long before they had set out on that unlikely quest, since all of their souls had been present at Mount Sinai.

Then, when the four sages opened their eyes, they saw that the stars had somehow formed themselves into another pattern, a great tree whose branches reached into every corner of existence. Rabbi Akiba was the first to recognize the shape of that immense tree, which filled the universe. Then one by one the others saw it, and it was a great revelation for them. For they saw once and for all that everything in the world is linked together like the roots and branches of that tree.

At that instant another veil was lifted, and the sages were able to recognize all of the generations of men in the branches of that tree, from the time of Adam to that of Noah, from Noah to Abraham, and from Abraham until that very day. And they saw how their own souls all followed the branch of Abraham. Then they understood that their souls were finally at home in that high place. For their souls had always been restless in the world of men, but here they knew a peace as great as the silence at the beginning of time, before the world was created.

Just then the sages heard the beating of wings, like a flock of doves, and an angel descended among them whose face bore an aura so bright that none of them could look upon it. And only Rabbi Akiba found his voice to address the glowing figure. "Who is it that so blesses us with his presence?" he asked.

The angel replied: "I am Raziel, the angel of secrets." And when the sages heard this, their hearts stood still, for that could be no other than the angel who had first brought the Book of Raziel to Adam. And when he was able to speak again, Rabbi Akiba said: "Then you know it is the Book of Raziel that we have been seeking for so long?"

"Yes," said the angel, "and I have been sent to serve as your guide in Paradise. Indeed, whenever you wish to call upon me, pronounce this name"—and the angel whispered a holy name for the sages to use in time of need.

Then the angel said: "Do you know what tree this is?" The sages said they did not. And the angel continued: "Know that this is the Tree of Souls. Every star in the heavens is a branch of this tree, and every tree and flower in this celestial Garden bears a soul of this Tree as well. The very place where you stand possesses a soul within it, as does everything you see and touch here."

Now this was a frightening revelation for the sages, and Ben Zoma was so concerned that he asked: "Do we, then, pose a danger to these souls in any way?"

Raziel replied: "Yes, each generation holds the trust and purity of these souls in their hands. And they must bear them carefully, and let their souls guide them, so that they may reach the next generation intact. For if a soul is refused, turned back, or harmed in any way, this too is passed down. Indeed, the greatest of all responsibilities is to bear a soul. For it is not only the living person whose soul is affected, but the past and future are dependent as well. For all generations exist at the same time in this Tree of Souls." And once more the four sages peered at that vast tree of all existence, and its image was imprinted on their souls.

Now in that celestial Garden there was a palace of stars, and when the angel guided them there, the sages found that they could peer into that palace, as if the wall of stars were invisible. And inside they saw a figure with a countenance so pure that the light it reflected almost blinded them. Now that being, so much like a man and yet so unlike one, left them filled with wonder. "Please," they all begged the angel, "reveal the identity of this pure being who inhabits this palace of stars."

"That," said Raziel, "is Adam Kadmon, the celestial Adam. Indeed, Adam Kadmon is the very soul of Adam who makes his home in this garden, in this very palace."

Then a great curiosity took hold of Elisha ben Abuyah,

and he found himself asking: "'The earthly Adam sinned and was expelled from the Garden. What was the fate of his heavenly soul?"

The angel replied: "Although Adam was compelled to depart from the earthly Garden, the soul of Adam has never left the celestial Paradise, for Adam's heavenly soul was not expelled from there. Indeed, it is because of Adam's soul that all other souls are still rooted here, for the soul of Adam contains all souls."

Ben Azzai said: "Please tell us more about Adam Kadmon."

And Raziel replied: "Before God created Adam as a man of flesh and blood, He created a dream Adam, whose name was Adam Kadmon. And God called forth this dream Adam and said: 'Alone among all creations, I am going to permit you to choose your own soul.' And God brought Adam Kadmon to the Treasury of Souls in heaven and opened its door. And when Adam looked inside, he saw a sky crowded with stars. And God said: 'Every one of those stars is a soul. Which one do you want?'

"And as he gazed out at that constellation of souls, scattered like sparks, Adam wondered how he could possibly choose one from among them. Every one glowed with a light of its own. Every one was equally beautiful. Then Adam saw that the constellation formed a great Tree of Souls, which branched out in every direction. And Adam said to the Holy One, blessed be He: 'I want the soul of the Tree of Souls from which all of the souls are suspended.' And God was delighted, and brought forth the soul of the Tree of Souls and gave it to Adam.

"And that is why the soul of Adam contained all souls and why all souls are a part of Adam's soul."

Now when the four sages heard this, they gasped, for now they understood how one soul could contain all others.

Just then the walls of the palace of Adam Kadmon were transformed into mirrors, and when the sages looked into those mirrors they saw something that few have witnessed in the history of men—they saw visions of the future generations that would arise from each one of them. Ben Azzai saw that his line had come to an end, and he grieved over this, but then, for an instant, he glimpsed his own heavenly reward, and it was so great that it left him overwhelmed, shedding tears of joy. Ben Zoma saw that his line continued for a great many generations into the future, so far that he could not see to the end of them. Elisha ben Abuyah saw his family mourning over him, and saw as well a fire burning above his grave. And he became very frightened, for he felt that, like Cain, sin was crouching at his door. But he did not share these fears with the others, nor did they know of them. As for Rabbi Akiba, what he saw there cannot be revealed, for it involved a secret so great that it could hasten the coming of the Messiah.

Now the sages were so curious about the visions of the future taking form in that mirror, that they moved closer to see them more clearly, and in this way they suddenly found themselves at the edge of the most beautiful garden imaginable, with an infinite number of flowers glowing like stars. Raziel explained that this was the Garden of Souls, in which all of the souls had their roots. Thus each flower in that garden was attached to a family of roots. Now as the sages stood before that garden, they wondered which one of those flowers represented the roots of their souls. It was Ben Zoma who asked about this, and Raziel said: "Close your eyes, and when you open them, the first flower you see will be the root of your soul." All of the sages did what the angel asked, and suddenly they found themselves plunged into the primal darkness that existed before the Creation of the world. And even though they only kept their eyes closed for a few seconds, it seemed to them that the darkness went on for an eternity. Then, as they opened their eyes, they each found themselves drawn to one of the glowing flowers in the Garden of Souls. Then each sage looked into the very center of that flower, and saw, for the first time in his life, the true root of his soul.

Now for three of the sages, this was the greatest experience they had ever known. This was true for Ben Azzai, Ben Zoma, and Rabbi Akiba. But unknown to them, Elisha's vision caused him great agony, for he learned that one of those destined to descend from his

seed would be a false Messiah. And this terrible revelation haunted him so much that he became blinded to
the glories of Paradise and instead saw everything from
a great distance. Still, he followed the others, remaining
silent, keeping his sorrow hidden.

9

The Heavenly *Genizah*

There in the Garden of Souls the four sages again glimpsed the golden dove. They had not forgotten how it had led them to the Academy of Shem and Eber, and once more they let it be their guide. In this way they reached a tree of unimaginable beauty, whose branches reached high into the heavens, while its roots extended all the way to the world below. That is where the golden dove made its nest. The sages marveled at this mysterious tree, and Raziel said: "This is the Tree of Life."

Now this greatly confused the sages, for did not it state in Genesis that the Tree of Life was in the midst of the garden? Then, all at once, Rabbi Akiba understood the meaning of the verse *the Tree of Life, also in the midst of the Garden, and the Tree of the Knowledge of Good and Evil.* Yes, both were in the Garden of Eden, but while the Tree of Knowledge was in the earthly garden, the Tree of Life was located in the celestial Garden, in the very heights of Paradise. And that tree grew directly before the most haunting of all the palaces they had seen in heaven, for it had the shape of a tear. The sages greatly wondered about it and were just about to ask Raziel when the golden dove began to sing.

Now the song of the golden dove was indescribably beautiful. None of them had ever heard a music so sublime. And Rabbi Akiba said: "Surely the palace that faces the nest of this golden dove must belong to the Messiah. For the song of this dove awakes in me a longing for the Messiah so sharp that I feel I cannot wait a day longer for the time of the Messiah to come." And when he said this, all of the other sages realized how powerful their longing for the Messiah had grown. Then Elisha said: "Indeed, the longing for the Messiah is palpable among us. But I also long to know more about this palace."

Raziel replied: "This palace is known as the palace of tears, for it was built out of the tears shed by those longing for the Messiah. This is where the Messiah waits for the sign to be given that the time has come for his footsteps to be heard."

When they learned this, all of the sages knew that they must somehow enter that palace, for they were drawn there by a longing far greater than any they had ever known.

The sages now saw a flock of angels entering the palace, and they understood that they, too, had been beckoned there by the song of the golden dove. And without hesitation the four sages followed those angels inside. There they saw that a host of angels had gathered to hear a teacher—an old man with a white beard whose face radiated a bright aura and whose eyes were filled with wisdom and loving-kindness. The sages pleaded with Raziel to tell them if that truly was the Messiah, and the angel confirmed that it was.

Then the old man began to speak, and he revealed secrets so profound that the seven veils of the Torah were lifted for each of the sages, and the depths of its truths revealed. And the last thing that the Messiah revealed was the purpose of the golden dove: "I have been waiting since before the creation for a sign that the world is ready. And that sign will come through the golden dove. For every year, on Rosh Hashanah, I send forth the dove as did Noah: to see if the world is ready. And if it is, the dove will perch on the gates of Paradise, as a sign that they should be opened, so that my footsteps might be heard in the world. But if the world is not ready, the golden dove comes back to its nest in the Tree of Life, and its silence lasts for three days."

Then the Messiah turned to the four sages and beckoned for them to approach. And as they did, the sages remembered the sparks they had gathered from the Garden of Eden and still carried with them. Then, one by one, they offered those sparks to the Messiah, who received them. And when he had gathered the sparks, the countenance of the Messiah glowed even brighter.

He smiled and thanked them and said: "Truly, you have gathered a veritable harvest of these precious sparks. Few are those who have gathered more. Tell me, what is it that you want to know?"

Then Rabbi Akiba spoke for all the others: "All we long to know is when your footsteps will be heard in the world." And the Messiah said: "When you find the Book you have come so far to seek, then this secret will be revealed." Thus spoke the Messiah, and the sages were elated to hear these words, for they not only confirmed that their quest might succeed, but that the most guarded of secrets, the time of the coming of the Messiah, might be disclosed. And before they took their leave, each of the sages thanked the Messiah and expressed the deeply felt wish that the time of his coming might be soon.

When they left the palace of the Messiah, the sages gathered together at the foot of the Tree of Life, in which the golden dove had built its nest. There Rabbi Akiba said: "Let us give thanks that we have been blessed to live until this moment, so that we might stand in the presence of the Messiah and hear these mysteries revealed. And now we must complete our quest to find the lost Book of Raziel. For the Messiah has revealed that it is destined for us to do so. And now that we are here in Paradise, we must discover exactly where it can be found."

Now all of the sages wanted more than anything else to complete their quest. And when Rabbi Akiba said this, Elisha replied: "We know that the Book of Raziel, which was handed down from Adam, was destroyed along with the Temple. And we know that the letters took flight when the pages of the book were burned. But where did they go? If those letters were pages of a book that had been worn or damaged on earth, we would have placed them in a *Genizah*. But where in heaven would such letters be found?"

"Where else but in a heavenly *Genizah*!" Ben Zoma cried out. "But where can we find it?"

Rabbi Akiba replied: "Both of you have spoken as if possessed by a blessed spirit who longs for this mystery to be revealed. For surely we will find a heavenly *Genizah* in the same place here as on earth, and that would be in the celestial Temple."

Only Ben Azzai was doubtful. "But how can there be a *Genizah* in heaven? A *Genizah* is intended for books that are torn or worn beyond use. But here in heaven everything is eternal. What purpose would a *Genizah* serve on high?"

This comment dashed the hopes of all the sages except for Rabbi Akiba, who said: "Remember that the earthly Temple was built as a mirror image of the Temple on high. And since there was a *Genizah* connected to the Temple in Jerusalem, then just as surely there must be one in heaven as well."

These words served to sway all of the others, even Ben Azzai, who said: "Surely the end of our quest may be close at hand. Now that we have deduced the existence of the heavenly *Genizah*, let us hasten to the Temple on high to find it."

And Rabbi Akiba said: "Yes, but first let us call upon the angel Raziel. For we dare not proceed any further without Raziel for our guide." Then Rabbi Akiba pronounced the secret name that summoned the angel, and Raziel appeared before them. They told the angel of their plan, and the angel replied: "Yes, the time has come for you to continue your ascent. But know that it is very dangerous for one of the living to ascend to those heights, and your only hope when you reach the heavenly Temple is, above all, to keep it in view at all times. Do not turn your eyes away from it for as long as a single instant. Otherwise you will be lost. Now come with me."

Then the sages gave themselves to that angel with complete trust, and all at once they found themselves seated inside a chariot of fire blazing its way across the heavens. And they had no time to wonder at this, as they marveled at the wonders before them. Before them they saw two kinds of luminaries. Those that ascended above were luminaries of light, and those that descended below were luminaries of fire. The fire resembled a river of fire that did not cease flowing, day or night. Ben Azzai asked Raziel to identify these luminaries, and he was told that those of light were the veil of the *Shekhinah* that the Holy One Himself draws up into Paradise, so that they can always be in contact, even while she is in Exile. For since the destruction of the Temple in Jerusalem and the exile of the *Shekhinah*, the Holy One has only been able to kiss His Bride through this veil. Each of the luminaries of fire, on the other hand, is an angel that has been newly created by the Holy One, blessed be He, to gather the prayers of Israel as they ascend on high.

Just then the chariot approached some kind of parting of the heavens, which resembled a line drawn across the cosmos. As they drew closer, they saw it was actually an opening through which an ethereal light emerged. Raziel recognized the question taking form in the mind of each sage, and he said: "We are approaching the place where the Upper Waters and the Lower Waters meet. This is where the Upper Worlds are separated from the Lower Worlds, and what belongs to the spheres above is divided from what belongs to the spheres below."

No sooner did the angel finish speaking than the chariot approached close enough to that place for the four sages to catch a glimpse of what lay on the other side. And what they saw was a magnificent structure suspended in space. And from that one glimpse they knew that no human structure could begin to compare with it. But then, before they had time to question the angel, the chariot passed through that very aperture, to the complete astonishment of all of the sages, for it was no higher than a hand's breadth. It was then that the four sages grew afraid, for they realized they were flying through space at a great height and dared not to look down. Then Ben Zoma said to the angel: "How is it possible that we have passed through a space no wider than three finger-breadths?"

Raziel said: "In the kingdom of men it is possible to contain a garden in the world. But in this kingdom it is possible to contain the world in a garden. How can this be? Because here, whoever opens his heart to the Holy One by as much as the thickness of a needle, can pass through any portal."

Even as Raziel spoke these words the sages had already been captured by the radiant vision that loomed ahead. So too did they now hear for the first time a faint, haunting music, which seemed strangely familiar. As they came closer, Raziel said: "The place we are approaching is so sacred that even this chariot is not permitted to come any closer. Therefore you must soon depart from it and remain suspended in space, like the Sanctuary you see before you."

And without any other explanation, all of the sages realized that the wonderful structure they saw must be the celestial Temple, after which the Temple in Jerusalem had been modeled, and with which it was identical in every respect, except for the fire surrounding the heavenly Sanctuary. For the marble pillars of this heavenly miracle were illumined by red fire, the stones by green fire, the threshold by white fire, and the gates by blue fire. And angels entered and departed in a steady stream, intoning an unforgettable hymn.

That is when the sages realized they were no longer within the chariot but suspended in space. And it was then, with their eyes fixed on that shimmering vision, that they were first able to distinguish the Divine Presence of the *Shekhinah* hovering above the walls and pillars of the Temple, illuminating them and wrapping them in a glowing light, which shone across all of heaven. It was this light they had seen from the other side of the aperture, before the chariot of fire had crossed into the Kingdom of Heaven. And so awestruck were the sages to witness the splendor of the *Shekhinah* that they suddenly experienced an overwhelming impulse to hide their faces, and they began to sway in that place, almost losing their balance. Had it not been for the angel Raziel speaking at that instant, they might have fallen from that great height. The angel said: "Remember my warning. Know that the Temple remains suspended by decree of the Holy One, blessed be He. Keep your eyes fixed on its glory, if you are not to become lost. So too should you know that no living man may enter into that holy dwelling place and still descend to the world of men. For no man could survive the pure fire burning there, through which only angels and purified souls can pass."

These words of warning served to assist the sages in regaining their balance. They focused all their attention on the shimmering Temple, and it was then that they finally discovered the secret of the celestial music. For as they followed that music to its source, their eyes came to rest on concentric circles of angels in the Temple courtyard. Then they realized that the music they had been hearing was being played by an orchestra of angels. And when they looked still closer they saw that each of the angels played a golden vessel cast in the shape of a letter of the Hebrew alphabet. And each one had a voice of its own, and one angel in the center of the circle played an instrument in the shape of the letter *Bet*.

As they listened to the music, Rabbi Akiba realized it was the long note of the letter *Bet* that served as its foundation and sustained all of the other instruments. He marveled at how long the angel was able to hold this note, drawing his breath back and forth like the Holy One Himself, who in this way brought the heavens and the earth into being. And at that moment Rabbi Akiba was willing to believe that the world only existed so that those secret harmonies could be heard. He was about to ask the angel Raziel, who had never left their side, and once more the angel read his thoughts: "The score of this symphony is the scroll of the Torah, which commences with the letter *Bet*, endless and eternal, and continues with each instrument playing in turn as it appears on the page, holding its note until the next letter has been sounded, and then breathing in and out a full breath."

And as the sages listened to that celestial music, they arrived at a new understanding of the Torah, and they realized that among its many mysteries there was one level on which it existed only as pure music. They were also aware that of all the instruments in that orchestra, only the letter *Bet* seemed to speak to them. Then the angel Raziel said: "The souls of all men draw their strength from one of the instruments in this orchestra, and thus from one of the letters of the alphabet. And that letter serves as the vessel through which the soul of a man may reveal itself. All of your souls draw their strength from the vessel of the letter *Bet*, which serves as a Foundation Stone and holds back the waters of the Abyss. That is why you were so drawn to the Mysteries of Creation, for it is these mysteries that are most important to your souls."

Then, while they hovered there, almost hypnotized by the glorious vision of the Temple, they saw a remarkable sight: a flock of glowing letters flying through the heavens. Rabbi Akiba pointed them out to the others, and they saw them fly toward the celestial Temple and disappear just outside the entrance. The four sages were transfixed by this sight. What could it mean? Rabbi Akiba was the first to speak: "Surely the heavenly *Genizah* can be found there! For that is the very place where the *Genizah* is found: beneath the step leading into the Temple!"

A shiver passed through each of the sages, for they knew that they must go there. And they approached the holy and eternal Temple on high, but only Rabbi Akiba remembered the dangers that existed there, and he warned the others: "Remember the vision of Ben Zoma in the palace of Moses: When you reach the stones of pure marble, do not say 'Water, water.' Remember, too, that none of us may enter that holy place."

As they drew nearer the chorus of the angels from inside the Temple seemed to beckon them closer, and the desire to see what was within the celestial Temple was as great as their longing for the Messiah, perhaps even greater. So too did they see a shimmering vision, in which the stones and pillars of the Temple resembled a celestial sea, with waves rising and falling, and they had to strongly resist crying out "Water, water!" The closer they came, the more were they swept up in the desire to enter that awesome Temple, and all that held them back from following the host of angels streaming inside was Rabbi Akiba's warning. That is when they reached the entrance of the Temple, and they glimpsed the secret place where the glowing letters had flown, which was indeed the heavenly *Genizah*. Peering into that miraculous place, the four sages saw a flock of letters forming themselves into prayers for the Holy One, as well as into holy names of unimaginable powers.

And there, in the luminous center of the heavenly *Genizah*, they saw a glowing jewel—a sapphire! And all of the sages remembered that the Book of Raziel was once said to have been engraved on just such a stone. They all held their breath as Rabbi Akiba reached down and picked it up. And when his hand touched it, it first turned into a glowing scroll, with letters of black fire on white fire, and, an instant later, it turned into a book. At last Rabbi Akiba held the Book of Raziel in his hands! His longing to open its pages was very great, but he remembered the words of Aaron that only he was permitted to read in the book. So Rabbi Akiba took his leave of the others and went behind a marble pillar of the Temple, where he might be alone with the book. And when he turned to the first page he saw that it was indeed the fabled Book of Raziel, which had once been read by Adam as well as by our father Abraham and the other Patriarchs.

The first thing Rabbi Akiba discovered was that the book consisted of four chapters, each beginning with one letter of God's ineffable Name. But even after making this discovery, he found that the words did not seem to form into sentences, and a veil of mystery concealed the meaning from him. All at once Rabbi Akiba had a searing insight—that those mysterious words were themselves the secret and ineffable Name of God. And at that instant he understood that the true secret of the book was to reveal that ineffable Name. And when he had read the last of those mysterious words, the true pronunciation of the Name was revealed to him in its entirety, and at the instant Rabbi Akiba pronounced it, he was blessed to see the world through the Eyes of God.

In that eternal instant, Rabbi Akiba saw everywhere at once, from one end of the world to the other, and nothing was hidden from his vision, not even what was in the hearts of men. He saw every child's first breath and every old man's last. He saw all those who were sleeping and each of their dreams. He saw a woman going to a well and saw how the spring that fed the well rose up under the earth. He saw the spirit of a tree beckon. He saw a thousand Arks being opened and the Torah being taken out of every one. He saw a thousand crowns of prayer ascending on high. He saw a valley of tears that had once been a beautiful Temple. He saw a white deer, a black swan, a golden dove. He saw the myriad angels, each of them face to face. He saw the hidden face of the Messiah, and learned the secret of when his footsteps would be heard in the world, and he wept. He saw the robe of the *Shekhinah*, hidden behind the *Pargod*, the heavenly curtain, and there he beheld the Lord of Hosts seated on a high and lofty throne. And, filled with awe and terror, he bowed low before the Throne of Glory. And he heard the Voice of the Lord say unto him: "*Draw Me after you.*" And Rabbi Akiba replied at once: "*The King hath brought me into His chambers.*" And from that moment on, Rabbi Akiba knew that he was forever after in the presence of the Lord.

In the long instant that vision lasted, every mystery was revealed to Rabbi Akiba, including the fate of his companions, for nothing is hidden from the Eyes of God. Then he cried out to God to spare him such knowledge. And at that instant the Holy One, in His infinite mercy, closed his eyes, and when he opened them again, Rabbi Akiba saw the world once more with the eyes of a man.

── 10 ──

The Fate of the Four

Meanwhile, the other sages waited for Rabbi Akiba, but as soon as they saw him step behind the pillar, both he and the pillar disappeared. Then Ben Zoma said: "Look, the pillar has vanished. All I can see is water above and below!" And at that moment the three sages forgot the warnings of Moses and Akiba, and they all looked up and saw that there were indeed two pools of water that had appeared there, above and below, and they saw Rabbi Akiba's reflection in both. Then Elisha said: "Look, you can see the letters of the book!" And as soon as he said this the three sages went into a trance, peering at those letters, which appeared backward in their sight, since they were reflected. Yet somehow they were able to read them as if they were not backward at all.

So it was that each of them read along with Rabbi Akiba. But what they did not realize is that the book they read there was not the true Book of Raziel, but the reflection of it as found in the *Sitra Ahra*, the Other Side. For of everything that God created, He created its counterpart, as it is written, *God hath made the one as well as the other*. And as they read those backward letters, each of them was unwittingly drawn into the *Sitra Ahra*, until it was too late to turn back.

Then, when Ben Azzai had read no further than the first chapter, he heard a song so beautiful he felt himself drawn to it like a moth to a flame. And he flew like an angel toward the entrance of the Temple, past all the guards who stood by their gates. Nor did they try to stop him, for they saw how his soul was burning and how it was drawn to that place. And all at once Ben Azzai entered into the celestial Temple that burned around him on every side. And there he saw a throne of diamonds, each of which glowed as if there were a fire burning within it. Seated upon that high and lofty throne was the very Bride of God, the *Shekhinah*, and Ben Azzai saw that she was singing, for it was her song that had led him to that place. And in her presence Ben Azzai recognized that the words she sang were from the Psalms. And the *Shekhinah* transformed them into the most beautiful song imaginable, whose melody, he now realized, had haunted him all his life. So it was that Ben Azzai understood that all of his dreams had come true, for he had been found worthy of entering the celestial Temple and of being received by the *Shekhinah*, whose song had sustained the eternal life of his soul. And Ben Azzai prostrated himself before the Bride and reveled in the glory of that immortal song. And when at last he raised his eyes, he saw that the *Shekhinah* had left her throne to embrace him, and as she did, she kissed him and gently brought his soul into Paradise. And all the angels witnessed how his soul was crowned in splendor as it was carried on high. Thus is it written *Precious in the eyes of the Lord is the death of His saints.*

So it was that Ben Azzai died by the kiss of the *Shekhinah*, as did Moses, and he was gathered to his forefathers, and all at once he found himself seated at the back of a heavenly academy. And when he looked up he saw none other than Moses the Redeemer speaking to all of those assembled there. And Moses reported to them all that God had revealed to him on Mount Sinai, not only during the day, when he wrote down the words of the Torah, but even at night, when God explained their meaning. And Ben Azzai perceived that every letter of every word he spoke was a world in itself, and all of the holiness of heaven was contained in each and every word.

And when Moses saw that Ben Azzai had joined them, he motioned toward him and said: "Rabbi Simeon ben Azzai, one of the pillars of the world, has joined us this day." And all of those present turned and welcomed the soul of Ben Azzai. And so it was that Ben Azzai received his heavenly reward.

As for Ben Zoma, when he read in those backward

letters, he was unable to proceed beyond the beginning of the second chapter before he found himself drawn as in a trance to the place where the upper and lower waters meet. Now when Ben Zoma peered into that crack between the worlds, he saw all the way to the beginning, remembered only the beginning, understood only the beginning. And there, in the beginning, Ben Zoma saw a distant star coming closer, until it suddenly exploded and the flames it cast up formed themselves into letters, beginning with the *Bet*. And as the letters of the Torah emerged in succession from within the letter *Bet*, the world was created as it was when God said *Yehi Or— Let there be light*. Then Ben Zoma found himself in a Garden, and he was approached by a woman who, like himself, was naked. In her hands there was a ripe fruit, a pomegranate. She gave it to him and he split it open and gave her one half. And Ben Zoma, who was Adam at that moment, forgot about everything that would come afterward, and as they each tasted one pomegranate seed, the world trembled and grew dark, and it was too late. Then Ben Zoma grieved because he knew that he too would fail at that fatal moment; the power of the *Yetzer Hara*, the evil impulse, was greater than he could bear.

Nor was the vision over, but Ben Zoma, in turn, relived the life of Seth, and as Enoch he was carried on high and transformed into the angel Metatron, burning as brightly as the sun. And for an instant Ben Zoma shared the knowledge of Metatron, the angel closest to

God, the heavenly scribe. And with Metatron he wrote down the words that he read as if he were Moses, receiving them for the first time. Nor did the heavenly Torah end there, but all past and future history was revealed, and Ben Zoma watched all of it, as if in the deepest trance. In this way Ben Zoma witnessed the words of the Torah firsthand, and the experience was overwhelming.

But it was what came next that left Ben Zoma unbalanced, for it was so unexpected. When the final words of the Torah had been read, there came a silence so still that it emptied the universe of every other sound, for the world had returned to the original chaos and void. So startled was Ben Zoma that he cried out at the sight of such chaos and at that instant he fell from that great height, a fall in itself that seemed endless, until his eyes closed and he fell into a deep, dreamless sleep.

And Ben Zoma slept for a very long time. And when he awoke, he found himself lying on the stone floor of the Cave of Machpelah, and there was a strangely sweet taste in his mouth, which he recognized as honey. Then he remembered Rabbi Akiba's warning, so long ago, only to eat enough, and he staggered up and returned to Jerusalem, but he was a broken man.

Not long after that Ben Zoma met his teacher, Rabbi Joshua ben Hananiah, who greeted him. But instead of returning the greeting, Ben Zoma only said: "Between the upper waters and the lower ones there are but three finger-breadths." And when he heard this, Rabbi Joshua said to his students: "Ben Zoma is gone." For the vision of chaos and void that Ben Zoma had witnessed had unhinged him. Nor did he live long after that.

Now Elisha was able to read no further in that backward book than to the third chapter, when he suddenly found himself far from the other sages, in a heavenly court. There he saw a mighty figure seated on a throne, and when he asked who this was, he was told that it was Metatron, chief among the angels, who once had been Enoch. Now he was the attendant of the Throne of Glory, the prince of the treasuries of heaven, and the ruler and judge of all the hosts of angels, as well as the heavenly scribe, who wrote down the merits of Israel. Elisha stared at Metatron with disbelief. How was it possible for him to be seated, since there is a tradition that there is no sitting on high, except for the Lord of Hosts. Then Elisha cried out: "God forbid—there must be two powers in heaven." And at that instant a heavenly Voice came forth and said: "*Do not let your mouth lead your flesh into sin.*" And at the same time the Holy One, blessed be He, commanded that Metatron be whipped with sixty fiery lashes for not rising up from the throne. But it was too late for Elisha, for his faith had already begun to waver, and at that instant he fell from that heavenly court back into the Garden of Souls, face to face with the flower that contained the very root of his soul.

Meanwhile, all the grief that Elisha had been holding back washed over him, for he could not bear the knowledge of what he had seen on high, nor that a false messiah would descend from his seed. All at once a terrible impulse came over him, and in an instant, before he had considered the full implications of his act, Elisha reached down and uprooted the flower of his soul. A great cry went up at that time, from all the souls whose birth had been denied, and all the angels broke out in sobs of grief. And at the same time a Voice spoke forth out of heaven and said: "*Return, ye backsliding children*—all except Elisha." These words struck Elisha like a fiery lash, and he realized that from that moment on he was an outcast, as was Cain. That is when he fell out of heaven, and found himself back on earth, alone in a desert. And he knew the desolation of that desert for many days before he found his way to Jerusalem. And from that time forward he found himself to be a fugitive and a wanderer in the eyes of men, no longer known by his name, but as Aher, the Other. For he had cut off all the generations that were tied to the root of his soul. And when at last he died, a fire rose up from his grave, for his torment had still not come to an end.

As for Rabbi Akiba, he closed his eyes and held the Book of Raziel close to his heart, and gave thanks to the Holy One, blessed be He, for all that he had witnessed when he saw the world through the Eyes of God. And when he opened his eyes, a Voice spoke from

Heaven and said: "*I have set My bow in the cloud.*" At that moment Rabbi Akiba witnessed one of the true miracles of heaven, the appearance of the rainbow of Noah, which has remained hidden in Paradise since the time it served to confirm the Covenant between God and Noah. That rainbow shimmered before Rabbi Akiba's eyes and illumined the signs that he had left behind in the heavens, to guide him back. And by following those signs he descended from the highest heavens back to the Garden and to the gate where the four had once entered. And when Rabbi Akiba reached that gate he discovered that it could always be opened from within, and he departed from there in peace.

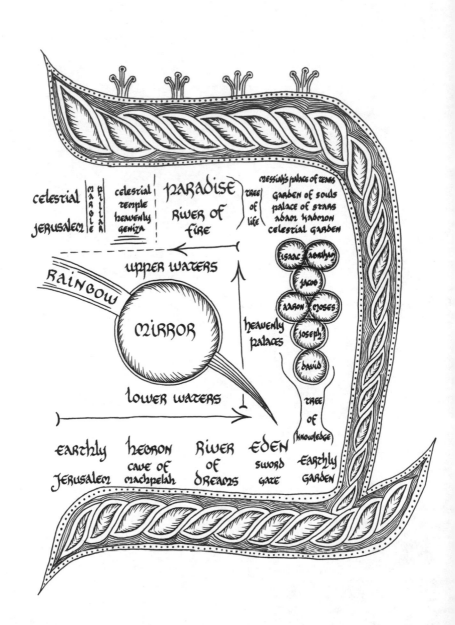

CELESTIAL | MAROR | CELESTIAL | PARADISE
JERUSALEM | PILLAR | TEMPLE | RIVER OF
| | HEAVENLY | FIRE
| | GENIZA |

TREE | MESSIAH'S PALACE OF TEARS
OF | GARDEN OF SOULS
LIFE | PALACE OF STARS
| ADAM KADMON
| CELESTIAL GARDEN

RAINBOW

MIRROR

UPPER WATERS

HEAVENLY
PALACES

ISAAC ABRAHAM
JACOB
AARON MOSES
JOSEPH
DAVID

LOWER WATERS

TREE
OF
KNOWLEDGE

EARTHLY | HEBRON | RIVER | EDEN | EARTHLY
JERUSALEM | CAVE OF | OF | SWORD | GARDEN
| MACHPELAH | DREAMS | GATE |

Thematic Commentary
Marc Bregman

THE LETTER *BET*

One of the most important themes that runs through Schwartz's *The Four Who Entered Paradise* is the motif of the *Bet*, the second letter of the Hebrew alphabet.[1] The singular importance of this letter stems from the fact that it opens the Torah in the word *Bereshit*, "In the beginning."[2] The sages of the talmudic period even interpreted the shape of the letter *Bet* ב, which suggested to them a kind of parenthesis that placed a limit on the legitimate areas of intellectual inquiry:

> Rabbi Yonah said in the name of Rabbi Levi: The world was created with the letter *Bet*. Just as the *Bet* is closed on all of its sides, but open on one of its sides,[3] so too you have no right to expound (*li-drosh*, or perhaps better in this context: "to investigate") what is above and what is below, what [comes] before and what after, except from the day that the world was created and on.[4]

It is significant that this comment is cited as part of the talmudic discussion of the restrictions on expounding "the work of creation" stated in Mishnah *Hagigah* (see the introduction, p. xiv). As we have seen, what led to Ben Zoma's demise was his passion for inquiring into and expounding the "Work of Creation"—in effect, daring to look beyond the three closed sides of the initial letter *Bet*.

In the opening chapter of the novella, the theme of the *Bet* is introduced as the denouement of Rabbi Akiba's dream of a previously undecipherable, ancient map: "Then, just before waking, he drew his eyes back and saw the map as if for the first time. And when he did, he could not comprehend how he had ever forgotten that the map was simply the letter *Bet*."

It is instructive to compare the contemporary storyteller's narrative revelation of the letter *Bet* as a map with a comment found in an exposition on the Hebrew letters by the contemporary hasidic scholar, Rabbi Yitzchak Ginzburgh:[5]

> The *beit* is composed of three connected *vavs* resembling a square, yet open on the left side. From the perspective of the Torah, the top line of the square faces east, the right side faces south and the bottom side faces west. The open side faces north—The Torah calls east "forwards" (*kedmah*, Genesis 28:14), south "towards the right" (*temanah*, Exodus 26:18, etc.), west "towards the [Mediterranean] sea (*yamah*, Genesis 18:14), which is also called "the sea behind" (*yam ha-aharon*, Deuteronomy 34:2), since it is behind one standing in the land of Israel facing east. Thus, if one imagines the *beit* lying on the ground, it assumes the orientation mentioned in the text.

It may well be that the *Bet* that Rabbi Akiba saw in his dream was the special form of the *Bet* found at the beginning of the Torah scroll. For not only is this particular *Bet* written larger than the following letters, but according to one halakhic source, it should be crowned with four short upward strokes (*tagim*).[6] Significantly, it was Rabbi Akiba who was particularly famous for his ability to interpret these "crowns" that God attached to the letters of the Torah just before giving it to Moses.[7] It would of course have been natural for Rabbi

Akiba to have interpreted the four strokes crowning the *Bet* of *Bereshit* as symbolically representing himself and his three companions who entered Paradise and as the river that went out of Eden to water the garden and from there divided into four heads.[8]

THE CAVE OF MACHPELAH

In the novella, the four sages also use their knowlege of rabbinic tradition to figure out that the entrance to paradise must be through the Cave of Machpelah. How this tradition developed is an object lesson in the way Jewish legend developed. Acccording to the biblical record, Abraham purchased the cave from the people of Hebron as a burial place following the death of Sarah (Genesis, chapter 23). After his own death, Abraham's sons Isaac and Ishmael buried their father in the same cave (Genesis 25:9–10). Subsequently, we learn that Isaac and his wife Rebekah and Jacob and his wife Leah are also buried in the Cave of Machpelah (Genesis 49:29–32, 50:13). Thus, Scripture records that three couples, the forebearers of the people of Israel,[9] were laid to rest in this family burial site. The Bible tells us that Hebron, where this burial cave was located, was also called Kiryat Arba (Genesis 23:2 and elsewhere); and it is quite explicit in explaining that this town (*kiryah*) was so named for Arba "the great man among the Anakim" (Joshua 14:13).[10] However, the word *arba* also means "four" in Hebrew. And so, it is only to be expected that *kiryat arba* would be understood not as "the town of Arba," but as "the town of four."[11] And since three couples were already known to be buried there, it was only natural for the midrashic imagination to supply a fourth couple—and what more appropriate couple than the forebearers of humanity, Adam and Eve![12] The exegetical motivation for the development of this legend within rabbinic Judaism may have been further strengthened by a separate tradition (possibly pre-rabbinic) that Adam was buried in a "cave of treasures." According to this tradition, Adam took treasures with him when he and Eve were expelled from Eden, after which they went to dwell in a cave near Paradise.[13]

But how did the first couple actually come to be buried specifically in the Cave of Machpelah? And how later did their descendants discover that it was this cave that was the entranceway to Paradise? The mythopoeic imagination of the *Aggadah* (Jewish legend) was quick to supply stories to answer these questions:

> When the angels visited Abraham,[14] he wished to prepare for them a great feast. So he ran to fetch a calf. But the calf fled from before him and ran into the Cave of Machpelah. When Abraham entered the cave he found Adam and Eve lying their on beds,[15] asleep, with lights burning above them.[16] And a sweet scent was upon them like pleasing scent (of a sacrifice). And therefore Abraham desired the Cave of Machpelah as a burial site.[17]

A medieval Jewish source clarifies the origin of this "pleasing scent": "When Adam went to bury Eve in the Cave of Machpelah, he wanted to dig deeper, because he scented the sweet fragrance of Paradise, near the entrance to which it lay, but a heavenly voice called to him, Enough!"[18]

Ultimately, the Cave of Machpelah came to be the passageway through which the souls of the deceased pass on their way to the celestial paradise. And, in medieval Jewish exegesis, this notion was anchored in sacred Scripture:[19]

> And Abraham buried Sarah his wife in the Cave of Machpelah . . . her death and burial were in a place that was destined to be the "house of God and there the gate of heaven"[20]. . . . "And Sarah died in Kiryat Arba which is Hebron" (Genesis 23:2). This city is called Hebron because the soul of anyone buried there unites (*mithaberet*) on high in the city of God with four (*arba*) camps of the *Shekhinah*.[21] And so the Patri-

archs had good reason to seek burial in this place, for from there souls merit to be reunited with their source which is the Throne of Glory. And this is the meaning of "Kiryat Arba which is Hebron."

Understandably, the descendants of the Patriarchs continued to seek burial in the Cave of Machpelah. The medieval traveler, Benjamin of Tudela, relates:

> If a Jew comes . . . and gives a special reward, the custodian of the cave opens unto him a gate of iron, which was constructed by our forefathers, and then he is able to descend below by means of steps, holding a lighted candle in his hands. He then reaches a cave, in which nothing is to be found, and a cave beyond, which is likewise empty, but when he reaches the third cave, behold there are six sepulchers, those of Abraham, Isaac, and Jacob, respectively, facing those of Sarah, Rebekah, and Leah. And upon the graves are inscriptions cut in stone [with the names of each]. A lamp burns day and night upon the graves in the cave. One finds there many casks filled with bones of Israelites, as the members of the house of Israel were wont to bring the bones of their fathers thither and to deposit them there to this day.[22]

In the novella (chapter 2), Schwartz seems to have projected the experience of the medieval travel back onto the four sages from Tannaitic times. When they come to the Cave of Machpelah they find:

> . . . its entrance guarded by an iron door that dated from the time of our forefathers. The doorkeeper was an old Jew[23] who assumed they had come to visit the burial place of the Patriarchs Abraham, Isaac, and Jacob and their wives. He directed them to cross two empty caves and then to descend twenty-four steps in a narrow passage, in order to come to the six tombs on which the names of the Patriarchs and their wives are engraved.
>
> Each of the sages purchased a candle from the old man and they passed through the outer caves as he had directed them. Inside they saw by the light of the candles that these caves were filled with stone boxes

containing the bones that had been brought there because the cave was
a holy resting place.

No wonder the four companions subsequently come to realize that
the beginning of their journey to Paradise through the Cave of
Machpelah is a passage "beyond the tomb" (pp. 19–20).[24]

THE THREE SOUL SISTERS

Following a somnial cruise down a subterranean River of Dreams,[25]
the four sages enter an enchanted realm (chapter 3).[26] Here they encounter one of a series of mythical figures who will serve as their guides
as they continue their mystical odyssey. The first of these spiritual
figures introduces herself as Neshamah. After the sages realize that
they have already found their way into Eden, Neshamah relates that
she and her sisters are daughters of "the Bride." This clearly refers
to the *Shekhinah*, the "Bride" of God.[27] Naturally, her maternal role
is also frequently described;[28] but more specifically the *Shekhinah*
is the Mother of the Soul.[29] Thus, in the novella, Neshamah and
her two sisters, Ruah and Nefesh,[30] are a narrative elaboration of
the notion of the tripartite soul.[31] This concept of the soul is reflected
in the *Zohar*, where *neshamah* is the highest aspect of the soul, *nefesh*
the lowest, and *ruah* plays some kind of intermediary role.[32] However, the essential unity of the three is also stressed by Rabbi Moses
de Leon, who is thought to be the author of at least the main part of
the *Zohar*.[33]

In the novella, characteristically it is Rabbi Akiba who first realizes
the essential unity of the three soul sisters, and significantly this realization is presaged in another of the dream sequences that are a leitmotif
of the novella:

... As for Akiba, he dreamed of a bird whose feathers were woven of moon rays, whose heart was a living opal, and whose wings in flight echoed the crystalline music of the stars.

Rabbi Akiba, wakened by the sound of wings, was the first to open his eyes the next morning. At first he thought he was still dreaming of the magical bird. Then he saw three young eagles circling above him, their soft feathers drawn around them, gray and white. As he watched, Akiba saw something quite strange: sometimes the three eagles seemed to blend into one eagle, while a moment later he saw all three again soaring side by side. This happened several times before the eagles landed on the other side of the rock that stood next to the pool of living waters, where the sages had first found Neshamah. Then Akiba saw Neshamah and two other young women who bore a close resemblance to her emerge from behind the rock and come toward the place where the other sages were still sleeping. . . . Akiba saw that the three sisters sometimes seemed to blend into one figure, who was somehow more complete than any one of the three by herself. This he linked to the three eagles, and he understood that the sisters had the power to alter their form. (chapter 4, pp. 41–42)

Rabbi Akiba's perceptive reverie, at the end of the sages' first night in Eden, is remarkably similar to a recurrent image found elsewhere in the writings of Rabbi Moses de Leon: "*Nefesh . . . Ruah . . . Neshamah . . .* fly out from the river that flows out of Eden."[34] The portrayal of the three aspects of the soul as flying creatures suggests the soul's power of ascent. At first glance, it may seem curious that Schwartz has chosen the eagle to represent the soul-bird.[35] While not every specific image in the novella necessarily has a precise analog in Jewish tradition, it is interesting that even this choice finds an echo, for example, in Eve's vision of a chariot of light, flying through Heaven, drawn by radiant eagles.[36]

THE INDIVIDUAL IDENTITY AND PERSONAL QUEST OF EACH OF THE FOUR SAGES

It is in one of the dialogues between the three soul sisters and the four sages that we learn what motivates each of them on their quest to enter Paradise (chapter 4, pp. 48–49).

First, Ben Zoma tells that he is seeking the Mysteries of Creation (*ma'aseh bereshit*). This is in line with a story about this sage found in a number of places in rabbinic literature:[37]

> Simeon ben Zoma was sitting and meditating when Rabbi Joshua passed by and greeted him once and twice but received no reply. The third time he answered hurriedly. Then he asked him: Where do the legs come from [i.e., what are you up to]?[38] He said: Nothing from nothing, Rabbi.[39] He [Rabbi Joshua] insisted: I call upon heaven and earth as my witnesses that I will not budge from here until you tell me where the legs are from. He answered: I was contemplating the Work of Creation (*ma'aseh bereshit*), and there was only a space of two or three fingers between the upper and lower waters, for it is not written "And the Spirit of God blew," but "hovered" (Genesis 1:2), like a bird flying and flapping with its wings, its wings barely touching [the nest]. Thereupon Rabbi Joshua turned to his disciples and remarked to them: Ben Zoma is gone [i.e., gone mad, lost his mind].

In the talmudic sources this story is brought to elucidate what is meant by the phrase "Ben Zoma looked and was stricken" in the core story of the four sages who entered Paradise [see introduction, p. xv].

In the continuation of the sages' dialogue in the novella, Ben Azzai relates a curious story about himself:

> Once, when I was studying Torah, a flame surrounded my body, and I heard the words of the Torah as they were spoken at Mount Sinai. And when I opened my eyes I saw the chariot in the vision of Ezekiel,

and a bolt of electrum passed through me, and for a long instant my soul flew from my body. And I heard a voice say: "Rise, for magnificent palaces and golden beds await you in Paradise." Ever since I have pursued the Mysteries of the Chariot, for they haunt me night and day.

Ben Azzai is indeed depicted as having been considered by his contemporaries, as an interpreter of the Mysteries of the Chariot of nearly supernatural power.

Ben Azzai was once sitting and expounding[40] and the fire was burning around him. They came and told Rabbi Akiba: Ben Azzai is sitting and expounding and the fire is burning around him. He came to him [to Ben Azzai] and said to him: Perhaps you are dealing with the Chambers of the Chariot.[41] He replied: No; rather I am stringing [like pearls] words of the Torah to the Prophets and words of the Prophets to the Writings,[42] and the words of Torah are as joyful as the day they were given from Sinai. And when they were originally given from Sinai were they not given with fire? So it is written, "And the mountain burned with fire to the heart of heaven" (Deuteronomy 4:11).[43]

The appearance of fire and flame, such as that seen at the Sinaitic revelation of Torah (see Exodus 19:18, Deuteronomy 4:15), is often associated with the Work of the Chariot (*merkavah*) described in the Book of Ezekiel, chapters 1 and 10, particularly when it was being expounded in the circle of Yohanan ben Zakkai.[44] It should also be noted that the voice heard by Ben Azzai in the novella seems related to what Rabbi Yohanan ben Zakkai is said to have related to Rabbi Yose Ha-Kohen: "In my dream you [plural] and I were sitting at a table on Mount Sinai[45] when a heavenly voice proclaimed from heaven: Come up to here, Come up to here! Large couches and comfortable cushions are spread out for you. You and your disciples and your disciples' disciples are invited . . ."[46]

The "bolt of electrum" that passed through Ben Azzai at the moment he saw the celestial Chariot also seems to reflect a related talmudic tradition: "Our masters taught: There is a story about a certain boy who was reading in his master's house in the Book of Ezekiel. And he understood the word *hashmal* ("electrum")[47] [in the prophet's description of the *merkavah* Chariot] and fire came forth from *hashmal* and burned him up."[48] Ben Azzai's explanation of what he personally is seeking in Paradise is thus a veritable collage of talmudic traditions concerning the *merkavah*.

Elisha ben Abuyah relates a different reason for seeking to enter Paradise: "I have always been drawn to seek knowledge of God, for God is the source of all knowledge." This follows the widely accepted notion that this sage was involved in some sort of Gnostic or similar type of heretical, dualistic speculation on the nature of the Godhead.[49] In talmudic tradition, Elisha (or Aher as he is often called) seems to represent the danger of external, particularly Greco-Roman, influences on traditional Jewish culture: "What about Aher? Greek song did not cease from his mouth. They said of Aher that when he used to get up (to leave) the study-house, many heretical books [*sifrei minin*] would fall from his bosom."[50]

The final speaker in the dialogue with the soul sisters is Rabbi Akiba, who reveals that his only longing is for the light of Torah. This is in line with the portrayal of Rabbi Akiba throughout rabbinic literature as the quintessential Torah scholar. Since the acquisition of Torah learning is such a primary value in rabbinic culture, it is no wonder that Rabbi Akiba is the only one of the four sages who "ascends and descends in peace." For only Rabbi Akiba's goal in entering Paradise— the passionate desire for Torah wisdom—is the correct one in the value system of the rabbis who told the story of the four sages in talmudic times. In this connection, it is interesting to note that of the four sages who entered Paradise, only Akiba is said to have been a fully ordained rabbi, while the other three are described as "disciples of the wise" (*talmidei hakhamim*).

This dialogue in the novella, in which each of the four sages explains his own personal goal, presents in narrative fashion a resolution of one of the fundamental enigmas of the talmudic tale of the four who entered Paradise: What do each of the four sages represent metaphorically? The answer given here is that Rabbi Akiba's three companions went astray because each mistook the part for the whole in a different way. Ben Zoma represents the disciple who is overly engrossed in the study of the Work of Creation, Ben Azzai the disciple who is overly engrossed in the Work of the Chariot. Elisha ben Abuyah represents the risk of being led astray by an overemphasis on theosophical wisdom (Gnosis). Rabbi Akiba succeeds where the others fail because he intuitively grasps that Torah contains all knowledge.[51] And it is Akiba who embodies the fundamental principle of rabbinic culture—the study and practice of Torah outweighs all else (talmud torah ke-neged kulam).[52]

GATHERING THE SPARKS

It is natural that the most prominent of the three sisters should introduce another theme that follows the sages on their adventure like a thread of light—the gathering of sparks. Before the sages bid farewell to the sisters who have escorted them through Eden, Neshamah says (chapter 4): "If you succeed in entering the Garden, see if you can find any sparks of the primordial light. . . . If you can, give them to the Messiah. For the more sparks that are gathered for him, the sooner his footsteps will be heard in the world."

The motif of primordial light is as ancient as the story of Creation, as described at the beginning of the Book of Genesis (1:2–3): "And God said: Let there be light, and there was light. And God saw that the light was good, and God divided the light from the darkness." In talmudic times the interpretation of this verse had already become part of esoteric lore:

"And God said: Let there be Light." R. Shimon bar Yehotzedek asked
Rabbi Shmuel bar Nahman, saying to him: Since I have heard about
you that you are a master of legendary lore (*ba'al haggadah*), [tell me],
How was this light created? He answered: The Holy One, blessed be
He, wrapped Himself in it like a garment and the brilliance of His splendor radiated from one end of the universe to the other. He [Shmuel]
said this to him [Shimon] in a whisper. He [Shimon] said to [Shmuel]:
This is stated fully in Scripture, "He wraps Himself in Light like a garment" (Psalms 104:2), so why relate it in a whisper?! He [Shmuel] answered: Just as I heard it in a whisper, so I said it in a whisper."[53]

This tradition about the origin of the primordial light seems to be
a fragment of the "Work of Creation" (*ma'aseh bereshit*), which was
not to be taught with so many as two as stated in the Mishnah.[54] In
the talmudic discussion on this Mishnah, we find another fragment of
the complex of traditions about the primordial light:

> Rabbi Eleazar [ben Pedat] said: The light which the Holy One, blessed
> be He, created on the first day, Adam saw by it from one end of the
> universe to the other. But when He saw that the subsequent behavior
> of mankind was corrupt, He arose and hid it from them, as it says, "But
> from the wicked their light is withheld" (Job 38:15). And for whom
> did He hide it? For the righteous in the World to Come.[55]

It is significant that elsewhere this primordial light is said to have had
the power to "eclipse the light of the sun,"[56] just as the primordial
Adam was so splendorous as to "eclipse the light of the sun." And in
size this primordial Adam extended "from one end of the universe to
the other,"[57] like the light that enabled him to see "from one end of
the universe to the other." So there seems to have been some connection between the conception of the primordial light and the idea
of the primordial man in the esoteric traditions about the "Work of
Creation" that developed already in talmudic times.[58]

These mythic motifs may have provided the basis for the development of the last major Jewish myth by Isaac Luria (called the "Ari") and his followers in the sixteenth century. According to the Ari, the primordial man (*adam kadmon*) is the source of the primordial light that was originally contained in "vessels" (*kelim*). However, due to a cosmic catastrophe there was a shattering of the vessels (*shevirat ha-kelim*), scattering the primordial light in sparks that fell to earth. The primary purpose of religious life, as seen in this myth, is to seek out and raise up these sparks to their celestial home through the process of repair and restoration (*tikkun*). The completion of this process will inevitably lead to the end of Exile, final redemption, and the coming of the Messiah.[59]

It is these sparks of light that the four sages gather in the Garden of Eden, prior to their heavenly ascent, in order to eventually restore them to the Messiah in the continuation of the novella (chapter 9).

AT THE ANGEL GATE

However, actually entering the Garden—which according to the novella is located within Eden[60]—proves a considerable challenge. Having traversed Eden led by the three soul sisters, the four sages arrive at a gate that is guarded by two angels, one of them spinning a sword of flame and the other guarding the way to the Tree of Life (chapter 4). This clearly is based on the verse, "And at the east of the garden of Eden, God placed Cherubim and a flaming sword that turned every way, to keep the way of the Tree of Life" (Genesis 3:24). Just as this gate and its guardians posed an obstacle for the four sages in the novella, so too the verse on which this episode is based has raised a number of difficulties for biblical interpreters thoughout the ages.

First, to what extent are these terrifying Cherubim stationed at the entrance to the Garden of Eden to be identified with the Cherubim

mentioned elsewhere in the Bible?[61] In most places these angelic beings
are represented as servants of God, as in the Genesis passage quoted
above.[62] Similarly, over the Ark was placed a golden representation of
two Cherubim between which God's presence was believed to dwell
(1 Samuel 4:4, 2 Samuel 6:2, 2 Chronicles 13:6). In one description it
is said that the two Cherubim face each other (Exodus 25:20). Although at first glance this description seems innocent enough, in rabbinic times it led to the remarkable idea that the two Cherubim were
locked in embrace.[63] "Rabbi Katina said: When Israel would come
on pilgrimage, they [the Temple functionaries] would unveil the curtain [in the Temple] and show the Israelite pilgrims the Cherubim
embracing one another. And they would say to them: 'Look! God's
love for you is like the love of man and woman.'" No wonder that in
the Talmud this statement arouses considerable discussion, which
concludes with an even more remarkable story that explains what
eventually became of this suggestive, and easily misunderstood, image.[64]

> Resh Lakish said: When the gentiles entered the Temple they saw the
> Cherubim embracing one another. They took them out to the market-
> place and proclaimed: "These Israelites, whose blessing is a blessing and
> whose curse is a curse—that they should be occupying themselves with
> such matters!" Then they cast them down [destroyed the Cherubim],
> as it is said, "All that honored her, cast her down, for they have seen
> her nakedness" (Lamentations 1:8).

However, another biblical description of these Cherubim states that
they faced "toward the House" (2 Chronicles 3:13), which was taken
to mean that the Cherubim were not facing, but rather turned away
from one another,[65] as Schwartz portrays them in the novella.

The Cherubim placed by God as guardians of the entrance to the
Garden of Eden are actually referred to in another biblical passage,
the Prophet Ezekiel's lamentation over the king of Tyre (Ezekiel

28:11 ff.).[66] Curiously, this passage became the focus of a strange legend in which the *Merkavah*—which elsewhere in the Book of Ezekiel (chapter 1) is depicted as God's divine chariot—becomes God's opponent, a kind of "anti-*Merkavah*."[67]

The changeable character of the Cherubim is also reflected in Ezekiel's *Merkavah* vision itself. In the first version of this vision, one face of the four "living creatures" (*hayyot*) is described as being that of an ox (Ezekiel 1:10). But in another description of the same four mythical beasts, this face is replaced by that of a Cherub (Ezekiel 10:14).[68] How this change took place was explained by Resh Lakish:[69] "Ezekiel begged for mercy concerning it [the ox face, a reminder of Israel's sin in connection with the golden calf] and transformed it into a Cherub [here obviously regarded as a more benevolent image]. [To accomplish this] Ezekiel said to God: May an accuser become an advocate?"

The ambivalent nature of the Cherubim was also related to the way in which they guarded the entrance to the Garden of Eden. This controversy relates to the "flaming sword that turned every way." The Hebrew expression used to describe the "flaming of the sword" (*lahat ha-herev*) is reminiscent of the word used to describe the sorcery of the Egyptian sorcerers (*be-lahateihem*, Exodus 7:11). To make matters more complicated, the same Egyptian magic is also referred to by a slightly different Hebrew expression (*be-lateihem*). In the rabbinic discussion of these seemingly similar terms it was argued that one term referred to the "work of magic" (*ma'aseh keshafim*) and the other to "the work of demons" (*ma'aseh shedim*). And this exegetical debate concerning the Egyptian sorcerers was transferred onto the discussion of the "flaming sword" that guarded the Garden—did it operate by "magic" or were the Cherubim actually "demons"![70]

The ambivalent and changing nature of the Cherubim is similarly reflected in Schwartz's treatment of the two angels who guard the entrance to the Garden of Eden and the way to the Tree of Life. At first they seem to pose an insurmountable obstacle for the sages. But

once the demonic magic of the sword–wielding angel has been overcome, thanks to Rabbi Akiba's resourcefulness,[71] the four sages receive a warm welcome into the Garden of Eden from the now more
"cherubic" angel[72] who guards the way to the Tree of Life.[73]

The way in which Rabbi Akiba helps his companions to enter the
Garden of Eden by tricking the guardian angels is reminiscent of the
story of another sage who accomplished a similar feat.

> The sages taught: Rabbi Yehoshua ben Levi was completely righteous.
> And when the time came for him to die, the Holy One, blessed be He,
> said to the Angel of Death: Do whatever he requires and whatever he
> asks of you. He went to Rabbi Yehoshua ben Levi and said to him:
> The time has come for you to die, but whatever you ask of me I shall
> do for you. When Rabbi Yehoshua heard this he said: I ask that you
> show me my place in the Garden of Eden. He replied: Go with me
> and I will show you. Rabbi Yehoshua said to the Angel of Death: Give
> me your sword so that you won't upset me with it. So the Angel of
> Death gave him the sword and the two of them went until they came
> to the walls of the Garden of Eden. When they were standing outside
> the wall, the Angel of Death took Rabbi Yehoshua, lifted him up, set
> him on the wall of the Garden of Eden, and said to him: Look at your
> place in the Garden of Eden! Rabbi Yehoshua ben Levi jumped down
> from the wall into the Garden of Eden. But the Angel of Death grabbed
> him by the corner of his garment and said to him: Get out of there!
> Rabbi Yehoshua swore by the Name [of God] that he would not now
> leave. And the Angel of Death had no authority to go in there after
> him.[74]

In the continuation of the story, as it has come down to us in a number of versions, Rabbi Yehoshua ben Levi's reward for outwitting the
Angel of Death is a guided tour of Heaven and Hell.[75] And similarly,
in the continuation of the novella, Rabbi Akiba and his companions
now are able to continue on their journey, guided by the angel

Shamshiel,[76] through the Garden of Eden on their way to Paradise.[77] It should be noted that both stories deal with the theme of mortal men (in both cases talmudic sages) who were able to enter Paradise alive by outsmarting the angelic guardians whose job it is to prevent this. Overcoming angelic opposition to the heavenly ascent is also a major theme of the *Hekhalot* literature. In *Hekhalot* literature the angelic guardians of the celestial palaces often put up fierce and even cruel oppostion to the ascent of the aspiring *Merkavah* mystic.[78] In the novella, on the other hand, the various celestial beings that the four sages encounter tend to take a more kindly and even helpful attitude to their mystical quest. In the continuation of their entry into Paradise, instead of having to overcome angelic opposition, the sages encounter a series of biblical personalities and remarkably humane angels who welcome them and assist them on their ascent through the celestial palaces. From this perspective, Schwartz's overall approach to the heavenly ascent represents a humanization of the *Hekhalot*.

THE ASCENT THROUGH THE HEAVENLY PALACES

At the end of their journey through the Garden of Eden, the sages pass through another gate, the Tree of Knowlege,[79] and now begin their heavenly ascent in earnest.[80]

First, the sages are carried aloft into the celestial realms in a cloud (chapter 6), in much the same way that the earliest heavenly travelers[81] are said to have ascended: "It came to pass, when Enoch had told his sons, that the angels took him onto their wings and bore him up on the first heaven and placed him on the clouds."[82] However, it is the description of Moses' heavenly journey that incorporates a specific scriptural prooftext for the notion of the cloud of ascent.

When the time came for Moses to ascend on high, a cloud came and
crouched before him. Moses did not know whether to mount it or to
take hold of it. Thereupon, the mouth of the cloud flew open, and he
entered into it, as it is said, "And Moses entered into the midst of the
cloud" (Exodus 24:18) [this was the cloud of which it was said, "When
Moses had ascended the mountain,] the cloud covered the mountain"
(Exodus 24:15). And the cloud covered Moses and carried him up.[83]

In the continuation of this text, Moses makes an extended tour through
the heavens until he reaches the throne of Glory and is shown the
celestial Temple by God, who opens the seven firmaments for him.
Moses' heavenly ascent is the archetype for the heavenly journey of
the *Merkavah* mystic through the celestial palaces (*Hekhalot*),[84] which
in turn supplies the model for the continuation of the four sages' journey through the celestial Paradise.

However, in the novella, the four sages' journey through the celestial
palaces takes an unusual turn. For, as noted above, the palaces are not
guarded by hostile angels but are governed by biblical figures who each
accord the sages a warm welcome. In the continuation of the narrative, the sages ascend through the dwellings of David, Joseph, Aaron,
Moses, Jacob, Isaac, and Abraham. These seven biblical personalities
are known in Jewish tradition as the *ushpizin*,[85] "guests" who are invited into the temporary dwelling, known as a *sukkah*, during the holi-
day of Tabernacles (Sukkot).[86] On each of the seven days of the holi-
day all seven guests are invited, but on each day one of the seven biblical
heroes is invited to be the special guest of honor, beginning with
Abraham. The invitation formula is in Aramaic, reminiscent of the
language of the *Zohar*:

Enter, O lofty and holy guests. Enter, O lofty and holy fathers, to sit in
the lofty shade of faith.[87] Enter, Abraham the beloved, and with him
Isaac who was bound,[88] and with him Jacob the innocent, and with

him Joseph the righteous, and with him Moses the faithful shepherd,[89] and with him Aaron the Holy Priest, and with him David the King Messiah. Let me invite to my feast the lofty guests. . . . I pray thee, Abraham my lofty guest, sit with me and with you the other lofty guests, Isaac, Jacob, Joseph, Moses, Aaron, and David.[90]

No wonder this invitation is phrased in such lofty, mystical language. This liturgical custom, or at least the idea behind it, seems to have originated with Moshe de Leon, the primary author of the *Zohar*. In one of his admittedly authored works[91] he writes:

And when one sits in the *sukkah*, seven righteous ones, the foundations of the world, are his guest (*ushpizo*) who took for their portion the seven days. And they are Abraham, Isaac and Jacob, Joseph, Moses and Aaron, David.[92] And when he eats he must invite them to his meal. And about them it says, "You shall dwell in booths (*sukkot*) seven days" (Leviticus 23:42).

In the *Zohar*, this custom is attributed to talmudic sages in typical zoharic fashion.[93] Elsewhere, the *Zohar*[94] cites "The Book of the *Aggadah*," to the effect that the four species represent the seven guests. The three myrtle sprigs stand for Abraham, Isaac, and Jacob, the two twigs of willow stand for Moses and Aaron; the palm branch is Joseph and the citron is David. The unusual order that puts Joseph after Moses and Aaron is necessitated by the connection of the seven "guests" to the seven lower *sefirot*,[95] which are arranged in a definite order. Abraham, Isaac, and Jacob represent *Hesed*, *Gevurah*, and *Tiferet*; Moses and Aaron represent *Netzah* and *Hod*; Joseph represents *Yesod*, and David *Malkhut*.[96] In the novella, this order is retained, though reversed, as the four sages ascend, as it were up through the sefirotic tree,[97] as they visit the celestial residences of David, Joseph, Aaron, Moses, Jacob, Isaac, and Abraham.[98] This reversal is entirely appropriate to Paradise, which is referred to in talmudic tradition as an "inverted world" in which those that were above will be below and those that were below will be above.[99] Indeed, such reversals are also typical of *Merkavah* literature, which paradoxically refers to those who undertake the heavenly ascent as *yordei merkavah*, literally "those who 'descend' to the Chariot."[100] In the novella we actually have a double reversal of the *ushpizin* tradition, since here it is the biblical "guests" who now repay the hospitality shown to them by inviting the four sages into their seven heavenly dwellings.[101]

IN THE CELESTIAL PARADISE

Upon leaving the palace of Abraham, the four sages continue their ascent into the celestial paradise above the seventh heaven. This cosmological arrangement is in line with the view that the celestial Garden of Eden is located above the seven firmaments.[102] As with the terrestrial and transitional portions of their mystic odyssey, in their journey through the celestial realms, the four sages continue to experience adventures based in traditional lore.

In the celestial Garden, guided now by Raziel himself, the sages are shown the Tree of Souls[103] and a Palace of Stars[104] occupied by Adam Kadmon.[105] This primordial man is not just the genealogical progenitor of the human race described in the first chapters of Genesis. According to rabbinic myth, prior to his final crystallization in recognizable human form, Adam filled the entire universe.[106] The mythopoeic imagination of the rabbis depicted Adamic ancestry in a very concrete way: "While Adam was still in primordial form [*golem*], the Holy One, blessed be He, showed him each and every righteous descendant from among his offspring. Some hung from his head and some from his hair, and some from his neck, and some from his two eyes, and some from his nose, and some from his mouth, and some from his ears, and some from his arm."[107]

But other rabbis conceived of our descent from Adam in a some-
what less physical way: "Rabbi Yohanan said: Concerning what Scripture says, 'He does great things without measure and wonders without number' (Job 9:10), know that all souls until the end of time are
from Adam; all were created in the Garden of Eden during the first
six days of creation."[108]

Elsewhere, this storehouse of souls is called the "body" (*guf*). "As
Rav Assi said: The son of David (i.e., the messiah) will not come until
all the souls have been depleted from the 'body.'"[109]

This complex of notions was extensively elaborated by the Lurianic
kabbalists of the sixteenth century who particularly expanded the idea
of Adam's supernal body. According to this conception, Adam's comprehensive soul was composed of 613 "major roots" (248 "limbs" and
365 "sinews"), which subdivided into "minor roots," each of which
constitutes a "great soul," which further subdivide into individual sparks
constituting the souls of individuals. In this way all individual human
souls (or "soul sparks") constitute together one unity, in the same way
that the various parts of a tree have their source in the root of the
tree.[110]

Like the kabbalists of Safed, Schwartz has continued to develop the
idea of the primordial Adam, but using the narrative mode through
which myth has traditionally been expressed as legend. In the novella
(chapter 8), in answer to Ben Azzai's question about Adam Kadmon,
Raziel explains:

> Before God created Adam as a man of flesh and blood, He created a
> dream Adam, whose name was Adam Kadmon. And God called forth
> this dream Adam and said: "Alone among all creations, I am going to
> permit you to choose your own soul." And God brought Adam Kadmon
> to the Treasury of Souls in heaven and opened its door. And when Adam
> looked inside, he saw a sky crowded with stars. And God said: "Every
> one of those stars is a soul. Which one do you want?"
>
> And as he gazed out at that constellation of souls, scattered like sparks,
> Adam wondered how he could possibly choose one from among them.

Every one glowed with a light of its own. Every one was equally beautiful. Then Adam saw that the constellation formed a great Tree of Souls, which branched out in every direction. And Adam said to the Holy One, blessed be He: "I want the soul of the Tree of Souls from which all of the souls are suspended." And God was delighted and brought forth the soul of the Tree of Souls and gave it to Adam.

And that is why the soul of Adam contained all souls, and why all souls are a part of Adam's soul.

In the continuation of their mystic odyssey, the sages find themselves in what Raziel explains is the Garden of Souls. It is here that each of the sages, for better or for worse, learns about the true root of his own soul.

The last celestial palace the sages visit is occupied by none other than the Messiah.[111] Again it is Raziel who explains: "This palace is known as the palace of tears, for it was built out of the tears shed by those longing for the Messiah. This is where the Messiah waits for the sign to be given that the time has come for his footsteps to be heard."

Moshe Idel has called attention to the importance of weeping as a mystical practice that could indeed even contribute to the coming of the Messiah.[112] One medieval mystical text specifically links the coming of the Messiah to celestial weeping:

When the Messiah goes out and takes hold of the four rings [connected to the four edges of the firmament] and gives forth his voice, then the whole firmament above the Garden [of Eden] trembles. Seven angels are summoned to him and say to him: Chosen of the Lord, be still! For the time has arrived for the Kingdom of Evil to be uprooted from its place. And the voice heard [coming] from the synagogues and study-houses [is that of Israel] reciting [Kaddish] with all their strength: Amen, May His great name be blessed for ever and to all eternity. Then the Holy One, blessed be He, shakes all the firmaments and lets fall two tears into the Great Sea. And the righteous and the Messiah enter into that Palace [hekhal] known as the Bird's Nest.[113]

The "Bird's Nest" (*ken tzipor*) is further identified in the same text as the innermost palace in which the Messiah resides. The *Zohar* refers not only to the "Bird's Nest,"[114] but also to the Bird and its song: "Then the Holy One, blessed be He, beckons the bird, and it enters its nest, and comes to the Messiah, and it calls what it calls, and stirs up what it stirs up, until the Bird's Nest and the Messiah are called three times from inside the Holy Throne, and all ascend."[115]

This supernal bird makes its appearance in the novella (chapter 9) in the guise of a golden dove. Characteristically it is Rabbi Akiba who makes the connection between this bird and the Palace of the Messiah.

> Now the song of the gold dove was indescribably beautiful. None of them had ever heard music so sublime.[116] And Rabbi Akiba said: "Surely the palace that faces the nest of this golden dove must belong to the Messiah. For the song of this dove awakes in me a longing for the Messiah so sharp that I feel I cannot wait a day longer for the time of the Messiah to come." And when he said this, all of the other sages realized how powerful their longing for the Messiah had grown.

The golden dove makes its nest in the Tree of Life, which stands by the Palace of the Messiah. It is here that the sages gather again when they leave the Messiah's palace. And it is here that the sages realize that the goal of their quest, the Book of Raziel, must be sought even further beyond, in the Heavenly Temple.

The notion of a heavenly temple is very ancient and widespread. In the Hebrew Bible, this motif forms the basis of the prophet Isaiah's vision (chapter 6) of "the Lord sitting upon a throne, high and lifted up, and his train filled the Temple (*hekhal*)." Not surprisingly, the existence of a Heavenly Temple located within a celestial Jerusalem is a basic assumption in postbiblical literature.[117] For the most part, both the heavenly city and its temple are understood to be celestial models of their earthly counterparts.[118] Moreover, Isaiah's vision of God sitting on His celestial Throne in his Heavenly Temple supplies one of the primary scriptural subtexts for early Jewish *Hekhalot* mysticism (also referred to as "Throne" mysticism), the central goal of which was to view and visit these celestial sites.[119] Like the *Merkavah* mystics, so too the four sages' mystic odyssey concludes with their vision of the Heavenly Temple.[120]

The sages' final discovery of the Book of Raziel in a *Genizah* located at the entrance to the Heavenly Temple demonstrates Schwartz's rare ability to integrate ancient and modern sources. The Bible mentions "royal treasuries" (*ginzei ha-melekh*) belonging to Persian rulers. These treasuries served not only as a repository for monetary wealth but also as royal libraries or archives.[121] Similarly, the Temple in Jerusalem contained a Treasure Chamber, which served for the preservation of both monetary deposits and priestly archives.[122] The Mishnah (*Shabbat* 9:6, 16:1) rules that sacred writings that have become unusable require *genizah* ("hiding away").[123] And indeed a characteristic feature of ancient synagogue architecture seems to have been a *Genizah*, for keeping worn-out sacred texts, which was usually located in the floor of the apse where the Torah ark was placed.[124] At least one talmudic tradition actually speaks of such a text repository located— like the *Genizah* in Schwartz's Celestial Temple—under one of the steps leading to the Jerusalem Temple. "Rabban Gamliel the Elder [who was President of the Sanhedrin before the destruction of the Temple] . . . was sitting on a step leading up the Temple mount when an [Aramaic] translation [*targum*] of the Book of Job was brought before him. And he said to a builder:[125] hide it away (*tignezo*) under the course [of building stones].[126]

In the novella, when Rabbi Akiba finally recovers the Book of Raziel from the Heavenly *Genizah* and reads this long-lost sacred text, he discovers that each of its four chapters begins with one letter of the Ineffable Name of God. ". . . and at that instant he was blessed to see the world through the Eyes of God. For an eternal instant, Rabbi Akiba saw everywhere at once, from one end of the world to the other. . . ."[127]

This remarkable vision reveals a more modern source of Schwartz's inspiration. Like Rabbi Akiba, the hero of Jorge Luis Borges' story "The Aleph" is granted a moment of God-like vision when he peers beneath a cellar step: "Then I saw the Aleph. . . . In that gigantic instant I saw millions of delightful and atrocious acts; none astonished me more than the fact that all of them together occupied the same point, without superposition and without transparency. What my eyes saw was simultaneous."[128] Here Schwartz recognizes and recovers the Jewish vision at the heart of Borges' story, which even in its title acknowledges its Jewish origins.

THE FATE OF THE FOUR

In his momentary vision of eternity, the last thing that Rabbi Akiba learns is the demise of his three companions. The denouement of the novella (chapter 10) narrates the respective fates of the four sages.[129] In this way, the conclusion of the novella brings us back to the core story of the four who entered Paradise found in talmudic sources. These sources (see the introduction, p. xv) deal primarily with the fate of the four sages by linking each to a suggestive biblical verse.

According to the Babylonian Talmud: "Ben Azzai looked and died; about him Scripture says, 'Precious in the eyes of the Lord is the death of His saints' (Psalms 116:15)." An anonymous commentary to the legend of the four sages elaborates on the death of Ben Azzai as follows:[130]

"Ben Azzai looked and died," for he gazed upon the splendor of the *Shekhinah*. And [this is] like a man who looks with his weak eyes at the full force of the sun's light and his eyes become dim and sometimes he is blinded by the strength of the light that overpowers him. This is what happened to Ben Azzai; the light he was looking at overpowered him. And [this was due to] his excessive desire; for he desired to cleave[131] to

it and enjoy it endlessly. But since he cleaved to it, he did not want to separate from that sweet splendor;[132] and he remained immersed and concealed within it. And his soul was crowned and wreathed[133] by that splendor and radiance that no creature can cleave to and thereafter live, as is written, "for no person may see Me and live" (Exodus 33:20).[134]
. . . And this death is the death of the righteous who separate their souls from all concern with the lower world and cause their souls to cleave to the ways of the upper world. And when their soul [leaves their bodies], there it is crowned.

It is instructive to compare Schwartz's vision of the death of Ben Azzai:

> . . . he heard a song so beautiful he felt himself drawn toward it like a moth to a flame. . . . And all at once Ben Azzai entered into the celestial Temple that burned around him on every side. And there he saw a throne. . . . And seated upon that high and lofty throne was the very Bride of God, the *Shekhinah*, and Ben Azzai saw that she was singing, for it was her song that had led him to that place. . . . And Ben Azzai prostrated himself before the Bride and . . . she left her throne to embrace him and . . . kissed him and gently brought his soul into Paradise. . . . Thus it is written *Precious in the eyes of the Lord is the death of His saints*.

Michael Fishbane has recently explored the theme of "death by a kiss" in Jewish tradition.[135] According to the Talmud, the Angel of Death had no power over Abraham, Isaac, Jacob, Moses, Aaron, and Miriam. The famous commentator Rashi explains that this means they died by a kiss from the *Shekhinah*.[136] The Italian kabbalist Menahem Recanati, in discussing the death of Jacob, mentions the way in which Ben Azzai's soul cleaved to the supernal soul.[137] According to Recanati, the separation of such a soul from the body is known as "death by a kiss," that is to say, the soul is united with the *Shekhinah* by the exchange of a kiss, as between lovers.[138]

According to the Babylonian Talmud: "Ben Zoma looked and was stricken; about him Scripture says, 'Have you found honey? Eat what is enough for you, lest you be filled with it and vomit it' (Proverbs 25:16)." Recanati[139] compares the deaths of Ben Azzai and Ben Zoma by citing a parable of two men, wandering hungry in a forest, who find a honeycomb, the inside of which is good and sweet but the outside "more bitter than death." One [Ben Azzai] knew to separate the good from the bad, but the more he ate of the honey the sweeter it became and so ate himself to death. The other [Ben Zoma] devoured as much as he could without even separating the good from the bad until his thoughts were confused, he lost his mind, and "he fell broken." As we have seen above ("The Three Soul Sisters"), Ben Zoma was declared by his teacher, Rabbi Joshua, to have lost his mind through overindulgence in contemplating the Work of Creation. A number of scholars have suggested that Ben Zoma's demise resulted from his becoming involved in different forms of syncretistic speculation,[140] that is to say, he failed to separate the "good from bad."[141] In the novella, Ben Zoma not only overindulges in speculation about creation of the world, but his fall is described as his actually falling back into the Work of Creation (ma'aseh bereshit) itself:

> . . . he found himself drawn as in a trance to the place where the upper and lower waters meet. Now when Ben Zoma peered into that crack between the worlds, he saw all the way to the beginning, remembered only the beginning, understood only the beginning. . . . For six days Ben Zoma witnessed the miracles that took place on every day of creation, and then he found himself in a Garden, like Adam, and once more he was approached by a woman who, like himself, was naked. In her hands there was a ripe fruit, a pomegranate. She gave it to him and he split it open and gave her one half. And Ben Zoma, who was Adam at that moment, forgot about everything that would come afterward, and as they each tasted one pomegranate seed,[142] the world trembled and grew dark, and it was too late. . . . But it was what came next that

left Ben Zoma unbalanced . . . for the world had returned to the original chaos and void. So startled was Ben Zoma that he cried out at the sight of such chaos and at that instant he fell from that great height . . . and he staggered up and returned to Jerusalem, but he was a broken man.

Ben Zoma's transformation into Adam and his meeting with an alluring female figure in the Garden recall Adam's vision of the "radiant appearance of the *Shekhinah* . . . under the Tree of Life" on the day he was expelled from the Garden of Eden.[143] The eating of the forbidden fruit from the tree in the Garden serves as the basis for one of the most important formulations of the problem of evil in kabbalistic literature:[144]

> Regarding the matter of the Tree of Knowledge, of which Adam was commanded not to eat . . . the Tree of Life and the Tree of Knowledge are one [tree] below but two [trees] above . . . the moment it [the Tree of Knowledge] is separated [from the Tree of Life], its strength is freed and Satan is able to act. . . . And this is the matter known as "cutting the shoots" (*kitzetz ba-neti'ot*), for had he been connected [with the Tree of Life], he would have been unable to do this thing. Moreover, had Adam not first separated the fruit, Satan would have been unable to separate him from the Tree of Life. . . . Hence, when Adam ate of the fruit of the Tree of Knowledge, which is of the side of evil, and separated it [through his awareness or his contemplation] from the Tree of Life, the Evil Urge dominated him in his eating and in his soul, for his soul took part in the eating of the fruits of the Garden. . . . This explains that by his eating he caused destruction above and below in the "shoots" . . . and that is why it is said of Adam that he "cut the shoots."[145]

The expression "cut the shoots" recalls, of course, the sin of Elisha. According to talmudic tradition: "Aher looked and cut the shoots; about him Scripture says, 'Do not let your mouth lead your flesh to sin,' etc. (Ecclesiastes 5:5). Who is Aher ['other']? Elisha ben Abuyah."

In the novella, just as Ben Azzai is drawn toward the light of the *Shekhinah* and Ben Zoma is drawn into the Work of Creation, so Elisha's fate is to be drawn into the Heavenly Court. Here he experiences his vision of Metatron seated on a throne, which leads him to the fatally erroneous conclusion that there must be "two powers in heaven" (see above, "The Three Soul Sisters"). This thought caused his faith to waver,

> . . . and at that instant he [Elisha] fell from that heavenly court back into the Garden of Souls, face to face with the flower that contained the very root of his soul. Meanwhile, all the grief that Elisha had been holding back washed over him, for he could not bear the knowledge of what he had seen on high, nor that a false messiah would descend from his seed. All at once a terrible impulse came over him, and in an instant, before he had considered the full implications of his act, Elisha reached down and uprooted the flower of his soul.[146] A great cry went up at that time, from all the souls whose birth had been denied,[147] and the angels broke out in sobs of grief. And at the same time a Voice spoke forth out of heaven and said, "*Return, ye backsliding children*—all except Elisha. . . ." And when at last he died, a fire rose up from his grave, for his torment had still not come to an end.[148]

The early kabbalistic commentary on the story of the four sages also links Elisha's erroneous conclusion with his fatal act, though in a more philosophical mode of interpretation:[149]

> And when Aher saw that among the [Heavenly] servants there is one who is seated, he thought that there is some other [heavenly] power [apart from God]. And he said: Perhaps there are two powers in heaven . . . one for Justice and one for Mercy. So he made from One, two. . . . And this is what is meant by "he uprooted the shoots";[150] he separated the shoot from the root. For the shoot and the root are one; but they appeared as two. . . . He uprooted the strength of the root which enters into the shoot, and thus caused the shoot to whither. . . .

According to talmudic tradition (in at least one of the versions): "R. Akiba ascended in peace and descended in peace; about him Scripture says, 'Draw me, we will run after you,' etc. (Song of Songs 1:4)." His lone successful completion of the mystical quest is actually alluded to only in the continuation of the verse, "the king has brought me into his chambers." This indeed helps us grasp, in more concrete terms, what is meant by "Rabbi Akiba ascended . . . in peace." The conclusion of the novella completes the task of imaginative interpretation, by depicting how Rabbi Akiba "descended in peace" by means of a concluding mystical vision:

> As for Rabbi Akiba, he closed his eyes and held the Book of Raziel close to his heart. . . . And when he opened his eyes, a Voice spoke from Heaven and said: "*I have set My bow in the cloud*" (Genesis 9:13). At that moment Rabbi Akiba witnessed one of the true miracles of heaven, the appearance of the rainbow of Noah, which has remained hidden in Paradise since the time it served to confirm the Covenant between God and Noah.[151]

The rainbow that Rabbi Akiba sees is not only the rainbow that appeared in the days of Noah. More allusively, it is also the rainbow that appears at the end of Ezekiel's vision of the celestial Chariot (1:28), heralding the verbal prophecy that was then communicated to him: "As the appearance of the bow that is in the cloud in the day of rain, so was the appearance of the brightness round about. This was the appearance of the likeness of the glory of the Lord. And when I saw it, I fell upon my face, and I heard a voice of one that spoke."

At least one rabbinic sage, Rabbi Yehoshua ben Levi, was said to have actually required rendering homage to the rainbow, in this rather extraordinary manner, whenever it was seen in a cloud.[152] Indeed, there seem to have been those in rabbinic times who regarded the rainbow as "comparable" to God in some way.[153] The existence of such a seemingly heretical view may underlie the halakhic opinion that one who gazes at the rainbow is in the category of "one who shows lack of concern for the honor (or 'glory') of his Maker (*kevod kono*)."[154] It should be noted that this warning against gazing at the rainbow is cited in the talmudic discussion of the Mishnah (*Hagigah* 2:1), which serves as the subtext for the story of the four sages who entered Paradise: "One may not expound . . . the Work of Creation with two, nor the Chariot with [even] one . . . and whosoever shows lack of concern for the honor of his Maker, it were better for him if he had not come into the world." And significantly, in this same discussion we find the Talmud's explanation of how Rabbi Akiba alone completed the heavenly ascent in peace: "The ministering angels tried to repel him as well [Rabbi Akiba, as well as his three companions]. [But] the Holy One, blessed be He, said: Let this elder be, for he [alone] is worthy to make use of my glory."[155]

In the concluding lines of the novella, Rabbi Akiba makes good use indeed of God's glory—the rainbow—in order to descend in peace as well:

> That rainbow shimmered before Rabbi Akiba's eyes and illumined the signs that he had left behind in the heavens, to guide him back.[156] And by following those signs he descended from the highest heavens back to the Garden and to the gate where the four had once entered. And when Rabbi Akiba reached that gate he discovered that it could always be opened from within, and he departed from there in peace.

THE LITERARY CHARACTER AND PSYCHOLOGICAL STRUCTURE OF THE NOVELLA

How can *The Four Who Entered Paradise* be characterized as a literary composition? A number of seemingly disparate possibilities suggest themselves, which taken together as an organic unity may supply the best answer to this question. Schwartz's retelling of the talmudic tale of Rabbi Akiba and his three companions could be characterized as contemporary *aggadah* (Jewish legend).[157] The novella, which is basically an extended narration of the four sages' heavenly ascent, could also be seen as a modern apocalypse.[158] It would also not be amiss to refer to the unfolding of the sages' spiritual odyssey as a mystical novella.[159] As noted in the introduction, the original story of four sages who entered Paradise fits the contemporary critical category of "fantasy."[160] Schwartz's retelling of this talmudic tale can be seen as a Jewish contribution to this popular genre of literary creativity.[161] The poetic quality of the writing gives the novella the rhetorical character of an epic prose-poem. As we shall see, the author's inspiration draws not only on traditional Jewish lore but on archetypal material as well;[162] we therefore have here a prime example of what the analytical psychologist C. G. Jung has called the visionary mode of artistic creation.[163]

The traditional motif of biblical and rabbinic personalities who entered Paradise naturally lends itself to various psychological interpretations. At the turn of the century, Wilhelm Bousset argued that ecstatic ascent to heaven during life was understood in texts from many different cultures as an "anticipation" of the ascent of the soul after death.[164] Gershom Scholem did not hestitate to offer a psychological explanation of the paradoxical term *yordei merkavah*[165] as "those who reach down into themselves in order to perceive the chariot."[166] David Halperin has offered a more strictly Freudian interpretation; the heavenly ascent is in effect an invasive assault that fundamentally reflects the deep-seated urge of the younger generation to usurp power from their fathers, both genetic and spiritual.[167] And Moshe Idel has suggested that a "nostalgia for Paradise," conceived of as a sublime psychological experience, may be assumed of the ecstatic Kabbalah.[168]

Despite the very graphic depiction of the sages' mystical odyssey in the novella, here too the heavenly ascent of the four can be understood as the spiritual ascent of the soul. There are a number of recurrent motifs that "cry out" for this kind of psychological interpretation. The first and perhaps most pervasive of these is the motif of the dream.[169] The novella opens with the report of Rabbi Akiba's strange and vivid dream in which he and his three companions attempt to decipher an ancient map indicating the location of a secret book written on sapphire.[170] This dream propels the narrative development of the entire novella, for it is this dream that motivates Rabbi Akiba to assemble the other sages who eventually undertake the quest to enter Paradise. When Rabbi Akiba reveals the reason he has brought them together, it turns out that each of the other three sages remembers a vivid dream that relates to the dream of Rabbi Akiba. The four dreams of the four sages fit together like a puzzle, which, when completed, points them on their way. Their journey to the Garden of Eden includes a mythical voyage down a river of dreams (chapter 2). During their first night in Eden (chapter 3), each of the four sages again has a vivid and poetically suggestive dream. Rabbi Akiba's dream concludes with a vision of three young eagles who resolve into the three soul sisters. Later, in their actual ascent through the seven palaces (chapter 7), the sages enter the Tents of Jacob and find the patriarch asleep: "Jacob was dreaming, his dreams rose up as visions, and each of the angels who witnessed one of those dreams then carried it off to deliver it to the world of men. And blessed would be he who received one of the dreams of Jacob. For when that person awoke he would find that his faith had been restored, for it bore the imprint of the faith of Jacob, which was perfect."

When the sages finally meet the angel Raziel in the celestial Garden (chapter 8), he reveals to them the secret of the creation of man: "Before God created Adam as a man of flesh and blood, He created a dream Adam, whose name was Adam Kadmon. And God called forth this dream Adam and said: 'Alone among all creations, I am going to permit you to choose your own soul.'" Humanity, at least in some spiritual sense, is thus portrayed as having originated in a divine dream of the heavenly Creator.

Not only do imaginative dreams represent a leitmotif that runs through the novella like a scarlet thread, but a personal dream actually served as one of the author's key sources of inspiration:

> Four men pass a tree at night on which fruit glitters like jewels. They discuss whether or not to pick it. One says that the fruit must be enchanted. To taste it might cause an enchantment to fall on them. Even to touch it is dangerous. The second says it is an illusion. It doesn't even exist. How can a fruit tree grow in the desert? The third says it may be a great blessing. It must not be ignored. The fourth one goes to the tree, plucks the fruit, tastes it, and is satisfied.[171]

Through this window into the author's unconscious, we can see how the talmudic tale of the four sages, along with a great deal of other traditional Jewish and mythic material, has "percolated" through the creative imagination of a natural storyteller, eventually resulting in a consciously created literary work. A comparison of the dream to the fully elaborated novella provides an object lesson in the visionary mode of artistic creation mentioned above.[172]

Another leitmotif that runs through the novella is the image of the mirror,[173] a nearly universal symbol of the soul.[174] At the conclusion of his opening dream (chapter 1):

> Akiba found his eyes tracing the familiar lines of the map. Sometimes it was a map, and sometimes a mirror. Once, when it was a mirror, Akiba saw himself wandering in a labyrinth, lost in a tangle of possible turns. Then, just before waking, he drew his eyes back and saw the map as if for the first time.

And when he did, he could not comprehend how he had ever forgotten that the map was simply the letter *Bet*.

In the sages' discussions, prior to setting out on their journey (chapter 1), Elisha ben Abuya suggests:

> But let me propose a way in which we might succeed in making this journey—it was suggested to me by Akiba's dream, in which the letter appeared not only as a map, but also as a mirror. Indeed, let us approach this map as if it were a mirror. Our task, then, is to peer inside the mirror to find out where we are intended to go. Our first problem is to find out how to look inside the mirror, and once we do, how to find our own reflection among all the mysteries it reveals.

The depiction of the map as a mirror appears repeatedly throughout the novella. More particularly the round *dagesh* in the middle of the letter *Bet* plays a central role in the duel of mirrors between the leader of the sages and the angel who attempts to prevent their entry into the Garden of Eden (chapter 4):

> Confronted with that fiery sword, the sages did not know what to do next. . . . Only Rabbi Akiba dared to look directly at it. There he saw a mirror that reflected the sages as they stood before the gate. This discovery gave Akiba an idea—he told Ben Zoma to give him the map of the letter *Bet*, and when Ben Zoma took it out they found the *dagesh*, the dot inside the letter *Bet*, glowing brightly, reflecting the light of the flaming sword as if it were a mirror. Akiba held up the map and the reflection from the flaming sword was directed back upon the angel that spun it.[175] Surprised for an instant, the angel stopped spinning the sword, and Akiba whispered for the sages to enter quickly, without hesitating, and they slipped beneath the sword into the Garden. . . .

Later, having arrived in the celestial Paradise (chapter 8), the sages encounter more mirrors that now reflect not only their discrete temporal existence, but their individual personas projected into the future: "Just then the walls of the palace of Adam Kadmon were transformed into mirrors, and when the sages looked into those mirrors they saw something that few have witnessed in the history of men—they saw visions of the future generations that would arise from each one of them." This near infinity of mirrored reflections, like the leitmotif of the dream, suggests that the novella is far more than a highly imaginative retelling of a talmudic tale. Schwartz's *Four Who Entered Paradise* may also be read as an archetypal allegory of four refractions of the human soul and their respective spiritual journeys.

In conclusion, I would suggest that the deep structure of the novella can be read as an interplay between the archetypal numbers: one, three, four, and seven. The most obvious numerical pattern—the fourfold structure of the story of the four sages who entered Paradise—is of course already inherent to the original talmudic tale on which the novella is based. The archetypal aspect of such fourfold structures has been analyzed by Jung and his followers; these analytical psychologists refer to the numerical symbolism of the number four as "quaternity," which represents the stabilizing power of divinity to bring order out of chaos. But, as Jung himself emphasized, "quaternity" (four) derives its psychic power from being in dynamic dialectic with the vitality of the previous number, three ("trinity"), the first and basic synthesis that reunites what has been split.[176] This archetypal rhythmic relationship (3 + 1 = 4) is reflected in the story of the four sages, three who fail and one who succeeds in the mystic quest. In the novella, however, this dynamic interplay between the three and the four is further elaborated in the meeting of the four sages with the three sisters (chapter 4), who themselves reflect a similar numerical relationship (3 + 1 = 4), since, as we have seen, these three figures together represent the triune aspect of one entity, the human soul.[177] A different uniting of three and four is found in the continuation of the novella when the sages encounter the seven biblical personalities who govern the seven celestial palaces through which the four make their heavenly ascent. According to Jung, the motif of seven stages, which

appears so frequently in various cultural traditions, symbolizes transformation.[178] Indeed, the four sages and other *Merkavah* mystics un-
dergo spiritual transformation as they ascend through the seven
Hekhalot. In this respect, it is interesting to note that the number seven
is frequently linked to an image of the soul.[179] Seven, being a combination of the ternary and the quaternary, is perhaps the most recurrent formulaic number, particularly in Jewish culture.[180] The symbolic
dynamism of the number seven finds expression in the idea that everything is determined by seven dimensions: the four cardinal directions (left, right, before, and behind), the two vertical dimensions
(upward and downward), and existence itself as a central point.[181] Significantly, this notion is linked to an imaginative interpretation of the
first word of the Hebrew Bible, *bereshit*, read as two words: *bara* ("He
created")[182] *sheit* ("six")[183]— the six extensions that stretched out from
the one primal point.[184] In the early mystical work *Sefer Yetzirah* ("The
Book of Creation," chapter 4), this idea is connected to the seven letters
of the Hebrew alphabet that are "doubled" or may have their pronunciation "hardened" by the addition of a *dagesh* point inserted in
the middle of the letter.[185] "There are seven doubled letters, *bet, gimmel,
dalet, kaf, peh, resh, tav*. Seven and not six; seven and not eight . . . cor-
responding to the seven extentions (*ketzavot*), consisting of six extensions—upward and downward, east and west, north and south—and
in the middle the Holy Temple directed [to the Holy Temple above],
which supports all of them."

It is tempting to visualize this complex of ideas as a depiction of
the letter that stands at the beginning of the Hebrew Bible, the *Bet*,[186]
extending out three dimensionally from the *dagesh* in its center. Plot-
ted on the plane of the *Bet* map, as it is in the novella, the traditional
motif of the heavenly ascent has likewise been extended, not only along
the vertical but also along the horizontal axis. By following the con-
tours of the three strokes of the *Bet* around its one central point, the
four sages circumscribe what is, in effect, a mandala—the Jungian sym-

bol of the self in the context of the cosmos.[187] Viewed in this way (see the map on page 124), Schwartz's retelling of the enigmatic story of the four who entered paradise explores the extent of archetypal mythic potential inherent in one typically terse talmudic tale.

NOTES

1. In the following comments, I have tried to trace some of the broader themes that appear in the novella back to their origins, for the most part in traditional Jewish sources. Needless to say, a more detailed analysis of all the traditional motifs on which the novella is based would have required a much more extensive line-by-line commentary, which the following "thematic commentary" does not claim to be.

2. For the legend of the controversy between the letters, won eventually by the *Bet*, about which letter God should pick to begin the Torah, see L. Ginzberg, *Legends of the Jews*, vol. 1, pp. 5–8, and notes, vol. 5, p. 6 n. 12; retold in picturesque manner in Ben Shahn's *The Alphabet of Creation*. A large selection of midrashim about the initial *Bet* of the Torah is found in M. Kasher's *Torah Shelemah*, I, secs. 1–38. Significantly, the *Quran* (not only the opening *fatiha*, but all the following suras as well) begins with the *basmalah* ("In the name of God, the merciful and compassionate"), which, like *bereshit*, begins with the letter *b*, the second letter of the Arabic alphabet with the numerical equivalent of two; see *Encyclopaedia of Islam*, s.v. basmala. On the numerical value of the *Bet*, see *Zohar* I, 240b: "The process of creation, too, has taken place on two planes, one above and one below, and for this reason the Torah begins with the letter "*Bet*," the numerical value of which is two. The lower occurrence corresponds to the higher; one produced the upper world, the other the lower world"; trans. Lawrence Fine, "Kabbalistic Texts," chap. 6, in *Back to the Sources—Reading the Classic Jewish Texts*, ed. Barry Holtz (New York: Summit Books, 1984), p. 325. See also *Zohar Hadash* 88c–d, which describes the *Bet* of *bereshit* as a "treasure-chest" (*kumtera de-askufa*) that contained all the other letters of the Hebrew alphabet from which God created the world. For *kamtera* as a specific kind of chest, see Mishnah, *Oholot* 9:15,

and Abraham Goldberg's commentary in *Mishnah Treatise Ohaloth Critically Edited* (Jerusalem: Magnes, 1955), p. 75. On *askufa*, meaning "treasury," particularly in Zoharic Aramaic, see Scholem, *Major Trends in Jewish Mysticism*, p. 165 n. 47. Lawrence Englander and Herbert Basser translate "something like a showcase"; see *The Mystical Study of Ruth: Midrash Ha-Ne'elam of the Zohar to the Book of Ruth* (Atlanta: Scholars Press, 1993), p. 141, which I understand to stress the idea that the *Bet* is open at one side through which the other letters pass and are seen within. My thanks to Professor Herbert Basser for calling my attention to this text. I would suggest that this text may also depict the *Bet* as an open "box" (*kamtera*) placed at the "threshold" (*askufah*) of the Torah; compare Mishnah *Shabbat* 10:2, which speaks of a basket (*kupah*) placed at the threshold (*askufah*) of a house. The association of the *Bet* with *bayit* "house" is well-known; for example, see below, n. 5.

3. This curious formulation may be a dim reflection of the more fully closed shape of the *Bet* in what the rabbis knew as the earlier form of the Hebrew script, in contrast to the more open form of the *Bet* in the script they actually employed; see Babylonian Talmud, *Sanhedrin* 21b–22a, and *Encyclopaedia Judaica*, vol. 4, col. 709, s.v. *Bet*. On the nearly square shape of the *Bet* see below.

4. Palestinian Talmud, *Hagigah* 2:1, 77c; *Genesis Rabbah* 1:10. Compare the elaboration of this theme in the modern "chain midrash" on "The Seven Lights of the Lamp" by Moshe ben Yitzhak HaPardesan, in *Gates to the New City*, ed. Howard Schwartz (Northvale, NJ: Jason Aronson, 1991), p. 112: "Now, it is forbidden to ask what was above, below or before the three strokes of the letter *Bet* of *Bereshit* that stands at the beginning of the Torah. But we may ponder the *Aleph* of *Or*, the Light that shone within the Bet, shining out through its open side and illuminating all that comes after." This modern midrash may help further illuminate the *Bet*, which glows mysteriously at various points in Schwartz's novella.

5. *The Hebrew Letters—Channels of Creative Consciousness* (Jerusalem: Gal Einai, 1990), pp. 41, 386. Rabbi Ginsburg seems to have drawn his inspiration for this comment from a midrashic tradition found in elaborated form in Hezekuni to Genesis 1:1; for parallels and sources see the notes by H. D. Chavel in his edition of the commentary (Jerusalem: Mosad HaRav Kook,

1980). See also Menahem Kasher's *Torah Shelemah*, vol. 1, sec. 30, citing *Midrash Ha-Ne'elam Shir Ha-Shirim* in the *Zohar Hadash* [ed. Margaliot, 60c]: "Bet is the 'house' of the whole world. . . ." However, none of these sources come as close as Rabbi Ginsburg to describing the initial letter *Bet* of the Torah as a map. It should be noted that the motif of the *Bet* map is already found in Schwartz's earlier sketch, "The Cave of Machpelah," in *Gates to the New City* (1991), p. 277. It therefore seems that the modern storyteller and the contemporary hasidic scholar have each developed this idea independently. See also Milton Steinberg's *As a Driven Leaf*, part 1, chap. 16, where ben Azzai says: "It is as though one wishes to see a great king and holds in his hand a map of the palace and keys to its doors. That map is Scripture, those keys the reason of man."

6. See *Massekhet Sofrim* 9:1 and the extensive notes in Menahem Kasher's *Torah Shelemah*, vol. 1, sec. 1.

7. See Babylonian Talmud, *Menahot* 29b.

8. Genesis 2:10. Note that these four headwaters are symbolically linked to the four sages who entered Paradise who are then linked to the four levels of interpretation known as PaRDeS in *Zohar* I, 26b (*Tikkunim*); see I. Tishby, *The Wisdom of the Zohar*, vol. 3, p. 1090 nn. 90 and 91.

9. Note that Jacob specifically requests to be buried in the cave of his forefathers (i.e., Abraham, Sarah, Isaac, and Rebekah); see Genesis 49:29. Jacob buried Rachel in Bethlehem where she died in childbirth (Genesis 35:18–19, 48:7).

10. See also Joshua 15:13–14 and Numbers 13:32–33, where the Anakim are described as giants. A visitor to Hebron in 1333 c.e. relates that there was to be found there a tremendous skeleton that was said to be that of one of these giants; see Zev Vilnay, *Legends of Palestine* (Philadelphia: Jewish Publication Society, 1932), p. 155.

11. Indeed, biblical scholars have suggested that originally *kiryat arba* referred to four towns (*kiryot*), hills, or quarters that were "united" (*haber*) to make up the city of Hebron; see the commentary of Yehudah Kil to Joshua 14:15 (in the *Da'at Miqra* series [Jerusalem: Mosad HaRav Kook, 1970]), p. 124.

12. "What does *machpelah* ('doubled-up') refer to? That [the Cave of Machpelah] was 'doubled-up' with couples. Mamre is Kiryat Arba (Genesis

35:27). Rabbi Isaac said: It is the town of the four couples [*kiryat ha-arba zugot*], Adam and Eve, Abraham and Sarah, Isaac and Rebekah, Jacob and Leah"— Babylonian Talmud, *Eruvin* 53a; compare *Sotah* 13a and *Genesis Rabbah* 58:4.

13. See, for example, *Testament of Adam* 3:6: "They buried Adam at the east of Paradise . . . [and this 'testament of Adam'] was put into the cave of treasures with the offerings Adam had taken out of Paradise, gold and myrrh and frankincense." On the *Testament of Adam* and the *Book of the Cave of Treasures*, see J. H. Charlesworth et al., *The Pseudepigrapha and Modern Research* (Chico: Scholars Press, 1981), pp. 70–73, 91–92.

14. At Mamre, which is identified with Kiryat Arba/Hebron (see above, n. 11). The biblical source for the story of Abraham and the three angels is Genesis, chap. 18.

15. The beds of Adam and Eve were still on display in Hebron in the Middle Ages, as reported by an Italian monk who visited the Holy Land in about 1485: "And one can still see their beds cut out of the rock and the cavern is called in Arabic *Magharat et-Tahatein*, that is, Cavern of the Two Beds"; see Zev Vilnay, *Legends of Judea and Samaria—The Sacred Land*, vol. 2 (Philadelphia: Jewish Publication Society, 1975), p. 36.

16. Note that according to the Christian Ethiopic *Book of Adam and Eve, Also Called the Conflict of Adam and Eve with Satan*, English trans. S. C. Malan (London, 1882) 2:9, Adam was buried in a cave with a lampstand burning in front of him. The motif of the lights burning in the cave where Adam is thought to be buried seems connected to the Muslim custom of lowering a lamp, which is continually lit, into the Cave of Machpelah; see *Encyclopaedia Judaica*, vol. 11, col. 673. On the identity of Adam's burial cave in nonrabbinic sources, see above, n. 13, on "the cave of treasures."

17. Paraphrased from *Pirke de Rabbi Eliezer*, chap. 36. A full text of the passage may be found in the English translation of this work by Gerald Friedlander, p. 275.

18. *Zohar Ruth* I, 97b, as cited by Ginzberg, *Legends of the Jews* I, pp. 288–289. On the importance of smell in such Jewish traditions, see Elliot Ginsburg, "The Olfactory Imagination in Jewish Mysticism" (lecture given at Association for Jewish Studies 25th Annual Conference, Boston, December 12, 1993; in preparation for publication).

19. Rabbenu Bahya (Spain, late thirteenth century) on Genesis 23:2.

20. Compare Genesis 28:17 referring to Beth-El/Luz.

21. On the camps of the four camps of the *Shekhinah*, see 3 Enoch 18:4 and the notes by Odenberg in his edition, p. 55.

22. *The Itinerary of Benjamin of Tudela: Travels in the Middle Ages*, introductions by Michael Signer, M. N. Adler, and A. Asher (Malibu, CA: Joseph Simon, 1984), pp. 86–87.

23. This figure may be a dim reflection of the Old Man (*sava*) who appears in the *Zohar*, and despite his lowly appearance turns out to be a great spiritual guide; see particularly the discourse of Rav Hamnuna Sava (*Zohar* I, 5a–7a) and the discourse on the doctrine of the soul in the *Sava de-Mishpatim* (*Zohar* II, 94b–114a); translated in Tishby, *Wisdom of the Zohar*, vol. 1, pp. 161–197. Note that in the continuation of the novella the four sages are led at various stages in their journey by a series of spiritual guides, or "psychopomps."

24. Note that when the four sages emerge from the Cave of Machpelah into Eden, they are said to have "crossed over to the World to Come" (chap. 3). See Fishbane, *The Kiss of God—Spiritual and Mystical Death in Judaism*, pp. 20–50: "For the religious seeker, the quest for true life requires death of some sort. . . . One must die somehow, in some measure, in order to pass the fiery sword that guards the gates of Eden, the eternal realm of God" and *passim*. On "death" as a metaphor for psychological shift in consciousness, see James Hillman, *The Dream and the Underworld* (New York: Harper & Row, 1979), pp. 64–67. On the heavenly ascent (during life) as an "anticipation" of the soul's ascent to heaven after death, see below, p. 156 (on Bousset).

25. On the possibility of such an underground river, see Philo, *Questions and Answers on Genesis*, I:12 (to Genesis 2:10 "And a river went out of Eden") (Loeb Classical Library, trans. Ralph Marcus), p. 8: ". . . perhaps Paradise is in some distant place far from our inhabited world, and has a river flowing under the earth." During the sages' passage to the Garden of Eden, Ben Azzai comes to the realization that they must be traveling south (chap. 2), despite the fact that Scripture (Genesis 2:8) suggests it is located to the east. On the view that the Garden of Eden lies to the south, see the commentary of Ibn Ezra to Genesis 2:12, who locates the Garden of Eden below the equator. For this view and for an extensive survey of the various opinions on the lo-

cation of the Garden of Eden (in the East, North, or West), see Shalom Rosenberg, "The Return to the Garden of Eden," *The Messianic Idea in Jewish Thought—A Study Conference in Honour of Gershom Scholem* 1977 (Jerusalem: Israel Academy of Sciences and Humanities, 1982), pp. 68 ff.

26. This further suggests that, in the novella, the mystical adventure of the four sages progressively becomes more a spiritual than a physical journey. On the psychological–spiritual interpretation of entering *pardes* in geonic and medieval Jewish thought, see introduction, n. 23. This approach to the story of the four sages has recently been clothed in more modern garb by J. P. Schultz, "The Heavenly Ascent and the Out-of-Body Experience of the Four Who Entered Pardes" (lecture given at the Twenty-Fifth Annual Conference of the Association for Jewish Studies, Boston, December 12, 1993). See 2 Corinthians 12:2–4 on the man who was caught up to the third heaven and Paradise "whether in the body or out of the body I do not know, God knows." On ecstatic experience as seeing oneself as if from outside, see Christopher Rowland, *The Open Heaven: A Study of Apocalyptic in Judaism and Early Christianity* (New York: Crossroad, 1982), pp. 214 ff.

27. See *Zohar* III, 115b (Tishby, *Wisdom of the Zohar*, vol. I, p. 421); *Zohar* I, 241a–241b (*Wisdom of the Zohar*, vol. 1, p. 381 n. 30); Gershom Scholem, "Shekhinah: The Feminine Element in Divinity," in *On the Mystical Shape of the Godhead*, pp. 182 ff.; *On the Kabbalah and Its Symbolism* (New York: Schocken, 1969), p. 139: ". . . the conception of the *Shekhinah*'s marriage to her Lord is a mystical symbol expressing something that transcends all images." On the *hieros gamos* enacted between God and the *Shekhinah*, see there, p. 148.

28. On the constellation of basic kabbalistic symbols: *shekhinah* ("the Divine Presence"), *knesset Yisrael* ("the community of Israel"), *matrona/matronita* ("mother, royal consort"), *kallah* ("bride"), see Gershom Scholem, *Kabbalah* (1974), pp. 111–112 [*Encyclopaedia Judaica*, vol. 10, col. 575, s.v. Kabbalah].

29. Tishby, *Wisdom of the Zohar*, vol. 2, p. 684.

30. The three Hebrew terms (*neshamah, ruah, nefesh*) are basically synonyms for what can be roughly translated by English "soul"; on the problem of terminology, see Tishby, *Wisdom of the Zohar*, vol. 2, p. 714 n. 17 and Goldstein's

comment on the translation/transliteration of these terms, p. 715 n. 46. In some places in rabbinic literature, the identity of the terms is stressed; see *Genesis Rabbah* 14:10 on Genesis 2:7–8 and *Genesis Rabbah* 32:11 on Genesis 7:21–22. However, there also seem to be preliminary attempts at differentiation: *Nefesh*, which relates to the "life-blood," represents that aspect of the soul that gives life to the physical body. *Ruah* relates to the moving "wind" and represents the soul's capacity to ascend to heaven (i.e., in sleep) and return to the body. *Neshamah*, which relates to "breath," is the least physical, most spiritual aspect of the soul (i.e., the content and nature of personality). See W. Hirsch, *Rabbinic Psychology—Beliefs about the Soul in the Rabbinic Literature of the Talmudic Period* (London: Edward Goldston, 1947), p. 152. Later Jewish philosophers, such as Sa'adia Gaon, employing Greek philosophical ideas, distinguish *nefesh* as the appetitive faculty, *ruah* as the emotive faculty (e.g., anger), and *neshamah* as the faculty of cognition. But the essential unity of these three aspects of the soul was generally stressed, especially by Maimonides; see Tishby, *Wisdom of the Zohar*, vol. 2, pp. 690–691. It is interesting to compare these ancient tripartite divisions of the soul with the "three stages of the anima" represented by three female figures, Lilith, Eve, and the *Shekhinah*, proposed by the Swiss Jungian analyst, Siegmund Hurwitz, *Lilith—the First Eve, Historical and Psychological Aspects of the Dark Feminine* (Zurich: Diamon, 1992), p. 233.

31. The relationship between the three sisters and the soul is elaborated in the novella in a more subtle manner in the motif of the fabulous pearl, which falls from Neshamah's hair into the waters of the pool and is eventually recovered by the sages. The pearl is a symbol of the soul, particularly in gnostic sources; see Hans Jonas, *The Gnostic Religion* (Boston: Beacon, 1963), p. 112, on "The Hymn of the Pearl," especially pp. 125–129. A. Altmann, "Gnostic Themes in Rabbinic Cosmology," in *Essays in Honor of J. H. Hertz*, ed. I. Epstein et al. (London: Goldston, 1943), pp. 26–27, has investigated the impact of this theme on various rabbinic traditions, particularly in relation to the "stones of pure marble," which are not to be mistaken for water in the Babylonian Talmud's version of the four who entered Paradise. On the symbolism of the *Shekhinah* and the feminine as a jewel, see Gershom Scholem, *Origins of the Kabbalah* (Philadelphia: Jewish Publication Society, 1987), pp. 162 ff., esp. 175.

32. See Tishby, *Wisdom of the Zohar*, vol. 2, pp. 684 ff.

33. See Rabbi Moses de Leon, *Sefer ha-Nefesh ha-Hakhamah*, quoted in Tishby, *Wisdom of the Zohar*, vol. 2, pp. 711 n. 202: "The mystery of the soul is that it is divided into three parts, but joined together in a single unity. Even though they appear to be separated from one another because of their separate names, they really form one mystery: *nefesh, ruah* and *neshamah*. . . . They are indeed a single mystery, without any division. . . ." It may be added that there is a striking similarity between the kabbalistic mystery of the tripartite soul and the Christian mystery of the triune Godhead or Trinity.

34. *Sefer Shekel ha-Kodesh*, quoted in Tishby, *Wisdom of the Zohar*, vol. 2, p. 694 nn. 108, 109.

35. Note that in the talmudic discussion of the eagle-face of the celestial Chariot (*Merkavah*) (Ezekiel 1:10, 10:14), it is said that the eagle is the king of the birds (Babylonian Talmud, *Hagigah* 13b).

36. See *The Life [Apocalypse] of Adam and Eve* 33:2. These eagles seem to relate to the "eagles of the *merkavah* (celestial chariot)" mentioned repeatedly in 3 Enoch; see there 2:1 (and H. Odenberg's note in his English translation, p. 5, and P. Alexander's note in his more recent English translation, *The Old Testament Pseudepigrapha*, ed. J. H. Charlesworth, vol. 1, p. 257, for additional references). Compare also Ezra's "Eagle Vision" in 4 Ezra, chap. 11 ff.

37. *Bereshit Rabbah* 2:4 following the reconstruction and translation of Saul Lieberman, "How Much Greek in Jewish Palestine?" in *Text and Studies* (New York: Ktav, 1974), pp. 230–232 (originally published in *Biblical and Other Studies*, ed. A. Almann [Cambridge, 1972], pp. 137–139). Compare Tosefta *Hagigah* 2:6; Palestinian Talmud, *Hagigah*, chap. 2 (77a); Babylonian Talmud, *Hagigah* 15a (these three sources are part of the "mystical collection." See introduction, p. xiv n. 6).

38. Compare the version of Rabbi Joshua's question to Ben Zoma in the Tosefta and the Babylonian Talmud: "Whence and wither?" According to Lieberman, *Tosefta Ki-Fshutah*, part 5 (*Mo'ed*), p. 1292, such a question was a typical way of addressing a person who was acting strangely. This interchange should be compared to Mishnah *Avot* 3:1: "Look to three things and you shall not come to sin. Know from whence you came, and whither you are going, and before Whom you will in the future have to render account."

39. That is, I am nothing who comes from nothing. This is the reading of the best manuscripts preferred by Lieberman ("How Much Greek," pp. 231–232), who notes that such formulations were current among the writers and intellectuals of antiquity.

40. "Sitting and expounding" (*yoshev ve-doresh*) is the typical rabbinic expression used to describe a sage in the act of giving a sermon (*derashah*) or engaged in some other formal teaching or preaching activity; see Marc Bregman, "The Darshan: Preacher and Teacher of Talmudic Times," *The Melton Journal* 14 (1982): 3 ff.

41. On this term, see Joseph Dan, "The Chambers of the Chariot," *Tarbiz* 47 (1978): 47–55 [Hebrew]. As Dan points out, this term (found only in this passage in ancient talmudic and midrashic literature) is related to Rabbi Akiba's success in entering Paradise unscathed, which in the story of the four sages is crowned with the verse "the King [God] brought me into His chambers."

42. On the use of "stringing" as an exegetical–homiletical term, see Joseph Heinemann, "The Proem in the Aggadic Midrashim," in *Studies in Aggadah and Folk Literature*, ed. Joseph Heinemann and Dov Noy [Scripta Hierosolymitana 22] (Jerusalem: Magnes, 1971), p. 101, and A. Goldberg, "Petiha und Hariza—Zur Korrektur eines Missverstaendnisses," *Journal for the Study of Judaism* 10 (1979): 213–218.

43. *Leviticus Rabbah* 16:4; see the parallels and notes cited by Margulies in his edition, p. 354.

44. See David Halperin, *The Faces of the Chariot*, pp. 13 ff.

45. Compare Exodus 24:9–11: "Then went up Moses and Aaron, Nadav and Avihu and seventy of the elders of Israel. And they saw the God of Israel and there was under His feet as a paved work of sapphire and like the very heavens for purity. And upon the nobles of the children of Israel he laid not his hand; also they saw God, and did eat and drink."

46. Babylonian Talmud, *Hagigah* 14b, in the "mystical collection."

47. Ezekiel 1:27; see also Ezekiel 1:4, 8:4. From the contexts, it would seem that something like lightning is being described. In the Septuagint and the Vulgate, *hashmal* is translated as "electrum" (amber, or a pale yellow combination of gold and silver). In Latin-based languages this word has yielded the modern word "electricity." In 1600 William Gilbert published his trea-

tise on magnetism and used "electron" to refer to the static charge created by rubbing amber. He then coined the term "electricity" [my thanks to Professor Eric Rabkin, English Department, University of Michigan, for this information]. Similarly, in modern Hebrew (apparently from the time of the nineteenth-century Russian Hebrew poet and journalist Yehuda Leib Gordon), *hashmal* has come to mean "electricity"; see the Ben Yehudah Dictionary, pp. 1805–1806.

48. Babylonian Talmud, *Hagigah* 14a, in the "mystical collection." See also in the continuation of the discussion there, "What does the word *hashmal* mean? Rav Yehudah said: Living creatures speaking fire (*hayyot esh memallot*)." For a discussion of the passage in its talmudic context and other danger stories about those who pursued the mysteries of the *Merkavah*, see David Halperin, *The Merkavah in Rabbinic Literature*, pp. 153 ff.

49. See the introduction, p. xvii, for the talmudic story of how Elisha came to the erroneous conclusion that there are "two powers in heaven." In subsequent Jewish tradition, Elisha ben Abuyah (or "Aher") became the archheretic. In the modern period he has been made the central character of several novels. For a partial list see Shmuel Safrai in *Encyclopaedia Judaica*, vol. 6, col. 670. See further, Yehudah Liebes, *The Sin of Elisha* (Jerusalem: Academon, 1990), pp. 20–22 [Hebrew]. In American Jewish fiction, the classic example is Milton Steinberg's *As a Driven Leaf* (1940), in which Elisha is portrayed as a kind of premature but failed Kant; see, for example, chap. 21, where Elisha states: "I am seeking a theology, a morality, a ritual, confirmed by logic in the fashion of geometry so that one need not forever wonder whether what he believes is true." As Howard Schwartz has noted, Cythia Ozick's classic story "The Pagan Rabbi" can be read as a modern retelling of the story of Elisha's apostasy; see *Gates to the New City—A Treasury of Modern Jewish Tales*, ed. and with intro. by Howard Schwartz (Northvale, NJ: Jason Aronson, 1991), pp. 286–310 for the story and pp. 676–677 for Schwartz's notes. On the other hand, Liebes argues that Elisha was not guilty of any particular ideological transgression, but rather that his sin was hubris; see particularly, pp. 23–24 for his interpretive retelling of the story of Elisha as a Greek tragedy.

50. Babylonian Talmud, *Hagigah* 15b.

51. See Mishnah *Avot* 5:22: "Turn it [Torah] and turn it again for everything is in it."

52. See Mishnah *Pe'ah* 1:1, *Avot*, chap. 6, and *Kiddushin* 4:14 (end): "with all" (Genesis 24:1) is interpreted to mean "Torah."

53. *Genesis Rabbah* 3:4 and parallels. On this enigmatic tradition, and particularly the "garment of light" mentioned in it, see Gershom Scholem, "Some Aggadic Sayings Explained by Merkabah Hymns. The Garment of God," in *Jewish Gnosticism, Merkavah Mysticism and Talmudic Tradition* (New York: Jewish Theological Seminary, 1965), pp. 56–64, and the response by Raphael Loewe, "The Divine Garment and Shi'ur Qomah," *Harvard Theological Review* 58 (1965): 153–160.

54. See in the introduction, p. xiv.

55. Paraphrased from Babylonian Talmud, *Hagigah* 12a, in line with the parallels (see for example *Genesis Rabbah* 12:6 and Theodor's notes p. 102 l. 2) according to the interpretation of Alexander Altmann, "Gnostic Themes in Rabbinic Cosmology," in *Essays Presented to J. H. Hertz* (London: Goldston, 1943), pp. 28–32, on "The Primordial Light Which is Stored Up for the Righteous."

56. *Genesis Rabbah* 3:6.

57. Babylonian Talmud, *Hagigah* 12a; *Genesis Rabbah* 8:1; and other parallels.

58. See the article by Altmann mentioned above, n. 55.

59. For a basic presentation of this highly complex set of ideas, see Gershom Scholem, *Kabbalah*, pp. 135–144 on "The Breaking of the Vessels" and "Tikkun" in the doctrine of creation in Lurianic Kabbalah. See further his discussion in *On the Kabbalah and Its Symbolism* (New York: Schocken, 1969), pp. 109–117, at the conclusion of discussion of "Kabbalah and Myth." Howard Schwartz has given his own presentation of the "myth of the Ari" in *Gabriel's Palace* (New York: Oxford University Press, 1993), introduction, pp. 16–17, and in his recent lecture "The Mythology of Judaism" (forthcoming as a published essay).

60. On the question as to whether the Garden contained Eden or Eden contained the Garden, see *Genesis Rabbah* 15:2 and notes and parallels cited by Theodore in his edition, p. 136.

61. See the article by Rabbi Louis Isaac Rabinowitz in *Encyclopaedia Judaica*, vol. 5, cols. 397–401, s.v. Cherub, for a convenient summary of the various sources and traditions.

62. See, for example, the depiction of God riding on a flying Cherub in 2 Samuel 22:11 and Psalm 18:11. The four "living creatures" (*hayyot*) that support the Divine Chariot described in Ezekiel, chap. 1, are identified as Cherubim supporting God's Throne in Ezekiel, chap. 10. This complex of prophetic visions is the basis for *Merkavah* ("Divine Chariot") and Throne mysticism; see Gershom Scholem, *Major Trends in Jewish Mysticism*, pp. 40–79, and the book-length study by David Halperin, *The Faces of the Chariot*. On *hayyot* and cherubim, see particularly pp. 39–44.

63. Babylonian Talmud, *Yoma* 54a.

64. Ibid., 54b.

65. Babylonian Talmud, *Baba Batra* 99a, Rashi ad loc. and Rabbi Louis Isaac Rabinowitz (see above, n. 61).

66. See *A Commentary on the Book of Genesis* by U. Cassuto, pp. 81–82, who regards this passage as preserving an ancient, pre-pentateuchal tradition about how the Cherub who dwelt in the Garden of Eden sinned in his pride against God and was driven out and cast down to earth.

67. See Halperin, *Faces of the Chariot*, pp. 241 ff.

68. In Ezekiel, chap. 10, the four mythical beasts are referred to as Cherubim rather than "living creatures" (*hayyot*), but the other three are still described as having the faces of man, lion, and eagle (Ezekiel 10:14), as in Ezekiel 1:10.

69. In the discussion of the *Merkavah*, Babylonian Talmud, *Hagigah* 13b.

70. See Babylonian Talmud, *Sanhedrin* 67b; *Exodus Rabbah* 9:11(2). But compare the version of the talmudic passage cited in the *Arukh*, s.v. *lat* (3). See also *Genesis Rabbah* 21:9: "which turned every way" (Genesis 3:24) sometimes turning into men, sometimes into women, sometimes spirits, and sometimes angels. It is significant that in the School of Rabbi Moshe Ha-Darshan, the Cherubim who guard the way to the Garden of Eden are specifically identified as "angels of destruction"; see *Pugio Fidei* (1687), p. 572. In the *Hekhalot* literature it is these "angels of destruction" who guard the various "heavenly palaces" and who attempt to prevent the *Merkavah* mystic's heavenly ascent. For a fuller discussion of these sources, see Marc Bregman, *The Tanhuma-*

Yelammedenu Literature—Studies in the Evolution of the Versions (doctoral dissertation, The Hebrew University of Jerusalem, 1991), chap. 3, sec. 37.2 [Hebrew], and Marc Bregman, *The Sign of the Serpent* (Tuebingen: Mohr-Siebeck, forthcoming).

71. Rabbi Akiba's stratagem of using the mirrorlike *Bet* map to reflect the light of the flaming sword back at the angel bears comparison with the Greek legend of Perseus who defeats Medusa by looking at her reflection in a mirrorlike shield and cutting off her terrifying head with a sickle. On this theme, see Tobin Siebers, *The Mirror of Medusa* (Berkeley, CA: University of California, 1983). Rabbi Akiba's mirror-duel with the angel who guards the entrance to the Garden of Eden also bears comparison with Don Quixote's encounter (part 2, chap. 12 et seq.) with the Knight of Mirrors, who is also called the Knight of the Grove. On this episode, see Robert B. Alter, *Partial Magic: The Novel as a Self-Conscious Genre* (Berkeley, CA: University of California, 1975), chap. 1 "The Mirror of Knighthood and the World of Mirrors."

72. The depiction of the Cherub as a child in late Christian art finds its forerunner in the talmudic discussion of the Cherub face of Ezekiel's celestial Chariot (*Merkavah*): What is the meaning of Cherub (*keruv*)? Rabbi Abbahu said: Like a child (*ke-ravia*). For in Babylonia a child is called a *ravia* (Babylonian Talmud, *Hagigah* 13b). Also in the *Zohar* I, 228b, the Cherubim have the faces of children and serve as the *Shekhinah*'s "boys"; see Tishby, *Wisdom of the Zohar*, vol. 2, p. 591.

73. See S. R. Hirsch on Genesis 3:23: The purpose of the Cherubim was to "preserve" for man the road to the tree of life, so that he might find it again.

74. "Ma'aseh Rabbi Yehoshua ben Levi," *Bet HaMidrash*, ed. Adolf Jellinick, vol. 2, p. 48. See also *Hibbur Yafeh MihaYeshuah*, ed. Hayyim Zeev Hirshberg, pp. 106–107. Compare Babylonian Talmud, *Ketubot* 77b, and *Berakhot* 51a; Moses Gaster, *The Exempla of the Rabbis*, p. 85, sec. 138 (and see pp. 214–215 for numerous additional parallels and references); on the various versions of this story see J. Dan, *The Hebrew Story in the Middle Ages* (Jerusalem: Keter, 1974)[Hebrew], p. 16, and the sources and bibliography listed on p. 273. The evolution of the tale of how Rabbi Yehoshua ben Levi

tricked the angel of death to enter the Garden of Eden alive, from its talmudic sources to the expansive versions found in later works, is a prime example of the Jewish art of retelling, comparable to the evolution of the story of the four sages who entered Paradise.

75. See the previous note and *Hibbur Yafeh Mi-Ha-Yeshuah*, pp. 6–7; Dan, *Hebrew Story*, p. 90; and the extensive bibliography listed by Martha Himmelfarb, *Tours of Hell—An Apocalyptic Form in Jewish and Christian Literature* (Philadelphia: University of Pennsylvania, 1983), pp. 32–33.

76. It is Shamshiel, "prince of the Garden of Eden," whom Moses finds sitting under the Tree of Life and subsequently serves as his guide through Paradise; see "Midrash Ke-Tapuah ba-Atzei Ha-Ya'ar" in *Batei Midrashot*, originally edited by Shelomo Aharon Wertheimer in the second enlarged edition by Abraham Joseph Wertheimer (Jerusalem: Ktab Wasepher, 1968), vol. 1, p. 284. On the relation of this text to *Gedulat Moshe* (Amsterdam, 1754), see Ginzberg, *Legends of the Jews*, vol. 2, pp. 304 ff., especially pp. 314–317, vol. 5, pp. 416–419. On Shamshiel, see Reuven Margaliot, *Malakhei Elyon* (Jerusalem: Mosad HaRav Kook, 1964), pp. 196–197. Shamshiel seems to be mentioned in 1 (Ethiopic) Enoch 6:7 and 8:3 (see *The Apocrypha and Pseudepigrapha of the Old Testament*, ed. R. H. Charles, vol. 2, pp. 191–192); in the latter passage Shamshiel teaches "the signs of the sun" and therefore may be connected with the sun-god Shamash. See also 3 Enoch 14:4, where Shamshiel is "appointed over the day." On the other angels whom the four sages learn of in the Garden of Eden, Sandalphon and Michael, see Margaliot, pp. 108–135, 149–154. On the connection between Sandalphon and sandal, see Gershom Scholem, *Encyclopaedia Judaica*, vol. 14, col. 828. For the motif of how Sandalphon weaves crowns for God from the prayers of the righteous, see Babylonian Talmud, *Hagigah* 13b. The theme of weaving crowns from the sandals of those who danced with the Torah on Simhat Torah is found in a story of the Baal Shem Tov; see Eliezer Steinmann, *Gan Ha-Hasidut* (Jerusalem: World Zionist Organization, 1957), pp. 103–104. This story has been retold by Howard Schwartz as "A Crown of Shoes," in *Gabriel's Palace*, pp. 194–195.

77. Later righteous men, even such as the Baal Shem Tov, were unable to proceed beyond the flaming sword gate when they encountered it; see Dov

ben Samuel, *Shivhei Ha-Besht*, ed. Samuel A. Horodezky (Berlin, 1922). This story is retold by Howard Schwartz in *Gabriel's Palace*, pp. 189–191.

78. On the cruel and arbitrary attitude of the angelic guardians of the seven palaces (*hekhalot*), see J. Dan's discussion of "The Dangers of the Mystic Experience," in *The Ancient Jewish Mysticism*, pp. 95 ff. On the other hand, Schaefer, *Hidden and Manifest God*, pp. 32 ff., takes note of the ambivalent task of these angelic gatekeepers, who on the one hand protect the divine sphere from unauthorized entry, but also provide help to those who are worthy of seeing God in His beauty.

79. According to *Seder Gan Eden* (*Otzar Ha-Midrashim*, ed. Eisenstein, pp. 85–89, especially p. 89), there is located in the middle of the Garden of Eden a tree with fifty gates through which the righteous pass and serves as their column of ascent. The same text (p. 88) speaks of a celestial ladder that appeared in Jacob's dream (Genesis 28:12); compare the heavenly ladder that the four sages encounter in chapter 7 of the novella. For additional sources and the relationship of this heavenly ladder to the column of ascent, see Ginzberg, *Legends of the Jews*, vol. 5, p. 10 n. 22, p. 91 n. 49, and A. Altmann, "The Ladder of Ascension," *Studies in Mysticism and Religion Presented to Gershom G. Scholem* (Jerusalem: Magnes, 1967), pp. 1–32. On the comparison of the Tree of Souls to a ladder of ascent, see below, n. 103. On the hollow pillar (or column) of ascent in the *Zohar*, see Tishby, *Wisdom of the Zohar*, vol. 2, pp. 592, 599. On the use of this column of ascent in Hasidism and various non-Jewish traditions, see Moshe Idel, *Kabbalah—New Perspectives*, pp. 94, 321 n. 133. On the shaman's ascent to heaven on a pole or tree, symbolic of the cosmic tree, see Mircea Eliade, *Myths, Dreams and Mysteries* (New York: Harper, 1960), p. 63, cited by Mario Jacoby, *The Longing for Paradise— Psychological Perspectives on an Archetype* (Boston: Sigo Press, 1985), p. 206. On passing through the Tree, see *Zohar* II, 51a (top), which interprets *derekh etz ha-hayyim* "the way of [or: to] the tree of life" (Genesis 3:24) as "the way through the tree of life" through which one proceeds from this tree to another [higher] tree. Compare *Zohar* III, 239b, which speaks specifically of a lower tree that was prepared "so that whoever enters into the upper tree should not do so without permission, but would find the lower tree [in his way], and then he would be afraid to enter unless he were first found to be worthy

enough." See *The Wisdom of the Zohar*, vol. 1, pp. 357 ff.; in n. 510 Tishby explains this passage in relation to the sefirotic system: "*Malkut* is the gate by which one enters the mystery of the divine, whose basis is in *Tiferet*. With the aspect of Judgment that it contains it repulses and punishes those who seek to enter without being sufficiently worthy."

80. On the heavenly ascent in apocalyptic and early Jewish mystical sources, see Itamar Gruenwald, *Apocalyptic and Merkavah Mysticsm* (Leiden: Brill, 1980), especially chap. 2, "The Mystical Elements in Apocalyptic," pp. 29–72.

81. On the cloud as a means of heavenly transport, see Geza Vermes, *Jesus the Jew* (London: Collins, 1973), pp. 186–188. Vermes argues that "one like a son of man" coming with the clouds in Daniel 7:13 is a person journeying upward.

82. 2 Enoch 3:1 (trans. Forbes and Charles, *Apocrypha and Pseudepigrapha*, ed. Charles, vol. 2, p. 432). F. I. Andersen, in *The Old Testament Pseudepigrapha*, ed. J. H. Charlesworth, vol. 1, p. 110 n. e, argues that the clouds here are a vantage point, not a vehicle. Compare 1 Enoch 14:8: "Behold, in the vision clouds invited me and a mist summoned me . . . and the winds in the vision caused me to fly and lifted me upward, and bore me into heaven" and 3 Enoch 24, 2–4 on the "Chariots (*Merkhavot*) of wind and clouds." On Enoch's cloud ascent, see Ginzberg, *Legends of the Jews*, vol. 1, pp. 126, 131.

83. *Pesiqta Rabbati* 20:4; compare the translation by William Braude (based on manuscripts, commentaries, and parallel texts), p. 405. A closely parallel text, titled *Ma'ayan Hokhmah*, was published by Jellinek in *Bet Ha-Midrash*, vol. 1, pp. 58–61. For an extensive discussion of this text and its various parallels, see David Halperin, *The Faces of the Chariot*, pp. 289–322; on the derivation of the image of the "elevator-cloud" from Exodus 24:18, see pp. 292 ff. For a broad selection of related traditions, see *Legends of the Jews*, vol. 7 (index), p. 89, s.v. Clouds, Moses in the. For Moses' cloud ascent in later kabbalistic interpretation, see Moshe Idel, *Kabbalah—New Perspectives*, pp. 95, 322 n. 144.

84. On this vast theme, see most recently Peter Schaefer, *The Hidden and Manifest God*, index, p. 191 s.v. Heavenly journey. For the evolution of this material in later Jewish mysticism, see Tishby, *The Wisdom of the Zohar*, vol. 2, pp. 587–621.

85. An Aramaicized form of the Latin, *hospes*, "guest."

86. See *Encyclopaedia Judaica*, vol. 16, col. 19 s.v. ushpizin; A. Z. Idelsohn, *Jewish Liturgy* (New York: Schocken, 1967), pp. 203–204; Yom-Tov Lewinsky, *Encyclopedia of Folklore, Customs and Traditions in Judaism* (Tel Aviv: Dvir, 1975), p. 13 [Hebrew]; *Sefer Ha-Moadim*, ed. Yom-Tov Lewinsky (Tel Aviv: Dvir, 1963), vol. 4 (Sukkot), pp. 152–163; J. D. Eisenstein, *Ozar Dinim u-Minhagim: A Digest of Jewish Laws and Customs in Alphabetic Order* [New York, 1917], pp. 12–13 [Hebrew].

87. On the *sukkah* as the "Shade of Faith," see Tishby, *Wisdom of the Zohar*, vol. 3, pp. 1248–1249.

88. At the time of the "sacrifice of Isaac," see Genesis, chap. 22.

89. On Moses as "The Faithful Shepherd," see Tishby, *Wisdom of the Zohar*, vol. 1, p. 5.

90. Paraphrased from the version found in *Sefer Ha-Moadim*, vol. 4 (Sukkot), p. 152.

91. *Sefer Ha-Nefesh Ha-Hakhamah*, sheet-signature 12, folio 1c (Basel, 1608), referred to by Tishby, *Wisdom of the Zohar*, p. 1275, n. 354. On the complicated question of Moshe de Leon's literary corpus, relative to the composition of the *Zohar* and the problem of relative dating, see Elliot R. Wolfson's introduction (pp. 4–9) to his edition of *The Book of the Pomegranate—Moses de Leon's Sefer Ha-Rimmon* (Atlanta: Scholars Press, 1988).

92. Note that here the seven "guests" are arranged in the order of their biblical chronology rather than in their "sefirotic" order as in the *Zohar* (see below), in which David (*Malkut*) is adjacent to Joseph (*Yesod*). This may be somehow related to the fact that here Moshe de Leon has identified all seven biblical guests as "the foundations of the world" (*yesodei olam*). Normally there is a strong connection of Joseph specifically to *Yesod*, the second to last of the seven lower *sefirot*, based on the verse "the righteous one is the foundation of the world" (*tzaddik yesod olam*) (Proverbs 10:25) and the traditional identification of Joseph as the archetypal "righteous one" (*tzaddik*); see James L. Kugel, *In Potiphar's House* (San Francisco: Harper, 1990), pp. 25–26, 126 ff.

93. *Zohar* III, 103b–104a (Tishby, *Wisdom of the Zohar*, vol. 3, pp. 1305–1308); see also *Zohar—The Book of Enlightenment*, trans. and intro. by Daniel Chanan Matt [1983], pp. 148–152: "Rabbi Abba said: Abraham, five righteous

ones, and King David make their dwelling with him . . . the custom of Rav Hamnuna Sava [was] after he had entered the *sukkah* he would say: Let us invite our guests. . . . Be seated, lofty guests, be seated, guests of faith. . . ." Both Tishby and Matt note that the righteous who appear in the *sukkah* are Abraham, Isaac, Jacob, Moses, Aaron, Joseph, and David, related to the "sefirotic" order of these biblical personalities; see below. Matt's translation of the entire passage from the *Zohar* is reprinted and presented for the novice reader of kabbalistic texts by Lawrence Fine, "Kabbalistic Texts," in *Back to the Sources—Reading the Classic Jewish Texts*, ed. Barry Holtz (New York: Summit Books, 1984), pp. 330–340.

94. I, 220a–221a (Tishby, *Wisdom of the Zohar*, vol. 3, pp. 1308–1314, esp. p. 1313 n. 355).

95. See Tishby, *Wisdom of the Zohar*, vol. 3, p. 1306 nn. 271, 272 (on the relationship of the "guests," the *sefirot*, and the [seven] clouds of glory that accompanied Israel in the Wilderness), and p. 1307, n. 283.

96. Tishby, *Wisdom of the Zohar*, vol. 1, p. 288. In Sephardi *mahzorim*, the order of inviting the *ushpizin* conforms to this "sefirotic" order (i.e., with Joseph adjacent to David). This liturgical custom is attibuted by J. D. Eisenstein, *Ozar Dinim u-Minhagim*, p. 13, to the Ari (Isaac Luria), whom he says arranged the biblical "guests" according to their importance. In most Ashkenazi *mahzorim* the order of the "guests" is made to conform to biblical chronology; see above nn. 92 and 93.

97. On the sefirotic tree, see Gershom Scholem, *On the Mystical Shape of the Godhead—Basic Concepts in the Kabbalah* (New York: Schocken, 1991), pp. 42–45.

98. In the *Zohar*, these seven "celestial residences" (*hekhalot*) or "firmaments" are related to the *sefirot*; see Tishby, *Wisdom of the Zohar*, vol. 2, pp. 591–593 and the seven *hekhalot* are indeed occupied by biblical personalities (*Zohar* I, 41a–45b; Tishby, *Wisdom of the Zohar*, vol. 2, pp. 597–614, esp. 610–611). However, here Moses occupies the sixth, *Tiferet* (counting down from the first, *Keter*), while *Netzah* and *Hod* are occupied by "the other prophets." Like a true kabbalist, Schwartz seems to have made a symbolic syllogistic analogy: the seven *hekhalot* are related to the *sefirot* and the *ushpizin* are also related to the (seven lower) *sefirot*; thus the seven "celestial residences"

must be occupied by the seven biblical "guests" in their sefirotic order. I have not been able to find this precise linking of the *hekhalot* and the *ushpizin* stated in a specific traditional text, although such may well exist. There are, however, a number of partial parallels. In Paradise, Moses is shown thrones by the angel Shamshiel, the greatest of which is occupied by Abraham followed by Isaac and Jacob. See *Batei Midrashot*, vol. 1, p. 284; *Legends of the Jews*, vol. 2, p. 314, vol. 5, pp. 418–419 (on this text, see above, n. 76). In *Merkavah* literature, it is Metatron who shows Rabbi Ishmael "the souls of the fathers of the world, Abraham, Isaac, and Jacob, and the rest of the righteous, who had been raised from their graves and had ascended into heaven"; see 3 Enoch 44:7. This conception may be related to the rather remarkable statement attributed to Resh Lakish: "The patriarchs are themselves the *Merkavah*" (*Genesis Rabbah* 47:6 and two internal parallel passages; see the Theodor-Albeck edition, p. 475); for the development of this idea in the *Bahir*, in which Abraham, Isaac, and Jacob represent the three divine *middot* of Love, Fear, and Truth, see Gershom Scholem, *Origins of the Kabbalah* (Philadelphia: Jewish Publication Society, 1987), p. 146. Note that the "seven shepherds" mentioned in Micah 5:4, according to rabbinic escatological tradition, include "David in the middle, with Abraham, Jacob, and Moses to his left" (Babylonian Talmud, *Sukkah* 52b and parallels cited by Ginzberg, *Legends of the Jews*, vol. 5, pp. 130–131). In later midrashic tradition, it is less clear precisely who these "seven shepherds" are; see *Numbers Rabbah* 14:1. According to Gershom Scholem, *Kabbalah*, p. 111 (*Encyclopaedia Judaica*, vol. 10, col. 575, s.v. Kabbalah), the "seven shepherds" are identified with the "seven guests" (*ushpizin*), who are also known as "the partriarchs of the Chariot" (see *Genesis Rabbah* cited above) in their being linked with the seven lower *sefirot*. Scholem does not specifically link the "seven guests" to the seven separate *hekhalot* in the way they are clearly linked in the novella. However, it is possible that Schwartz's creative imagination was stimulated by Scholem's discussion.

99. See Babylonian Talmud, *Pesahim* 50a, for the story of how Rav Yosef the son of Rabbi Yehoshua ben Levi, in a near-death experience, had a glimpse of the World to Come.

100. On this paradoxical terminology, see Schaefer, *The Hidden and Manifest God*, pp. 2–3 n. 4 and the additional bibliography cited there.

101. The seven heavens or firmaments are actually referred to as "dwellings" (*me'onot*); see for example *Sepher Ha-Razim*, ed. Margalioth, p. 108 l. 1 and p. 109 l. 25; *Seder Rabbah di-Bereshit* in *Batei Midrashot*, vol. 1, ed. A. J. Wertheimer (1968), p. 24 (see n. 14). This seems based on the view, attributed to Resh Lakish, that there are seven firmaments, one of which is called *maon*, "dwelling" (Babylonian Talmud, *Hagigah* 12b, in the "mystical collection"); compare 3 Enoch 38:1 and the comments of Ithamar Greenwald (Gruenwald), "Yannai and Hekhaloth Literature," *Tarbiz* 36 (1966): 269–270. *Midrash Konen* (*Otzar Ha-Midrashim*, ed. Eisenstein, vol. 1, pp. 253–260) similarly describes a celestial cosmography composed of seven "houses" (*batim*). When Rabbi Yehoshua ben Levi surveys these seven celestial "houses," after he bests the Angel of Death (see above, n. 74), he reports back to Rabban Gamliel that the third house is occupied by specific biblical personalities, including Abraham, Isaac, and Jacob, Moses, Aaron, David, Solomon, and Caleb; see *Aggadat Rabbi Yehoshua ben Levi*, *Otzar Ha-Midrashim*, vol. 1, p. 212 (*Ma'aseh deRabbi Yehoshua ben Levi*, *Bet Ha-Midrash*, ed. Jellenick, vol. 2, p. 49; Graves and Patai, *Hebrew Myths*, pp. 71–73). On the possible link between rabbinic cosmography and the Gnostic notion that the earth is surrounded by seven circles of *Archontes* (planetary Powers), see A. Altmann, "Gnostic Themes in Rabbinic Cosmology" in *Essays in Honor of J. H. Hertz*, p. 20. On the conception of the seven heavens, see Ginzberg, *Legends of the Jews*, vol. 1, p. 9, and vol. 5, pp. 9–11 nn. 21–22. This conception is already found in ascent apocalypses that date from the first century C.E. or later; Martha Himmelfarb, *Ascent to Heaven*, pp. 32, 127 n. 14. See further Adela Yarbro Collins, "The Seven Heavens in Jewish and Christian Apocalypses," in *Death, Ecstasy, and Other Worldly Journeys*, ed. John J. Collins and Michael Fishbane (Albany: SUNY, 1995), who argues that the seven planetary spheres of Greek cosmology are not the source of this picture, but rather points to the prominence of the number seven for heavens in Sumerian and Babylonian magic (as cited by Himmelfarb).

102. See *Seder Gan Eden* (*Otzar Ha-Midrashim*, ed. Eisenstein, vol. 1, p. 88). The same text states that there are 390 firmaments. *Massekhet Hekhalot*, chap. 7 (*Otzar Ha-Midrashim*, vol. 1, p. 111) speaks of 955 firmaments; compare 3 Enoch 48A:1 and Odenberg's n., pp. 154–155. However, *Seder Gan Eden* goes on to state that the Upper Heavens have no measure and they also seem

to be, in some way, beyond place and time. This seems related to the view that "Eden has no measure" (Babylonian Talmud, *Ta'anit* 10a; *Song of Songs Rabbah* 6:9:3). Compare the novella, chapter 5: "At last they came to realize that the Garden of Eden was infinite from the inside, even though it appeared to be much smaller from without. That is when they understood that they had truly reached the *Olam Ha-Ba*, the World to Come. For there time and space are infinite and eternal, as is the Holy One Himself, Blessed be He." And see the beginning of chapter 8, on the celestial Garden, which is described as a "garden of stars as vast as the universe."

103. According to *Seder Gan Eden* (*Otzar Ha-Midrashim*, ed. Eisenstein, pp. 85–89, esp. p. 89), in the middle of the Garden of Eden is located a tree from which the souls blossom. Compare *Midrash Konen* (*Otzar Ha-Midrashim*, ed. Eisenstein, vol. 1, p. 255): "And from the tree of life the souls of the righteous ascend to heaven and descend from heaven to the Garden of Eden like a man who ascends and descends a ladder." The early kabbalistic text *Sefer Ha-Bahir* (Scholem, *Das Buch Bahir* [Leipzig, 1923], sec. 14, ed. Margaliot [Jerusalem, 1951], sec. 220) contains the following mythical reading of the verse "I am the Lord that maketh all" (Isaiah 44:24): "It was I who planted this tree, so that all the world could delight in it, and I engraved all within it, and called its name 'the All'; for all hangs from it and all comes from it and all need it, and all look upon it and set their hopes upon it, and from thence all souls emanate." See furthermore, Gershom Scholem's essay on "Tsaddik" in *On the Mystical Shape of the Godhead—Basic Concepts in the Kabbalah*, pp. 95–98. Elsewhere in *Sefer Ha-Bahir* (ed. Scholem, sec. 67), the crown and heart of this tree are said to be occupied by Holy Israel, and its fruit is described as "the soul of the righteous" (sec. 87); see Gershom Scholem, *On the Kabbalah and Its Symbolism* (New York: Schocken, 1969), pp. 91–92. On the use of the motif of the tree of souls in a hasidic story, see Moshe Idel, *Kabbalah—New Perspectives*, p. 397 n. 94. For a fuller and very different development of this motif, see Howard Schwartz, "Tree of Souls," in *Adam's Soul* (Northvale, NJ: Jason Aronson, 1992), pp. 79–80.

104. Compare the place of stars in the firmament shown to Rabbi Ishmael by Metatron according to 3 Enoch 46:1.

105. See Gershom Scholem, *Encyclopaedia Judaica*, vol. 2, cols. 248–249, s.v. Adam Kadmon (Primal Man).

106. See *Genesis Rabbah* 8:1; Babylonian Talmud, *Hagigah* 12a; and Ginzberg, *Legends of the Jews*, vol. 1, pp. 58 ff.; vol. 5, pp. 22 ff.; A. Altman, "The Gnostic Background of the Rabbinic Adam Legends," in *Essays in Jewish Intellectual History* (Hanover/London, 1981), pp. 1–16. On the notion that Adam contained the whole world, see Moshe Idel, *Kabbalah—New Perspectives*, pp. 117 ff.

107. Tanhuma, *Ki Tisa* 12; *Exodus Rabbah* 40:3.

108. Tanhuma, *Pekudei* 3.

109. Babylonian Talmud, *Yevamot* 62a, 63b. On this and the passage cited in the previous note, see Ginzberg, *Legends of the Jews*, vol. 1, p. 56; vol. 5, p. 75 n. 19. Compare the extensive discussion of the different versions of this passage in Theodor's comment in his commentary to *Genesis Rabbah* (24:4), p. 233, and A. Marmorstein, in *Metzudah* (1944), p. 94 ff.

110. See Gershom Scholem, "*Gilgul*: the Transmigration of Souls," in *On the Mystical Shape of the Godhead*, pp. 228–234. Compare Howard Schwartz's narrative retelling of this complex of ideas in *Adam's Soul*, p. 3.

111. Similarly the Baal Shem Tov's "soul ascent" leads to his finally entering the palace of the Messiah: "So I ascended degree by degree, until I entered the palace of the Messiah" (from the epistle to his brother-in-law, *Shivehei ha-Besht*, ed. J. Mondshine, pp. 235–236, Koretz version, cited by Moshe Idel, *Kabbalah—New Perspectives*, p. 94). Compare "The Besht in the Messiah's Heavenly Palace," *In Praise of the Baal Shem Tov*, trans. and ed. Dan Ben-Amos and Jerome R. Mintz (Northvale, NJ: Jason Aronson, 1994), pp. 54–58. For an extensive discussion of the Messiah in Jewish mysticism, including a number of motifs mentioned below, see Yehudah Liebes, *Studies in the Zohar* (Albany: SUNY, 1993), chap. 1, "The Messiah of the Zohar," pp. 1–84.

112. See *Kabbalah—New Perspectives*, pp. 75–76, 197–199, on "theurgical weeping" particularly in Lurianic Kabbalah. Babylonian Talmud, *Berakhot* 32b, speaks of the "gates of weeping" (*sha'arei dim'ah*), which are never closed, even when the "gates of prayer" are; see also the Yiddish "*Tkhine* of the Gates of Tears," in Tracy Guren Klirs et al., *The Merit of Our Mothers—A Bilingual Anthology of Jewish Women's Prayers* (Cincinnati: Hebrew Union College, 1992), pp. 90–98.

113. *Seder Gan Eden* (*Otzar Ha-Midrashim*, ed. Eisenstein, vol. 1, p. 86).

According to Gershom Scholem, in *Le-Agnon Shai*, ed. Dov Sadan and Ephraim Urbach (Jerusalem: World Zionist Organization, 1966), p. 294 ff., *Seder Gan Eden* must have been written at the end of the thirteenth century in kabbalistic circles that produced the *Zohar*; see Yosef Dan, *Encyclopaedia Judaica*, vol. 12, cols. 1457–1458. Compare *Zohar* III, 172b, which similarly mentions God's letting fall two tears into the Great Sea. The source of this image is found in Babylonian Talmud, *Berakhot* 59a: "When the Holy, Blessed be He, calls to mind His children, who are plunged in suffering among the nations of the world, He lets fall two tears into the Great Sea, and the sound is heard from one end of the world to the other." On this talmudic passage, see Michael Fishbane, "'The Holy One Sits and Roars': Mythopoesis and the Midrashic Imagination," *Journal of Jewish Thought and Philosophy* 1 (1991): 1–21, especially pp. 10 ff.

114. See *Zohar* II, 7b, and the additional references cited by Margulies, ad loc., n. 3. This zoharic image is referred to also in another version of the Baal Shem Tov's ascent to heaven in which the Messiah says to him: "I do not know whether you will open the gate, but if you do, redemption will certainly come to Israel. He said further that this was the gate of the palace of the Bird's Nest through which no one has ever passed save the Messiah, as it is said in the holy *Zohar*"; see *In Praise of the Baal Shem Tov*, p. 58, and the editors' notes on p. 319.

115. *Zohar* II, 8a.

116. Compare the beginning of chapter 3, "A Faint Melody," on sound as scent luring the four sages to their meeting with the soul sisters. On music as a source for inspiration, see Moshe Idel, "Music and Prophetic Kabbalah," *Yuval* 4 (1982): 150–169.

117. This motif has been extensively surveyed by A. Aptowitzer, "Bet Ha-Mikdash shel Ma'alah al pi Ha-Aggadah," *Tarbiz* 2 (1931): 137–287. A much-abridged English adaptation by Aryeh Rubinstein of this classic discussion, "The Celestial Temple as Viewed in the Aggadah," may be found in *Binah* (Studies in Jewish Thought), ed. Joseph Dan, vol. 2 (New York: Praeger, 1989), pp. 1–29.

118. For sources, see secs. 2 and 3 of the article by Aptowitzer (in the previous note): "The Heavenly Temple as a Counterpart to the Earthly

Temple," and "Correlation between the Plans of the Earthly and Celestial Temples." See also Jon D. Levenson, "The Jerusalem Temple in Devotional and Visionary Experience," in *Jewish Spirituality from the Bible through the Middle Ages*, ed. Arthur Green (New York: Crossroad, 1986), p. 39, who notes that the "holy palace" mentioned in Psalms 11:4 is both the Temple (e.g., Psalms 79:1) and the supernal archetype that it manifests; both "places" are in effect the same. Martha Himmelfarb, "From Prophecy to Apocalypse: The *Book of the Watchers* and Tours of Heaven," in the aforementioned volume, pp. 150–151, notes that the idea of a heavenly archetype for the earthly temple appears explicitly in the Bible in the instructions for the building of the tabernacle in the wilderness (Exodus, chaps. 26–27).

119. See Scholem, *Major Trends in Jewish Mysticism*, pp. 40 ff.; Schaefer, *Hidden and Manifest God*, pp. 11 ff.

120. On the motif of the vision of the Temple in biblical religion, see the article by Jon D. Levenson cited above, n. 118.

121. Esther 3:9, 4:7; Ezra 5:17, 6:1, 7:20. It is not clear whether the biblical term is derived from the Hebrew root *gnz*, meaning to hide away, or from a Persian word meaning treasury.

122. See Saul Lieberman, "The Temple: Its Lay-Out and Procedure," in *Hellenism in Jewish Palestine* (New York: Jewish Theological Seminary, 1962), pp. 169–172. Lieberman notes the similarity between this feature of the Jerusalem Temple and the *opisthodomos* (back chamber), which commonly served as treasury and archival library in Greco–Roman temples.

123. According to Babylonian Talmud, *Megillah* 26b, worn-out Torah scrolls are to be buried in pottery vessels in the grave of a Torah scholar. The same passage also mentions a similar means of dealing with worn-out Torah covers made of cloth. The Palestinian Talmud, *Yoma* 7:3 (44b), preserves a Tannaitic tradition according to which the special garments worn by the High Priest in the Temple on the Day of Atonement (see Leviticus 16:4) when they become worn out are to be "hidden away there" (i.e., in the Temple); compare *Leviticus Rabbah* 21:12 and the parallels cited by Margulies, p. 492.

124. See *Encyclopaedia Judaica*, vol. 15, col. 598, s.v. synagogue; vol. 4, col. 710, s.v. Bet Alfa. Other examples have been discovered at Masada and at Dura Europos in Syria.

125. See Lieberman, *Tosefta Ki-Fshutah*, part 3, Order *Mo'ed*, p. 204, who demonstrates that the reading *le-banav*, "to his son," is an obvious error for *le-bana'i*, "to a builder," and that the background description of the story is one of Rabban Gamliel supervising the Temple builders.

126. See Tosefta, *Shabbat* 14:2, ed. Lieberman, [13:2] p. 57, and the parallels cited there. My thanks to my colleague, Professor Michael Klein, Dean of the Hebrew Union College in Jerusalem, for calling this important source to my attention. Note also the mention of a "Syrian book" of Job in the addition at the conclusion of the Septuagint version of Job. It should be noted that in the case of the translation of the Book of Job the "hiding away" of the text was not to preserve it but rather to suppress the book by removing it from circulation, at least in written form. Compare the statement: the sages sought to "hide away" (*li-gnoz*, i.e., to remove from circulation and thereby exclude from the biblical canon) the Book of Ecclesiastes because it was found to be self-contradictory (Babylonian Talmud, *Shabbat* 30b); or in another formulation, because they found in it statements that tend to heresy (*Leviticus Rabbah* 28:1). On the near suppression of the Book of Ezekiel, see Babylonian Talmud, *Hagigah* 13a.

127. On the notion that time is collapsed when seen through the "eyes of God," see Psalm 90:4: "For a thousand years in Your eyes are like a day." Compare the rabbinic tradition cited above attributed to Rabbi Eleazar [ben Pedat] according to which Adam saw from one end of the universe to the other by the light which the Holy One, blessed be He, created on the first day. This primordial light was subsequently "hidden away" and is referred to in later Jewish tradition as "the hidden light" (*or ha-ganuz*). For an extensive discussion of the motif of the hidden light, see Freema Gottlieb, *The Lamp of God—A Jewish Book of Light* (Northvale, NJ: Jason Aronson, 1989), pp. 142–152, 345–347. My thanks to Professor Michael Klein for pointing out the link between the theme of the motif of the *or ha-ganuz* and the Heavenly *Genizah*.

128. *The Aleph and Other Stories 1933–1969*, translated by Norman Thomas di Giovanni in collaboration with the author (New York: Dutton, 1970), pp. 149–150.

129. Apart from Rabbi Akiba, the three other sages read the Book of

Raziel backward in mirror-image. This motif has perhaps been suggested by the halakhic discussion of reading various texts "backward" (*le-mafre'a*); see Mishnah, *Berakhot* 2:3, *Megillah* 2:1; Tosefta *Megillah* 2:1 and the commentaries cited in Lieberman's *Tosefta Ki-Fshutah*, vol. 5, p. 1141.

130. MS Vatican 283, folio 72, recently published by Moshe Idel, "An Early Kabbalistic Commentary on Entering Paradise," *Mahanaim* 6 (1993): 32–39 [Hebrew]; the passage translated here is found on p. 34. An abridged version of the passage is cited by I. Tishby, *Commentary on Talmudic Aggadoth by Rabbi Azriel of Gerona* (Jerusalem: Magnes, 1982), introduction, p. 19; for a translation of this text and a discussion of the death of Ben Azzai, see Michael Fishbane, *The Kiss of God: Spiritual and Mystical Death in Judaism* (Seattle: University of Washington Press, 1994), pp. 34–38.

131. On the idea of *devekut* ("cleaving to God"), see Scholem, *Major Trends*, pp. 140–141, and the important corrective of Moshe Idel, *Kabbalah— New Perspectives*, pp. 62 ff.

132. *Ha-ziv ha-matok*; on a similar expression in the poetry of Shelomoh ibn Gabirol, see Idel (above, n. 130), p. 36 n. 54.

133. *Mukhteret u-mu'etert*; for the use of this phrase among the kabbalists of Gerona, see Idel (above, n. 130), p. 37.

134. Compare the death of Ben Azzai in Milton Steinberg's *As a Driven Leaf* (chap. 20): "The veil is lifting. The wall is breaking through. Light flows over me and an intoxication as of wine. There is sweetness, too, sweetness within and everywhere. 'And God saw all which He had made and behold, it was good.' It is good, all good, aglow with light. The whole world is aglow with light . . . brighter and brighter . . . too bright to see, too dazzling, for no man may see Thee and live. I have asked after Thee, sought Thee in the night watches, and called out of the depths. Now do I, Simeon the son of Azzai—see—I see. . . ."

135. *The Kiss of God: Spiritual and Mystical Death in Judaism* (Seattle: University of Washington Press, 1994), particularly chap. 1 on "Death and Desire in Jewish Spirituality." As noted by Fishbane, the idea for death by a kiss emerges partly through a midrashic interpretation of the expression "And Moses died . . . according to the word of (*al pi*) God" (Deuteronomy 34:5), taken literally to mean "by the mouth of" God (i.e., by a divine kiss). See

Avot deRabbi Natan, version A, chap. 12 [*The Fathers According to Rabbi Nathan*, trans. Judah Goldin, p. 65]; *Deuteronomy Rabbah* 11:10 (end): "Then the Holy One, Blessed be He, kissed him and took his soul with a kiss of the mouth (*neshikat peh*)." On this passage, see Aliza Shenhar, "Concerning the Nature of the Motif 'Death by a Kiss,'" *Fabula* 19 (1978): 62–73. On the rich midrashic tradition on the death of Moses, see Judah Goldin, "The Death of Moses— An Exercise in Midrashic Transposition," in *Studies in Midrash and Related Literature* (Philadelphia: Jewish Publication Society, 1988), pp. 175–186 [originally published in *Love and Death in the Ancient Near East. Studies Presented to Marvin H. Pope*, ed. John Marks and Robert Good (Guilford, CT: Four Quarters Press, 1987]. Compare Maimonides, *Guide for the Perplexed* 3:51 (end), who interprets "death by a kiss," mentioned in talmudic sources, as meaning death resulting from comprehension of God, which results from an overabundance of desire for God and the knowledge of God. Also note that Maimonides regards the rabbinic derivation of "death by a kiss" from Scripture (see above) as an example of their well-known tendency to "poetic rhetoric" (*melitzat ha-shir*). For a discussion of this passage, see Fishbane, *The Kiss of God*, pp. 24–30. In the *Zohar* (III, 144a–b), three of the companions of Rabbi Shimon bar Yohai also die by a kiss; see the translation and commentary on this passage by Daniel Matt, *Zohar*, pp. 167–168, 283–284.

136. Babylonian Talmud, *Baba Batra* 17a; Rashi, ad loc, s.v. *she-lo shalat be-hen malakh ha-mavet*. See *Zohar* I, 125a, which includes Sarah. Compare *Song of Songs Rabbah* 1:16 on the verse, "Let him kiss me with the kisses of his mouth, for thy love is better than wine" (Song of Songs 1:2). See Menahem Recanati, *Perush al Ha-Torah* (Venice, 1523; Jerusalem, 1961), p. 38b. "And know that just as when the fruit is ripe it will fall from the tree since it no longer needs to be connected, so too is the connection between the soul and the body. For when it [the soul] comprehends what it is able to comprehend (of God) and cleaves to the supernal soul [*nefesh ha-elyonah*], it casts off its earthly garment, detaches itself and cleaves to the *Shekhinah* and this is 'death by a kiss.'"

137. *Perush al Ha-Torah* (Venice, 1523; Jerusalem, 1961), pp. 37d–38b. For a discussion of this passage, see Fishbane, *Kiss of God*, pp. 36–38.

138. Ibid., 37c.

139. *Perush al Ha-Torah* 38a in the *Be'ur Ha-Levush Even Yekarah* citing *Sefer Pelah Ha-Rimon* [The Book of the Pomegranate Slice].

140. See Lieberman, *Tosefta Ki-Fshutah*, vol. 5, pp. 1292–1294 (Gnosticism); Henry A. Fischel, *Rabbinic Literature and Greco Roman Philosophy* (Leiden: Brill, 1973), pp. 1–89 (Epicurean Philosophy); Samson H. Levey, "The Best Kept Secret of the Rabbinic Tradition," *Judaism* 21 (1972): 454 ff. (Christianity); compare the rejoinder to Levey by Solomon Zeitlin, "The Plague of Pseudo-Rabbinic Scholarship," *Jewish Quarterly Review* 63 (1972–1973): 187 ff.

141. Compare the interpretation of Ben Zoma's sin in the early anonymous kabbalistic commentary published by Idel (see above, n. 130), p. 34: ". . . and because his mind tended to become involved with the ways of the inferior (*shafel*) world his thinking became confused, sometimes tending one way and sometimes tending the other way. And neither of the two ways became clear with him but were confused, for the opinions were confused with each other—like one who wishes to eat honey and eats to satiety and beyond satiety and what he overate causes him to vomit up everything."

142. One of the various identifications of the "forbidden fruit" that Eve gave Adam to eat in the Garden of Eden, see Ginzberg, *Legends of the Jews*, vol. 5, p. 97 n. 70. Here, Schwartz's poetic imagination has reversed the Greek myth of Hades' giving Persephone a pomegranate seed in the underworld by refracting it through the biblical legend. On the symbolic significance of the "pomegranate" in Jewish mystical lore, see Elliot R. Wolfson, *The Book of the Pomegranate—Moses De Leon's Sefer Ha-Rimmon* (Atlanta: Scholars Press, 1988), introduction, pp. 17–20.

143. See 3 Enoch, chap. 5, ed. Odenberg, pp. 13–14; note that according to some versions it is "Adam and Eve" together who experience this vision. And see Idel (above, n. 130), p. 36 n. 52 and the additional bibliography mentioned there, particularly Ira Chernus, "Nourished by the Splendor of the Shekinah," in *Mysticism in Rabbinic Judaism* (Berlin: Walter de Gruyter, 1982), pp. 74–87.

144. Paraphrased from *Sod 'Etz Ha-Da'at* (The Secret of the Tree of Knowlege), attributed to Rabbi Ezra ben Solomon of Gerona; see Gershom

Scholem, "Sitra Ahra: Good and Evil in the Kabbalah," in *The Mystical Shape of the Godhead*, pp. 64 ff., and Idel (above, n. 130), p. 39, especially n. 61.

145. Compare *Genesis Rabbah* 19:3: "[And the woman said to the serpent . . .] but of the fruit of the tree which is in the midst of the garden [God hath said: Ye shall not eat it . . .]" so that he will not fall and "cut the shoots."

146. On the idea of soul roots, see above, n. 110 (Scholem, "Gilgul").

147. Compare *Genesis Rabbah* 42:3, where those who wished to destroy the people of Israel are characterized in a parable of three enemies of a king who did various kinds of damage to what was growing in his vineyard.

148. On the smoke that rose from the grave of Aher (Elisha) as a sign of his purgative punishment in the fires of Gehenna, see Babylonian Talmud, *Hagigah* 15b.

149. Idel (above, n. 130), p. 35 (text), and Idel's analysis, p. 39.

150. In the Kabbalah, Aher's act of "uprooting the shoots" is generally interpreted as separating the Godhead into two divine powers, symbolized as "shoots." See Liebes, *The Sin of Elisha*, p. 22. According to Liebes, Elisha's fundamental sin was hubris; see there, pp. 23–24, for his reading of the story of Elisha as a Greek tragedy.

151. On the primordial creation of the rainbow, see Kasher, *Torah Shelemah* to Genesis 9:13, para. 81. Furthermore, on the times when the rainbow was not visible, see Ginzberg, *Legends of the Jews*, vol. 5, p. 189 n. 55. See the extensive commentary of Rabbenu Bahya ben Asher on Genesis 9:13, particularly his comment that the sign of the rainbow appears only during times of culpability and generations lacking righteousness. Compare *Midrash Ha-Gadol* on Genesis 9:14: "It is told of Rabbi Shimon bar Yohai that the rainbow was not seen during his lifetime. [When he was asked about this, he said: The rainbow] is only for [averting] divine punishment (see Genesis 9:11–17), and I am sufficient to advert divine punishment"; *Lekah Tov* to Genesis 9:14: "The bow shall be seen in the cloud"—this teaches that Satan only accuses in a time of danger. And in the same work on Genesis 9:16: "And the bow shall be in the cloud, and I will see it"—for I drew my bow and brought a deluge upon it [the earth]; but from now on I shall see it [the rainbow] so that [the bow of divine wrath] shall not be drawn.

152. See Babylonian Talmud, *Berakhot* 59a, and the following warning

against behaving in this way: "They curse him in the West [Palestine], because he seems to be bowing to the rainbow." This is then followed by a discussion of the appropriate blessing to be recited upon seeing a rainbow. See Ithamar Gruenwald, *Apocalyptic and Merkavah Mysticism* (Leiden: Brill, 1980), p. 84 n. 31. For an extensive discussion of the relationship between the rainbow and the *Merkavah*, and particularly the role of Rabbi Yehoshua ben Levi as one who proposed the rainbow as an object of worship, see David Halperin, *The Faces of the Chariot*, pp. 250–261.

153. See *Genesis Rabbah* 35:14: "My bow (*kashti*)" (Genesis 9:13)—something that is "comparable" (*mukash*) to Me. Medieval commentators, like the Ramban (to Genesis 9:12), regarded this midrash as an "esoteric secret" (*sod ne'elam*). Recanati, in his commentary on the Torah (Jerusalem, 1981) on the same verse (20a), prefaces his explanation of this midrash with the following disclaimer: "The secret of the *keshet* ("rainbow") is most awesome for it is connected to the word *koshi* ("conundrum") and it connotates (*remez*) the supernal Glory [of God] (*kavod shel ma'alah*) . . ."

154. See Babylonian Talmud, *Hagigah* 16a (and see there further that the punishment for doing so is that one's eyes become dim). According to Rabbi Isaiah di Trani (ad loc.) shimmering, alternating colors of the rainbow are suggestive of the glory of the *Shekhinah*. Compare *Kiddushin* 40a and *Shulhan Arukh, Orah Hayyim* 229:1: "It is forbidden to gaze at it [the rainbow] intently (*le-histakel bo be-yoter*)."

155. Babylonian Talmud, *Hagigah* 15b. Compare the version represented in several *Hekhalot* texts: "Rabbi Akiba said: When I ascended on high I left a sign on the passageways to the heavenly firmament more than the passageways to my home. And when I arrived behind the celestial curtain, the angels of destruction came and sought to push me away until the Holy One, blessed be He, said to them: My sons, leave this elder alone for he is worthy to gaze at My glory." See Rachel Elior, *Hekhalot Zutarti* [Jerusalem Studies in Jewish Thought, suppl. 1 (1982)] [Hebrew], pp. 23, 38, 77, and Elior's comments, p. 63; Schaefer, *Synopse* §346. On the similarity of the expressions "worthy to make use of My glory" and "worthy to gaze at My glory," see I. Gruenwald, "New Fragments of Hekhalot Literature," *Tarbiz* 13 (1969): 366. On the similarity of the words "glory" (*kavod*) and "*merkavah*," see Lieberman, *Tosefta*

Ki-Fshutah, vol. 5, p. 1288; see also Schaefer, *Hidden and Manifest God*, p. 57 n. 13. On the phraseology of these passages within the larger context of the fate of Rabbi Akiba, see the extensive discussion by Liebes, *Sin of Elisha*, pp. 85–91; according to Liebes, Rabbi Akiba succeeds due to his modesty, where Elisha fails due to his immodesty (hubris).

156. On the "signs" that Rabbi Akiba left in the heavens, see the introduction, p. xix.

157. According to the now classic definition of Rabbi Samuel Ha-Nagid, *Aggadah* [an Aramaic term; "*Haggadah*" in Hebrew] is "all commentary in the Talmud that deals with something other than *mitzvah* [here in the sense of Jewish law]." For this definition and a more extensive evaluation of "The Nature of the Aggadah," see the essay by Joseph Heinemann, trans. Marc Bregman, in *Midrash and Literature*, ed. Geoffrey H. Hartman and Sanford Budick (New Haven: Yale University Press, 1986), pp. 41–55. On Schwartz's technique of expansively retelling traditional sources, see my survey review, "The Art of Retelling," in *The Jerusalem Post* Magazine, August 12, 1994, p. 20. This technique bears much in common with traditional forms of Jewish storytelling, such as the compositional genre known in contemporary scholarship as "rewritten Bible." What I refer to as "contemporary *Aggadah*" has sometimes been called "Modern Midrash." Personally, I would reserve this latter term for contemporary imaginative interpretations of biblical verses or stories.

158. For an attempt to define the literary genre of "apocalypse," one feature of which is detailed descriptions of such heavenly ascents, see *Apocalypse: The Morphology of a Genre, Semeia* 14 (1979), particularly the introduction by the guest editor John J. Collins; Ithamar Gruenwald, *Apocalyptic and Merkavah Mysticism* (Leiden: Brill, 1980), particularly chap. 1, "Two Essential Qualities of Jewish Apocalyptic," pp. 1–28; Martha Himmelfarb, *Ascent to Heaven in Jewish and Christian Apocalypses*, pp. 6 ff.; *The Old Testament Pseudepigrapha*, vol. 1—*Apocalyptic Literature and Testaments*, intro. by J. H. Charlesworth, pp. 3–4.

159. Borrowing and adapting a phrase from Gershom Scholem, who characterized the *Zohar* as a "mystical novel"; see *Major Trends in Jewish Mysticism*, p. 157.

160. See introduction, n. 18 (on Todorov) and David Stern's Introduction to *Rabbinic Fantasy—Imaginative Narratives from Classical Hebrew Literature*, ed. David Stern and Mark Jay Mirsky (Philadelphia: Jewish Publication Society, 1990), pp. 3–30.

161. See Eric S. Rabkin, *The Fantastic in Literature* (Princeton, NJ: Princeton University Press, 1976). More specifically *The Four Who Entered Paradise* could be regarded as one example of a Jewish subcategory of what has been termed "religious fantasy," previously noted examples of which are primarily Christian in orientation. See the annotated bibliography to Rabkin's anthology, *Fantastic World—Myths, Tales and Stories* (New York: Oxford University Press, 1979), pp. 472–473. On Christian fantasy, see Colin Manlove, "The Bible in Fantasy," in *Fantasy and the Bible, Semeia* 60 (1992): 91–122; see also the additional bibliography by the guest editors of this issue of *Semeia*, Tina Pippin and George Aichele, pp. 123–128. Other authors of Jewish religious fantasy in the modern period would include, for example, Rabbi Nachman of Bratzlav, I. L. Peretz, Franz Kafka (particularly his parable "Before the Law" from his novel *The Trial*), I. B. Singer (particularly his novel *Satan in Goray*) and S. Y. Agnon (particularly his novella *In the Heart of the Seas*).

162. For a brief survey of the Jungian notion of "archetype," see Andrew Samuels et al., *A Critical Dictionary of Jungian Analysis* (New York: Routledge & Kegan Paul, 1986), pp. 26–28, s.v. For a more extensive discussion, see Jolane Jacobi, *Complex/Archetype/Symbol in the Psychology of C.G. Jung* (Princeton, NJ: Bolligen Series LVII, 1971). On the application of Jungian archetypal thinking to Jewish myth, see Gershom Scholem's comment on the kabbalistic idea that the righteous live in Paradise in caves, in *On the Mystical Shape of the Godhead*, p. 289 n. 58. And see the review of this book by Elliot R. Wolfson in *The Journal of Religion* 73 (1993): 655–657. Wolfson suggests (p. 657) that Scholem's orientation is a kind of contextual archetypalism, that is, archetypal structures are linked to specific philological anchors that are passed on through oral or literary means of transmission in any given culture, although the possibility always exists that the motif will pass from one tradition to another. However, Scholem surely would have opposed the notion that there are timeless archetypes that are free of cultural mediation. On the application of Jungian analytical psychology to Jewish material, there is an

extensive literature; for example, see *Modern Jew in Search of a Soul*, ed. J. Marvin Spiegelman and Abraham Jacobson (Phoenix: Falcon, 1986); R. Kluger-Schaerf, *Psyche and Bible* (New York: Spring, 1974); Siegmund Hurwitz, *Lilith—The First Eve: Historical and Psychological Aspects of the Dark Feminine* (Einsiedeln: Daimon, 1992); Gustav Dreyfus and Judith Riemer, *Abraham—Man and Symbol* (Wilmett: Chiron, forthcoming).

163. See the essay, "Psychology and Literature," in *The Collected Works of C. G. Jung*, trans. R. F. C. Hull (New York: Pantheon, 1957) (Bolligen Series 57), vol. 15; reprinted in C. G. Jung, *The Spirit in Man, Art and Literature* (Princeton, NJ, Princeton University Press, 1971), pp. 84–105. Jung contrasts the "personalistic" mode (of the so-called "psychological novel") with what he terms the "visionary" mode of artistic creation. Ironically it is the latter that supplies a more interesting object for psychological analysis, particularly of the sort Jung engages in to illustrate his concept of the archetypal nature of the human psyche. Jung notes that the visionary mode of literary creation "cries out for interpretation." Compare the Jewish exegetical notion that allusive texts say "interpret me" (*darsheini*) to the reader; see Rashi's commentary to Genesis 25:22.

164. "Die Himmelsreise der Seele," originally published in 1901. For this summary of Bousset's article, detailed publication data, subsequent discussion of the essay, and additional bibliography on the ascent of the soul, see Martha Himmelfarb, *Ascent to Heaven*, p. 51, 134 n. 17.

165. Literally "those who descend to the chariot," which refers to *Merkavah* mystics who undertake the heavenly ascent (spiritual and/or physical) to view and hopefully even visit the celestial Chariot of God (*Merkavah*).

166. See Scholem's article on Kabbalah in *Encyclopaedia Judaica*, vol. 10, col. 494, and the critical comment of Schaefer, *The Hidden and Manifest God*, p. 3 n. 4. However, Schaefer notes (p. 146) that the protagonist of the heavenly journey and the subject of the associated adjuration, at least in the *sar hatorah* traditions, is "everyman."

167. *The Faces of the Chariot*, pp. 445–446; David Halperin, "Ascension or Invasion: Implications of the Heavenly Journey in Ancient Judaism," *Religion* 18 (1988): 47–67, especially. pp. 58–59. See also Halperin's article, "A Sexual Image in Hekhalot Rabbati and its Implications," in *Proceedings of the*

First International Conference on the History of Jewish Mysticism, ed. Joseph Dan (Jerusalem: The Hebrew University), English section, pp. 117–132; and most recently his monograph *Seeking Ezekiel—Text and Psychology* (University Park, PA: Pennsylvania State University Press, 1993), especially pp. 13–15, 219–220 on Ezekiel's *Merkavah* vision.

168. *Kabbalah—New Perspectives*, p. 183; see also p. 58 for the comment of R. Menahem Mendel of Premyshlyany that R. Isaac Luria saw "with mental eyes" like the four sages who entered *pardes*, and pp. 88 ff. for Idel's discussion of the "ascent of the soul." For a Jungian treatment of the motif of "nostalgia for paradise," see Mario A. Jacoby, *Longing for Paradise—Psychological Perspectives on an Archetype* (Boston: Sigo, 1985); on p. 193 the author attributes to Jung the view that the various descriptions of Paradise justify the psychological interpretation that what is involved is a set of symbols for the "self."

169. According to Sigmund Freud, *The Interpretation of Dreams*, sec. VII E, the interpretation of dreams is the "royal road" to a knowledge of the unconscious activities of the mind. For a Jungian perspective on the importance of the dream, see for example Hurwitz, *Lilith*, p. 26: "Just as the dream of an individual can be described as his *individual myth*, so the myth of a whole people can be described to a certain extent as the *dream of this collective*."

170. The additional specific image of diving for lost treasure, in Akiba's dream (see p. 4), can itself be read as a metaphor for dipping down into the unconscious.

171. My thanks to Howard Schwartz for his willingness to permit publication of this dream, which he recorded as having on December 11, 1977, in Jerusalem. As he notes in his preface to Appendix I, this dream served as a direct inspiration for his earlier story, "The Four Who Entered an Orchard" (also reprinted in the same Appendix). Much of Schwartz's highly imaginative writing is motivated by his own personal dreams. Additional examples of the author's dreams may be found in his *Dream Journal 1965–1974* (Berkeley, CA: Tree, 1975).

172. Specifically on the relationship between the dream and the work of art, see Jung, "Psychology and Literature" (above, n. 163), para. 161.

173. On the symbolic significance of the mirror in traditional Jewish sources, see Daniel Chanan Matt, "David ben Yehudah Hehasid and his *Book*

of Mirrors," *Hebrew Union College Annual* 51 (1980): 133–135; *The Book of Mirrors: Sefer Mar'ot ha-Zove'ot by R. David ben Yehudah he-Hasid*, ed. Daniel Chanan Matt (Chico, CA: Scholars Press, 1982), pp. 8–10.

174. For a detailed examination of beliefs concerning the mirror, see James G. Frazer, *Taboo and the Perils of the Soul*, vol. 3 of *The Golden Bough*, 3rd ed. revised and enlarged (New York: Macmillan, 1951); G. F. Hartlaub, *Zauber des Spiegels* (Munich: R. Piper, 1951). For a brief survey, see B. A. Litvinskii, "Mirror" in *The Encyclopedia of Religion*, ed. Mircea Eliade (New York: Macmillan), vol. 9, pp. 556–559 and especially pp. 556–557 on "mirrors and the soul."

175. On the use of mirror imagery in this episode, see above, n. 71.

176. For a brief discussion of "quaternity," see the article by George R. Elder in *The Encyclopedia of Religion*, ed. Mircea Eliade, vol. 12, pp. 133–134. For a fuller discussion of the dialectic relationship of three and four, see Edward F. Edinger's *Ego and Archetype* (New York: G. P. Putnam's Sons, 1972), especially pp. 179–193. The classic divine quaternity in Jewish sources is Ezekiel's vision of the four faces of the celestial Chariot, which clearly influenced the apocalyptic vision of God's throne surrounded by "four living creatures" in the New Testament (Revelation, chap. 4). David Halperin, *Faces of the Chariot*, pp. 190–191, specifically notes the Jungian notion of the interplay between quaternity (four) and trinity (three) in his analysis of a highly mythical midrash (*Exodus Rabbah* 43:8) in which one member of God's—or Helios's (!)—four-horse chariot is removed from the other three.

177. Similarly in the celestial Paradise, the four sages encounter the Messiah, Metatron, and the *Shekhinah*, who together represent the triune aspect of another entity, that of the Godhead.

178. *Collected Works*, vol. 12, p. 76, cited by Jacoby, *Longing for Paradise*, p. 204 n. 3.

179. H. Von Beit, *Symbolik des Marchens* (Berne: Francke, 1960), p. 258, cited by Jacoby, *Longing for Paradise*, p. 204.

180. See Annemarie Schimmel, "Numbers: An Overview," in *Encyclopedia of Religion*, vol. 11, pp. 15–16; Ginzberg, *Legends of the Jews*, index, pp. 426–428, s.v. seven, etc. In her discussion of a liturgical text from Qumran, Carol Newsom, *Songs of the Sabbath Sacrifice: A Critical Edition* (Atlanta: Scholars Press,

1985), p. 49, comments: "The entire composition seems at times to be a rhapsody on the sacred number seven"; cited by Martha Himmelfarb, *Ascent to Heaven*, p. 127 n. 17. See also *Zohar Hadash, Bereshit* 3a (*Midrash Ne'elam*): "Rabbi Shimon taught . . . everything depends on seven; there are seven pillars of heaven, seven firmaments, seven planets, etc." For seven as a cross-cultural formulistic number, see Stith Thompson, *Motif Index of Folk-Literature* §Z71.5.0.1.

181. See Ginzberg, *Legends of the Jews*, vol. 5, p. 9 n. 21.

182. Note that this is the second word of the Hebrew Bible.

183. In Aramaic, *sheit* means "six."

184. See *Zohar* I, 15b (the text is translated in Tishby, *Wisdom of the Zohar*, vol. 1, p. 313). Note that elsewhere in the *Zohar* (I, 24a; compare I, 38a–39b) this midrashic interpretation is related to the seven *hekhalot*. Compare the midrash (Babylonian Talmud, *Sukkah* 49a) where *bereshit* read as *bara' shit* is related to *shitin*, the primeval foundations of the world. See also *Midrash Ha-Gadol* to Genesis 1:1, ed. Margulies, pp. 11–12 and the parallels cited there.

185. See *Gesenius Hebrew Grammar* §12–13 on the use of the *dagesh* to "double" (i.e. strengthen) or "harden" the pronunciation of these letters, for example, the "hard" pronunciation of the *beit* as *b* (instead of the "soft" pronunciation *v*) at the beginning of a word.

186. See above, nn. 2 and 3.

187. On the archetypal significance of the mandala, in Jungian thought, as a symbolic expression of the psyche or more particularly the self, see *A Critical Dictionary of Jungian Analysis*, p. 90; C. G. Jung et al., *Man and His Symbols* (London: Aldus, 1964), index, s.v. mandala. On the Jungian concept of "self," see Jacoby, *Longing for Paradise*, pp. 194–201. On the cosmic symbolism of the mandala, see Erich Neumann, *The Origins and History of Consciousness* (New York: Harper, 1962) (Bolligen Series XLII), part I, p. 37: "The symbol of the circular mandala stands at the beginning as at the end. In the beginning it takes the mythological form of paradise; in the end, of the Heavenly Jerusalem . . . it is the paradise where the four streams have their source, and in Canaanite mythology it is the central point where the great god El sits, 'at the source of the streams. . . .'" Similar to the shape of the *Bet*, Navajo sand paintings, which are thought to be examples of mandalas, are often

bordered on three sides only; the fourth (eastern) side is left open, since evil cannot enter there. Compare the comment of Rabbi Yitzchak Ginsburg, cited above, p. 126, in which the open side of the *Bet* is said to face north. Rabbi Akiba can be seen as the one who "squares the circle"; by descending in peace from the heavenly ascent he alone completes the quest and, as it were, succeeds in closing the open side of the *Bet*.

Appendix I

This appendix collects several earlier tales by Howard Schwartz on the theme of the four who entered Paradise and some related material. "The Four Who Entered Pardes" is a brief view of the entire journey. "The Four Who Entered an Orchard" was based on a dream and portrays the entry into the orchard as a directive of Rabbi Nachman of Bratslav. "The Doors of Pardes" offers a series of metaphors about the nature of the concept of Pardes.

1

THE FOUR WHO ENTERED PARDES

Four sages, Ben Azzai, Ben Zoma, Elisha ben Abuyah, and Rabbi Akiba, made their way to the Cave of Machpelah, and by following the scent of cedars that bore a hint of Paradise, they discovered the route the souls of the righteous follow in order to reach the Garden of Eden. They knew that once every hundred years the gates of the Garden were opened for as long as the blink of a eyelash, and by many signs they had become convinced that the time was soon approaching for the gates to open in that generation.

In this they proved to be correct. Due to the vigilance of Rabbi Akiba, who alone among them had his eyes open at the instant the gates flew open and pulled in the others behind him, they managed to make their way into the earthly Paradise. There they hurried to seek out the tree in the center of the Garden. Which tree was this?—the Tree of Knowledge, for this tree forms a hedge around the Tree of Life. And the only pathway from the one tree to the other is hidden somewhere in the massive trunk of the Tree of Knowledge, which takes five hundred years to encircle.

Therefore it was necessary to choose the correct passage around this tree. Those who started in the wrong direction were unlikely ever to return. But on this matter the sages could not agree. Ben Azzai argued that they must cleave to the right, since the letters of the Hebrew alphabet are written that way. But Ben Zoma argued that they must cleave to the left, since the Tree of Life had been created first of all things in the Garden, and therefore their direction was backward, into the past, and not forward, into the future. Elisha, too, preferred to cleave to the left, for he had always sought to comprehend the secrets of creation. Yet Akiba insisted that they must cleave to the right, for that is where the Throne of Mercy can be found, while the Throne of Justice belongs to the left.

So it was that the four sages parted ways for the first time, and Ben Zoma and Elisha ben Abuyah followed the way that led to the left. Little did they know that in that direction lay an intricate labyrinth, impossible to penetrate. It was there that Ben Zoma lost his mind and Elisha abandoned his faith. And what of Ben Azzai and Rabbi Akiba, who cleaved to the right? They soon found the sole path that leads to the Tree of Life.

But what they did not know was that the Tree of Life is only visible from one side. From where they were, the two sages could see nothing but two paths branching from the one that had brought them to that place. Ben Azzai observed that if he took the one path and

Rabbi Akiba took the other, one of them might eventually arrive at the Tree of Life. Rabbi Akiba concurred. Then Ben Azzai chose the way that led to the left, for he said that it was necessary in order to seek out the balance. But Akiba continued to cleave to the right, for he believed that one must remain unwaveringly on the same path in order to reach the goal.

Ben Azzai soon discovered that he had made his way into a mirage that stretched like an endless desert on every side. And when he looked into that Abyss, he lost his life. But Rabbi Akiba made his way to the threshold of the Tree of Life and found himself standing before the *Pargod*, the curtain that hangs before the Throne of Glory. Inscribed there in black fire on white were the letters that spelled out the first word, *Bereshit*, in the beginning.

Slowly, with all of time still to unfold, Akiba began to read the letters of that word from right to left, starting with the first letter, *Bet*. And he saw that the path led from the circumference of the letter to the dot in the center, and because he never wavered from that path, he inevitably found himself standing before the gates of the Garden of Eden, which can always be opened from the inside, and he departed in peace.

2

THE FOUR WHO ENTERED AN ORCHARD

Reb Nachman was once walking at night with four of his Hasidim. They asked him to speak to them of the Mysteries of Creation. Reb Nachman agreed to their request, but asked them first to enter the orchard they were passing and to bring back the fruit of the first tree they came across.

Anxious to hear what Reb Nachman would have to say, the four entered the gate of the orchard and hurried to the first tree they saw in the distance, illumined by the light of the moon. As they approached it, they saw that the tree bore a unique jewellike fruit, which glittered in the night like precious gems and glowed with a light from within. The four Hasidim were dumbfounded to see such a tree, and at a loss as to whether they should pick such precious fruit.

One of the four turned to the others and warned them: "Most certainly this tree has been enchanted, and so must be the fruit. If we attempt to pick it we too may become enchanted. Even to touch it is dangerous." The second Hasid nodded his head in agreement: "Yes, it is possible we have stumbled on the tree that bears the forbidden fruit. If we pluck it we may bring a great sin down on ourselves." But the third Hasid protested this conclusion: "Reb Nachman has directed us to bring back the fruit of the first tree we come across. This is the tree, whose fruit is no doubt a great blessing that must not be ignored." For a while after this there was silence. Then the fourth Hasid spoke: "I, for one, do not believe this tree and its fruit exist in this world; therefore, it is an illusion, and we must be dreaming."

In this way the four Hasidim fell into a dilemma, and each argued for his own theory, and each was like a ram butting his head against the wall of the others' explanations. At last, with nothing decided, they came back to Reb Nachman empty-handed. They found him waiting outside the orchard, his features lined with grief. He asked them, knowing the answer in advance, "Did any one of you bring back the fruit of the Tree of Life?"

3

THE DOORS OF *PARDES*

The first door leads to a desert in which an occasional oasis may be found. In order to reach it and quench one's thirst, it is necessary to pass through the second door. There the oasis is recognized at once as a garden worthy of Eden, where the very air you breathe seems to provide enough sustenance to sustain you. Leaning over the pool of those pure waters to drink, you step through the third door and into another world that resembles this one in many ways, but all of these turn out to be illusions. However, by the time you discover this, you have already passed beyond the fourth door, and it no longer matters at all.

Appendix II

This appendix consists of the parable "The Four Who Sought to Re-enter the Orchard" by Marc Bregman, originally published in *Gates to the New City*. For a discussion of this parable, see page xxvi.

THE FOUR WHO SOUGHT TO RE-ENTER THE ORCHARD

Once, long ago, there were four ancient sages who longed to return to a famous garden, to again ponder and partake, each in his own way, of the wondrous fruits they knew grew there. After wandering for many years, they arrived at the awesome wall that surrounded the garden and followed it for many months until they found the gate, massive and impenetrable. In joy and expectation they gave thanks that they had been permitted to return to the entrance of the garden. After praying that they be found worthy to enter the garden and partake of its fruits, they arose together and, as one man, with great reverence, solemnly knocked upon the gate three times. The sound of their wordless plea could be heard echoing cavernously through the vast reaches of the great garden. However, the gatekeeper did not appear to let the sages enter. For he was tending and nurturing, with great love, the Tree that bore the wondrous fruits that grew in the garden.

Now the gatekeeper did hear the knocking of the sages on the gate. Indeed, it is said that it was he who, disguised sometimes as a poet, sometimes as a storyteller, had faithfully directed their steps to the gate. However, when they finally arrived, the gatekeeper was far within the garden, and the journey back to open the gate would be long and arduous. Moreover, a younger master of Torah, whom the gatekeeper had already admitted into the garden, had partaken of the fruits and become intoxicated with their sweetness. Tormented by their supernatural succulence, it was he who distracted the attention of the gatekeeper by telling him stories pregnant with deep but hidden meaning. So when the gatekeeper finally heard the three knocks of the four ancient sages, although he wanted to hurry to let them in as well, he was detained, torn between tending the fruits of the Tree and unraveling the mysteries they had inspired. So the four ancient sages continued to wait, reverently, standing at the entrance to the garden, fervently praying that the gatekeeper might appear. And, some say, they are still waiting there until this very day.

Glossary

Bereshit   lit. "in the beginning." The first word of the Torah.

Bet   the second letter of the Hebrew alphabet and the first letter of the first word of the Torah, *Bereshit*.

Dagesh   the dot in the center of some Hebrew letters, including *Bet*.

D'var Torah   lit. "a word of Torah." A Torah lesson that often accompanies a social or festive occasion.

Hekhalot   lit. "palaces." Refers to the visions of the Jewish mystics to the palaces of heaven. The texts describing these visions and the ascent into Paradise are known as *Hekhalot* texts.

Ma'aseh Bereshit   lit. "the work of creation." The mystical doctrine of the secrets of creation.

Ma'aseh Merkavah   lit. "the work of the chariot." The mystical doctrine associated with the vision of Ezekiel.

Olam ha-Ba   lit. "the World to Come." The world that follows this one. It is the most common Hebrew term for Paradise, and also refers to a messianic age that will exist on earth.

Rosh Hodesh   festival of the new moon.

Sheheheyanu   A blessing of thanksgiving for certain things when they are enjoyed for the first time, such as the eating of the first fruit of a new season.

Shekhinah   lit. "dwelling." The Divine Presence, usually identified
as a feminine aspect of the Divinity, which evolved into an inde-
pendent mythic figure in the kabbalistic period. Also identified as
the Bride of God and the Sabbath Queen.

Simhat Torah   the last day of the festival of Sukkot, on which the
cycle of reading from the Torah is concluded and begun again.

Sitra Ahra   the side of evil in kabbalistic terminology.

Sopher   a scribe. One who write holy texts, especially the Torah.

Tagin   designs used in the writing of the letters of the Torah, which
together form the crowns of the letter. Rabbi Akiba was said to be
able to interpret every crown and letter of the Torah.

Tohu ve-Bohu   lit. "chaos and void." The condition of the world
prior to creation. See Genesis 1:2.

Tzaddik   an unusually righteous and spiritually pure person.

Ushpizin   lit. "guests." The seven patriarchs who are said to visit the
sukkah during each night of Sukkot. They are Abraham, Isaac, Jacob,
Moses, Aaron, Joseph, and David.

Yetzer Hara   the Evil Inclination.

Selected Bibliography

This selected bibliography, prepared by Marc Bregman, is a compilation of previous studies on the story about the four who entered Paradise.

Alexander, P. S., "3 Enoch and the Talmud," *Journal for the Study of Judaism* 18 (1987): 54–68 [see the critique of C. R. A. Morray-Jones, "Hekhalot Literature and Talmudic Tradition: Alexander's Three Test Cases," *Journal for the Study of Judaism* 22 (1991): 17–36].

Bacher, Wilhelm, *Die Agadah der Tannaiten* (Strassburg: Trübner, 1884), vol. 1, pp. 333–334 [*Aggadot Ha-Tannaim*, 2nd ed., Berlin-Jerusalem: Dvir, 1922), vol. 1, part 2, pp. 74–76].

Baumgarten, Joseph M., "The Book of Elkesai and Merkabah Mysticism," *Journal for the Study of Judaism* 17 (1986): 216–223.

Bietenhard, H., *Die Himmlische Welt im Urchristentum und Spätjudentum* (Tübingen: J. C. B. Mohr, 1951), pp. 91–95.

Blau, Ludwig, *Das altjüdische Zauberwesen* (Berlin: Louis Lamm, 1914, first published 1898), pp. 115–116.

———, *Jewish Encyclopedia* (New York: Funk and Wagnalls, 1903), vol. 5, pp. 683–684, s.v. Gnosticism.

Bousset, W., "Die Himmelsreise der Seele," *Archiv für Religionswissenschaft* 4 (1901): 147–157.

Dan, Joseph, *The Ancient Jewish Mysticism* (Tel Aviv: MOD Books, 1993), pp. 29 ff., 81 ff., 93 ff., 108 ff.

———, "The Religious Experience of the *Merkavah*," in *Jewish Spirituality from the Bible Through the Middle Ages*, ed. Arthur Green (New York: Crossroad, 1986) [vol. 13 of *World Spirituality: An Encyclopedic History of the Religious Quest*], pp. 293–294.

Efros, Israel Isaac, *Ancient Jewish Philosophy* (Detroit: Wayne State University Press, 1964), pp. 56–59.

Fischel, Henry A., *Rabbinic Literature and Greco-Roman Philosophy* (Leiden: Brill, 1973), Part One: The "Four in Paradise"—Anti-Epicurean Stereotype, Biography, and Parody, pp. 1–34. [See the critique of A. Wasserstein, in *Journal of Jewish Studies* 25 (1974): 456–460.]

Fraenkel, Jonah, Lecture given at the Tenth World Congress of Jewish Studies, Jerusalem, 1989 [did not appear in the *Proceedings* of the Congress published in 1990]; critique of Liebes [first edition]. For summary of Fraenkel's views, in this lecture and in an earlier lecture [both in Hebrew] given in Jerusalem, 1985, and for a response, see Liebes [below], pp. 7–8 n. 19 and pp. 157–160.

Friedländer, Moriz, *Der vorchristliche jüdische Gnosticismus* (Göttingen: Vandenhoeck & Ruprecht, 1898), pp. 101 ff.

Ginzberg, Louis, *Jewish Encyclopedia*, vol. 5, pp. 138–139, s.v. Elisha ben Abuyah.

Goldberg, Arnold, "Der verkannte Gott: Prüfung und Scheitern der Adepten in der Merkawa-mystik," *Zeitschrift für Religions- und Geistesgeschichte* 26 (1974): 17–29.

Goshen Gottstein, Alon, "Four Entered Paradise Revisited," Lecture given at the Society of Biblical Literature, Annual Meeting, Washington, D.C., November 21, 1993 [in preparation for publication]. For reference to Goshen Gottstein's views, expressed in an earlier lecture given in Hebrew, see Liebes [below], p. 19, n. 12.

Grätz, Hirsch, *Gnosticismus und Judenthum* (Krotoschin: Monasch, 1846), pp. 55–101.

Gruenwald (Greenwald), Ithamar, *Apocalyptic and Merkavah Mysticism* (Leiden: Brill, 1980), pp. 50, 86–97, 108, 146–148.

————, "Yannai and Hekhaloth Literature," *Tarbiz* 36 (1966): 259–266 [Hebrew].

Halperin, David J., *The Faces of the Chariot—Early Jewish Responses to Ezekiel's Vision* (Tübingen: Mohr-Siebeck, 1988), pp. 7, 31–37, 194–210, 362.

————, *The Merkabah in Rabbinic Literature* (New Haven, CT: American Oriental Society, 1980), pp. 3, 78–79, 86–94.

Heschel, Abraham Joshua, *The Theology of Ancient Judaism* (London: Soncino, 1962), vol. 1, sec. 14, "Roundabout the Pardes," pp. 242 ff., especially pp. 242–246, "Rabbi Akaba was fit to gaze at My glory" [Hebrew].

Idel, Moshe, "An Early Kabbalistic Interpretation of the Story of Entering Pardes," *Mahanaim* 6 (1993): 32–39 [Hebrew]. [In the opening note, Idel indicates that this article is part of a comprehensive study of the medieval interpretations of the legend of the entry into *Pardes*, which is in preparation.]

————, *Kabbalah—New Perspectives* (New Haven, CT: Yale University Press, 1988), pp. 90, 92, 95, 124–125, 183, 301.

Jacobs, Louis, *Jewish Mystical Testimonies* (New York: Schocken, 1977), pp. 21–25.

Joël, Manuel, *Blicke in die Religionsgeschichte*, vol. 1 (Breslau: S. Schottlaender, 1880), pp. 163–164.

Lieberman, Saul, *Tosefta Ki-Fshhutah*, part 5, *Order Mo'ed* (New York: Jewish Theological Seminary, 1962), pp. 1289–1290.

Liebes, Yehudah, *The Sin of Elisha—The Four Who Entered Pardes and the Nature of Talmudic Mysticism* (second edition, corrected and expanded, Jerusalem: Academon, 1990) [Hebrew].

Levey, Samson H., "Akiba: Sage in Search of the Messiah; A Closer Look," *Judaism* 41 (1992): 334–345.

————, "The Best Kept Secret of the Rabbinic Tradition," *Judaism* 21 (1972): 454–469. [See the critique of Solomon Zeitlin, "The

Plague of Pseudo-Rabbinic Scholarship," *Jewish Quarterly Review* 63 (1972–1973): 187–203.]

Maier, Johann, "Das Gefährdungsmotiv bei der Himmelsreise in der jüdischen Apokalyptik und 'Gnosis,'" *Kairos* 5 (1963): 18–40.

Morray-Jones, C. R. A., "Paradise Revisited (2 Cor 12:1–12): The Jewish Mystical Background of Paul's Apostolate, Part 1: The Jewish Sources," *Harvard Theological Review* 86 (1993): 177–217.

Neher, André, "Le voyage mystique des quatre," *Revue de l'Histoire des Religions* 140 (1951): 59–82.

Neumark, David, *Geschichte der jüdischen Philosophie* (Berlin: Reimer, 1907), vol. 1, pp. 48–95.

Ostow, Mortimer, "Four Entered the Garden: Normative Religion versus Illusion," in *Fantasy, Myth, and Reality: Essays in Honor of Jacob A. Arlow, M.D.*, ed. Harold P. Blum (Madison, CT: International Universities Press, 1994), pp. 287–301.

Rowland, Christopher, *The Open Heaven: A Study of Apocalyptic in Judaism and Early Christianity* (London: SPCK, 1982), pp. 309–340.

Schäfer, Peter, *The Hidden and Manifest God—Some Major Themes in Early Jewish Mysticism*, trans. Aubrey Pomerance (Albany, NY: SUNY, 1992), pp. 69, 117–121, 145 ff.

———, "New Testament and Hekhalot Literature: The Journey into Heaven in Paul and in Merkavah Mysticism," *Journal of Jewish Studies* 35 (1984): 19–35.

Scholem, Gershom G., *Jewish Gnosticism, Merkabah Mysticism, and Talmudic Tradition* (New York: Jewish Theological Seminary, 1965), chap. III, "The Four Who Entered Paradise and Paul's Ascension to Paradise," pp. 14–19.

———, *Major Trends in Jewish Mysticism* (New York: Schocken, 1954), pp. 52–53.

Schultz, J. P., "The Heavenly Ascent and the Out-of-Body Experience of the Four Who Entered Paradise," lecture given at the Twenty-Fifth Annual Conference of the Association for Jewish Studies, Boston, December 12, 1993.

Schwartz, Howard, *Gabriel's Palace* (New York: Oxford University Press, 1993), pp. 3, 28–31, 51–52, 280–281.

Tabor, James D., *Things Unutterable: Paul's Ascent to Paradise in its Greco-Roman, Judaic and Early Christian Contexts* (Lanham, MD: University Press of America, 1986).

Urbach, E. E., "The Traditions about Merkabah Mysticism in the Tannaitic Period," in *Studies in Mysticism and Religion Presented to Gershom G. Scholem,* ed. E. E. Urbach et al. (Jerusalem: Magnes, 1967), pp. 1–28, especially pp. 12–17 [Hebrew section].

Weinstein, N. I., *Zur Genesis der Agada* (Göttingen: Vandenhoeck & Ruprecht, 1901), p. 198.

Wewers, Gerd A., *Geheimnis und Geheimhaltung in rabbinischen Judentum* (Berlin: de Gruyter, 1975), pp. 171–188.

Young, Brad H., "The Ascension Motif of Corinthians in Jewish, Christian and Gnostic Texts," *Grace Theological Journal* 9 (1988): 77–80.

Index

Howard Schwartz is Professor of English at the University of Missouri-St. Louis. He has published three books of poetry, *Vessels*, *Gathering the Sparks*, and *Sleepwalking Beneath the Stars*, and several books of fiction, including *The Captive Soul of the Messiah* and *Adam's Soul*. He has also edited four volumes of Jewish folktales: *Elijah's Violin & Other Jewish Fairy Tales*, *Miriam's Tambourine: Jewish Folktales from Around the World*, *Lilith's Cave: Jewish Tales of the Supernatural*, and, most recently, *Gabriel's Palace: Jewish Mystical Tales*. He has also collected the tales of Rabbi Zalman Schachter-Shalomi in *The Dream Assembly*. In addition, he has edited the anthologies *Imperial Messages: One Hundred Modern Parables*, *Voices Within the Ark: The Modern Jewish Poets*, and *Gates to the New City: A Treasury of Modern Jewish Tales*. He has also edited two children's books, *The Diamond Tree* (which won the Sydney Taylor Book Award in 1992) and *The Sabbath Lion*. He lives in St. Louis with his wife Tsila, a calligrapher, and his three children, Shira, Nathan, and Miriam.

Marc Bregman is Associate Professor of Rabbinic Literature at the Hebrew Union College in Jerusalem. He has also taught at The Hebrew University in Jerusalem, Ben-Gurion University in the Negev, and Yale University. He has published numerous articles in Hebrew and English in journals such as *Tarbiz*, *Journal of Jewish Studies*, *Journal of Theological Studies*, and *Revue de Qumran* and is the author of a forthcoming monograph, *The Sign of the Serpent and the Plague of Blood—The Tanhuma-Yelammedenu Midrashim to Exodus 7:9–25*.

Devis Grebu is an award-winning painter and illustrator. He was born in Romania in 1933 and left in 1964 because of the Communist regime. He later lived in Israel and France, and he now makes his home in Westchester, New York. A monograph of his work, *Devis Grebu: Through an Artist's Eyes*, was published in 1988. He has also illustrated more than forty books for adults and children, including *A Children's Haggadah* and *Joseph Who Loved the Sabbath*. His artwork has been exhibited internationally in one-man shows in the United States, France, Germany, Israel, and Switzerland. An important retrospective will take place in November 1995 at the Jewish National Museum in Washington.